Colored
Television

Also by Danzy Senna

Caucasia

Symptomatic

*Where Did You Sleep Last Night?:
A Personal History*

You Are Free: Stories

New People

COLORED TELEVISION

Danzy Senna

RIVERHEAD BOOKS
NEW YORK
2024

RIVERHEAD BOOKS
An imprint of Penguin Random House LLC
penguinrandomhouse.com

Copyright © 2024 by Danzy Senna
Penguin Random House supports copyright. Copyright fuels creativity, encourages diverse voices, promotes free speech, and creates a vibrant culture. Thank you for buying an authorized edition of this book and for complying with copyright laws by not reproducing, scanning, or distributing any part of it in any form without permission. You are supporting writers and allowing Penguin Random House to continue to publish books for every reader.

Riverhead and the R colophon are registered trademarks
of Penguin Random House LLC.

Library of Congress Cataloging-in-Publication Data

Names: Senna, Danzy, author.
Title: Colored television / Danzy Senna.
Description: New York : Riverhead Books, 2024.
Identifiers: LCCN 2024005082 (print) | LCCN 2024005083 (ebook) |
ISBN 9780593544372 (hardcover) | ISBN 9780593544396 (ebook)
Subjects: LCGFT: Novels.
Classification: LCC PS3569.E618 C65 2024 (print) |
LCC PS3569.E618 (ebook) | DDC 813/.54—dc23/eng/20240206
LC record available at https://lccn.loc.gov/2024005082
LC ebook record available at https://lccn.loc.gov/2024005083

International edition ISBN: 9780593854952

Printed in the United States of America
1st Printing

Book design by Amanda Dewey

This is a work of fiction. Names, characters, places, and incidents either are the product of the author's imagination or are used fictitiously, and any resemblance to actual persons, living or dead, businesses, companies, events, or locales is entirely coincidental.

We have met the enemy and he is us.

—Pogo Possum

**Colored
Television**

1.

Jane had to remind herself it was February. There had been no winter this year, not even the mild wet days they called winter out here. Just blazing dry heat for months on end.

Last night she and Lenny had watched *Soylent Green* together in bed. Movies were the new sex. The movie was supposed to be set in New York City but seemed to Jane to be set in Los Angeles. Every story about the apocalypse was really about Los Angeles. Jane had no urge to return to the East Coast, not anymore—but on days like this, she did miss it, the drama of the seasons, the changing mood ring of the sky, even the statues of old white men, something solid she could rail against.

She'd noticed recently that LA had two faces. By day it was as hopeful and effervescent as a hummingbird, by night it was terrifying, doomed. The flowers could fool you in the daytime. They could make you believe you weren't floating in outer space. But at night, you knew.

The brightness of the sky stared back at her now, unrelenting. Neither she nor Finn were wearing sunblock. But could she stop pushing him? Finn was most calm when he was swinging or jumping. This was, according to the doctors, a symptom of the problem.

The pediatrician they met with last spring, that terrible spring, had told her she needed to "face the elephant in the room." She would have preferred a less hackneyed metaphor, but she had to take what she could get these days. Jane had accepted his referral and called the special clinic, which, astoundingly, had no openings for many weeks. Apparently, she wasn't the only parent trying to get some answers here. She would have to wait in line to learn what her son was, exactly. Who he was. She would have to wait to learn what they would become.

Jane had been given a form to fill out before the appointment. It asked if Finn liked to swing. She was supposed to rate how much he liked to swing. She filled in the third circle: *The problem is severe in degree.* She'd never thought of his swinging as a problem, just something he liked to do, the way he liked books about bugs, YouTube videos about baking, whirlpools, and tunnels.

The doctor had not exactly blamed her and Lenny for Finn's problem, but he had suggested that their many moves had not helped. He said all that displacement had encouraged Finn to become best friends with the contours of his own mind.

Jane had been pushing Finn for what felt like an hour. She found weekends unbearable. They interrupted her momentum, so come Monday she would have to reacquaint herself with the story she was trying to tell. Weekends were when she and Lenny fought the most too. During the week, when they had hours with the kids at school to hide away from each other, they were happy to reunite at the end of the day. But on weekends they kept tabs on who was getting time to look at a book, who was scrolling on a phone and only pretending to be going to the bathroom, who had gotten an hour in their studio while the other cooked dinner.

There had been a particularly rough patch the previous year when they were fighting over money and Jane's not getting her book finished and Lenny's continuing to create art that he could not sell. And Finn too. They were fighting over Finn. Lenny refused to embrace the diagnostic language. He called it another system of capitalist thought they had to resist. It had been Jane's idea to go see a couple's therapist. They'd charged her to Jane's credit card, then, when that maxed out, to Lenny's.

In the second session, Heidi had told them she didn't think they were incompatible, they were both just too rigid and self-absorbed. They needed to learn how to compromise in the ways that were necessary to sustain a marriage. She'd given them a series of assignments that were supposed to help them accomplish this.

But they'd stopped seeing Heidi months ago before they'd completed the homework. In fact, doing the homework had made them realize that they hated her, which had been convenient, given that they could not afford her. Jane had seen their mutual hatred as a good sign, really—a remaining strength in their marriage. Together they still hated so much.

"I have to stop pushing," Jane said to Finn now. "My arms hurt."

"No, keep pushing," Finn said. "I want to reach the top."

"There is no top," Jane said, still pushing.

Someone was watching them from across the playground. A lone white woman in the park full of Latina nannies. The woman sat on the other side of the structure. Beside her was a bright, modernist stroller—the expensive kind with the thick tires as if meant for going off road. She moved it back and forth with one hand as she watched Jane and Finn. Jane wondered if the woman could tell from looking that Finn had been assessed—that he'd shown risk factors according to the doctor. Could she see he liked to swing too much?

"Let's agree on a number of pushes," she said to Finn now, remembering how one of the books she'd read in the aftermath of the assessment had told her to forecast everything for her child. She couldn't just stop pushing because her arms hurt. She had to tell him she was going to stop long before she stopped. He needed things broken down. She had to act like a computer or a wire mother out of an experiment. "How many more pushes should we do?" she said.

"Infinity," Finn said.

"That's too much for Mommy. Ten."

"Twenty," he said.

"Okay, twenty."

He was silent, peaceful, a little absent then, enjoying his last twenty pushes. He understood the logic of numbers.

In the distance, Jane saw that the white woman had taken her baby out of the stroller. The baby—in a pink onesie—had dark brown skin and a sprouting of curly black hair. She did not look biracial, Jane noted—she did not look like she could have come out of the mother's pale body. She had to be adopted, Jane decided. A child carried from another land to assuage this woman's desire to experience mother love.

On one of their first dates, Jane and Lenny had teased each other about their various strains of Blackness. Jane said Lenny was Caviar Black, which meant, she explained, riffing on Steve Martin's line in *The Jerk*, that he was born a rich black child. Lenny said Jane was *Pinky* Black. As in the kind of Black you can't see unless you're squinting. This baby, the one in her mother's pale arms, Lenny would have deemed Motherland Black. As in untainted. As in, she had come on an airplane just a few months ago, not once upon a time across the sea on a ship, stacked on top of others like herself.

It seemed like a long-gone era, when she and Lenny had joked like that, obsessed like that about color. She sometimes thought she was losing Lenny, or that he was losing her, she couldn't say which. They used to play a game they called Forensics. They would read strangers, guess everything about them just by looking. She could hear Lenny's read on the woman over there. Rich lesbian, Ethiopian baby, Bugaboo stroller, home in Silver Lake, film editor, Design Within Reach.

Watching the woman give the baby a bottle, Jane recalled an old photograph, a tintype she'd seen in a book many years ago, of a Black wet nurse with a white baby. The enslaved woman sat with her breasts exposed, staring out at the camera with a harrowing kind of sadness. Before Jane now was a new kind of daguerreotype: the white woman smiling brightly, the pampered dark baby nestled in her arms. It was a detail she could include in her novel, the one she was still trying to finish. She'd been writing it for so long.

Jane finished counting to twenty and pulled the swing to a stop. She lifted Finn off the seat, trying to meet his gaze. He looked away, toward the slide. She tried to hug him, but he squirmed out of her arms and began to bunny hop across the playground.

AT THE ASSESSMENT in the spring, the specialist had brought out a family of dolls for Finn—a mother, a father, a baby boy, and a little girl—along with some toy furniture and a toy truck. She'd also brought out a small flat disc that she announced to Finn was supposed to be a pizza.

"Would you like to play with me, Finn?" the specialist had asked in a singsongy voice.

Finn had not answered. He'd been too busy spinning the tires on the truck, watching the way they moved. Jane had found it interesting, which now she wondered was maybe the problem. That she could see his point. Whirlpools and tunnels were interesting. Cooking shows on YouTube were fun to watch. Maybe not two hours of them in a row, but still, she could see his point.

The specialist had begun to play in an animated fashion with the dolls. She pretended to be the mother doll speaking to the father doll. "Baby looks hungry. Shall we have some pizza together?" She placed the disc on the tiny table.

Finn picked up the little girl doll and turned her to the side so he was staring at her profile. Her blonde hair fell down her back. "Her hair makes a tunnel against her neck," he said.

The specialist glanced at Jane. "Does he notice shapes like that very often?" Jane shrugged, swallowed against the tightness in her throat. He did. She'd admitted that he did. Tunnels were everywhere if you knew how to look.

JANE TURNED ONTO the narrow winding road toward the house where they were staying this year. She and Lenny had lived in a lot of different spaces in the greater Los Angeles area since the kids were born. Lenny joked that Ruby and Finn were growing up like Jason Bourne, with no identity. It hadn't really been a choice, to raise them this way. They had simply discovered at some point that they were living in a city they couldn't afford. And so they had moved—from Venice Beach to Mid-City to Eagle Rock they had wandered, dragging their children behind them. A few times over the years they'd rented from actual landlords, with actual leases, but the places they could afford were not just overpriced but ugly, smelly, and dark. So they'd learned to find more temporary arrangements. They'd lived in the dank apartment in Silver Lake with the stash of female-oriented porn on the bookshelves beside the Judith Butler and Gayatri Spivak. They'd lived in the one-room back house in Venice behind the Rwandan genocide scholar who made Jane watch reality dating shows with her at night.

Jane had discovered somewhere along the way that if you did not have money there were benefits to hanging around with people who did. Rich friends got divorced, or they got restless; they went away on sabbaticals and film shoots and retreats. They didn't stay in one place, and they needed people to watch their possessions or pets or plants. Jane and Lenny and the kids were those people. They were those friends.

The current house belonged to Brett, who had been Jane's friend since graduate school. He and his wife, Piper, and their son, Max, had all gone to Australia for the year so Brett could be on set for a show he'd written. "It would be just for the school year, from August until June," he'd told Jane over tacos last spring. "To be honest, it's mostly to keep Max's bearded dragon alive. They don't have kennels for lizards."

They had been living at Brett's for six months now—long enough that every time Jane drove up its long winding driveway, she felt a surge of house pride, as if she owned the place.

To be sure, there were oddities about the house—for example, the fact that it had no windows overlooking what would have been a spectacular view. It sat at the peak of a mountain above the city, and yet the architect who had designed it, sometime in the sixties, had mysteriously decided to make the exterior a semicircle of unbroken wood, like a blind face. Only when you came into the junglelike courtyard, where lizards flitted across your path, did you discover that inside the semicircle the house was all glass, staring into its own navel.

Despite this strange design choice, or maybe because of it, Jane loved the house. It was a special house, witty and whimsical, historically significant in the architecture world. Inside, the kitchen was so stocked with gadgets and fancy Scandinavian pans and gleaming counters, it almost made Jane want to cook. Brett and Piper even had a wine refrigerator, with separate temperature-controlled zones, that they'd left stocked with wine. It hadn't taken Jane and Lenny long to start dipping into the assortment. At first, Jane had justified the uncorking of each new bottle with the vague sense that she'd replace them before Brett came back, and she had kept the empties apart from the rest of the recycling in that determination. But, of course, the wines were expensive. Or at least they tasted expensive. She had drawn the line at opening any of the next level of wine bottles, the dust-covered ones in their own special room, a glass-encased, temperature-controlled wine pantry off the dining room. At least she and Lenny had not opened any of those.

AN OPAQUE FILM hung over the basin of the city. Lenny would be bringing Ruby back from dance class. Or maybe they were there already, fixing dinner, doing homework, playing jazz.

Ruby was almost eight, two years older than Finn. When she was born, Jane and Lenny had vowed to keep her protected from the toxins of the world, cultural and otherwise. For the first few years, they'd shown her only a handful of television shows and movies, each of them educational and socially aware, parsed out carefully. They'd fed her only the purest of foods—kale chips and dried mango for snacks, nothing but water to drink. Her T-shirts had no corporate logos, and her dolls were all brown-skinned and curly haired, like herself.

Then came Finn. He cried all the time. The tiny apartment they were living in then was filled with the sound of his screams. Jane had paced back and forth, jostling his writhing body in her arms, whispering a goofy mantra: "Finnegan begin again." He seemed like a computer with a virus—something that needed to be rebooted. But he'd already been started, and she didn't know how to begin again.

One afternoon when they'd finally gotten Finn down for a rare nap, Ruby had approached Jane and Lenny where they lay on the bed, staring up at the ceiling in a kind of shock at the momentary calm. "Mama, Papa," Ruby had said in a small voice. "Can I watch a movie?" Jane had been about to say no, it wasn't screen time, but Lenny spoke first. "Sweetie," he said. "You can watch twelve."

These days, Ruby liked to change into her Elsa costume as soon as she got back from school—Elsa from *Frozen*—complete with the platinum blonde wig. It was Lenny, not Jane, who had taken her to see the movie, so Jane could at least say that in her own defense if it ever came down to a trial. But she hadn't brought Ruby anywhere special in months, so who was she to say what was toxic and what was not?

Jane eyed Finn now in the rearview mirror. His lips were moving.

He was whispering something to himself. He caught her gaze in the mirror.

"On the Finn planet," he said, "they have a machine that can turn glass back into sand. Did you know that already, Mama? Have you ever been there?"

She shook her head no.

There was this picture Finn drew everywhere, a character he drew on any paper he could find. A stick figure with a big head he called Baby Blue. In the drawings, Baby Blue was always in a situation of danger—standing tiny beneath a dinosaur or at the edge of a cliff—but no matter what, his expression never changed. He wore the same invisible flat smile in every image no matter what terrible thing was about to happen.

The doctor had said that the drawings were another symptom of the problem.

Everything that she had once found charming or special about their child was, it turned out, a symptom of something else.

Finn had another explanation for his behaviors. He told Jane about it when she was stroking his back late at night, in the darkness of Max's bedroom, surrounded by Max's toys, with Max's star stickers glowing above them, that he was from another planet. Finn told her he remembered his home planet so clearly. One day he'd fallen asleep, and the next he woke to find himself living in a strange, bright place, being held by strangers who called him by the wrong name. His name was not Finn. It was We. He wanted them to call him We. He said the people in this new land spoke a language he could not understand. He said the ground in this new land felt like spikes cutting into his feet, and this was why he walked on his tiptoes.

JANE'S FIRST NOVEL had not been a bestseller, but it had received high praise from the critics. Its young protagonist became the pawn in her seventies-era parents' social experiment. One reviewer said that it was as if the main character had been *born not of parents but of the American soil itself, with all its varied and tangled roots*. It had come out nine years ago—back when Jane seemed poised to be deemed a major American author. Her agent, Honor, had advised her to produce another novel as soon as possible. "Don't make it too ambitious," she'd told Jane over drinks. "Just bang it out and get it over with. Second novels are always a disappointment. You just have to move past them."

Jane had not followed Honor's advice. She'd tried. The book she was writing hadn't started out so sprawling. It had originally been the story of a 1950s actress who was passing as white, loosely inspired by the life of Carol Channing. But over the past eight years it had swelled and swelled, and she'd somehow ended up writing a four-hundred-year history of mulatto people in fictional form. There were five interwoven story lines from different historical moments. The 1950s actress had been joined by Thomas Jefferson and Sally Hemings, then by an ongoing thread on the Melungeons of Appalachia, who were believed to be the first tribe of triracial Americans to self-isolate and procreate, creating generations of future Benetton models. There were sections on Booker T. Washington and Slash from Guns N' Roses. The latest addition was a family of modern-day mulattos living in a town Jane called Multicultural Mayberry. The throughline was that all the characters were racial nomads and they were all related to one another through various strains in their ancestry. Lenny called it her "mulatto *War and Peace*." It had been so long in the making, but here in Brett's house, with its peace and calm and space, it had suddenly come into focus. For the first time, she was working with steadiness and conviction.

Lenny didn't have problems working with steadiness and conviction. He was a painter who made abstract paintings that didn't sell. He made paintings that steadfastly refused to depict Black bodies, Black faces, Black suffering.

Jane had half joked over the years that adding a little emblem of Blackness—anything really—in the corner of his paintings would go a long way. They'd sell like hotcakes! But Lenny wasn't that kind of artist. He wasn't that kind of person.

Like Jane, Lenny taught—and like Jane, he didn't have tenure. But unlike Jane, he had no possibility of tenure because he'd managed to teach at one of those art schools that didn't offer tenure. Which meant that only trust-fund babies with a cushion to fall back on could afford to work there for any length of time, and apart from Lenny, the school was unrepentantly white. A white hipster playground, as Lenny put it. But Lenny was stuck there because he was a Black painter who didn't paint Black themes. Or, as one bewildered reviewer put it, "You'd never know the painter was Black."

The review had been of a group show downtown. Lenny's piece, the only painting included in the show, had sat couched between an inflatable penis and a hologram of a mammy. He'd painted series of shapes and colors colliding and intersecting. You could see a second painting creeping out beneath the surface, a more figurative painting, like faces emerging from a calamity. It was the only piece in the show that hadn't sold.

Over the years, Lenny had become obsessed with the idea that his art would be better embraced outside the United States. For a long time, as for countless Black artists before him, it had been France that held his imagination. But the few times he'd visited, he had been put off by the French fetishization of Black Americans, along with their hatred of the Arabs in their midst.

So his focus had turned to Japan. His work was taken seriously there, and he had a solo show in Tokyo coming up in the fall. He had sabbatical this year, and he was spending all his time preparing. Which had turned out to mean not only working on the paintings but also learning Japanese, and not only fantasizing about living in Japan but also embarking on a long, strange correspondence with the Japanese embassy—excruciatingly formal and polite on both sides—in which he was requesting asylum from American racism, as if that were something on offer.

Jane had no such urge to leave the country. In her decidedly unscientific sampling, all the Black people who left the country in their desperate quest to "escape the American obsession with race" only became more obsessed with race themselves. Or rather, became obsessed with *not* being obsessed with race. Once you declared you didn't believe in race, it seemed, you had to declare this rather banal idea everywhere you went—so it became a way of believing in race even as you pretended not to believe in race. It was an "out damn spot" situation—the more you tried to wash your hands of race, the more the bloody spots emerged. Jane knew better. And Lenny knew better too, deep down. He wasn't one of those neoconservative Negroes they dragged out every few years to make white people feel good. They'd be richer if he was. So Jane pretty much ignored his Japan fixation, the same way he ignored her *Intervention* fixation (she was on season eighteen). The most successful couples, she knew, learn how to ignore each other's obsessions most of the time. And they had children to raise.

So they weren't leaving the country. Not yet, anyway. Jane was on sabbatical too, and she had promised Professor Mischling, the chair of her tenure committee, that she would finish her book. Which meant that Brett's offer couldn't have come at a better moment. Even Lenny could see the advantages. The kids could attend the blue-ribbon public school up the street, the one with the chicken coop. They could live cheaply and glamorously, and maybe even make a dent in the massive credit card debt they'd been dragging behind them all these years. Their last living situation, an accessory dwelling unit—really a converted garage—behind the mansion of a retired actress named Linda had grown untenable. Linda's demands on them had progressed from Lenny's doing odd bits of "men's work"—tightening cabinet doors and killing bugs—

to middle-of-the-night calls for Jane to talk her down from her panic attacks. Lenny said Jane was becoming Linda's mammy—that he felt like Benson, or worse, Kunta Kinte. Moving to Brett's would get them out from under Linda's antebellum thumb. And best of all, it would let them live as working artists together, the way Lenny had always dreamed—Jane in one space, Lenny in another, creating.

In their wedding vows so many years earlier, Lenny had quoted Rilke: "I hold this to be the highest task of a bond between two people: that each should stand guard over the solitude of the other." On Brett's property, there were two separate work studios—Brett's writing space, a converted garage, which was the perfect place for Jane to finish her novel; and Piper's architectural studio, where Lenny could paint. Lenny said yes.

So Jane and Lenny had put all their belongings in a storage facility in Koreatown, trash bags filled with stained cotton sheets and towels, boxes crammed with old letters and photographs, Jane's notebooks, scratched-up pots and pans, stainless steel silverware from Target, a Melitta coffee maker, a tank for the goldfish who had eaten each other alive, the keyboard for the piano lessons the kids had stopped taking, three lumpy mattresses, a stained pleather sofa, paintings and more paintings, books and more books. An IKEA Billy bookcase they'd dismantled and would, Jane suspected, never put back together again.

This was the year they were living in Brett's house. Eating off Brett's plates. Shitting in all five of Brett's special water-conserving toilets. Jane hadn't been about to miss out on the opportunity to pretend they were rich Black artists who lived in the hills. She had been determined to be that couple this year. She wanted it, and Lenny knew how badly she wanted it.

This was the year she would finish the book she'd been writing for so long. She'd publish it and get tenure, and they'd be middle class and maybe even have the money to buy a house of their very own. Lenny had played up the martyrdom, but she could see he was enjoying the use of Piper's studio at the far end of the lawn. He was plainly enjoying all of it. He just wouldn't admit it to her.

That first day in Brett's office, Jane had made herself dizzy swiveling circles in his Herman Miller Aeron chair. Then she'd taken a La Croix from the mini fridge, enjoying the crack and sizzle as she popped it open, imagining this would be how she'd start every day. A writer's call to prayer.

Brett had once been, like Jane, a writer of that most doomed of genres, literary fiction. He had written and published just one book, a pithy short story collection called *Lemon Rock*. He had also, like Jane, been the product of an unsuccessful interracial marriage that had ended in divorce. In the graduate workshop where they met, they had been the only two people of color. The white kids in their cohort used to say that he and Jane looked like siblings. It wasn't true—their hair textures and features were quite different—but to the untrained Caucasoid eye, light brown equaled beige, 3B hair texture was identical to 2B curls. Potato, potahto, mulatto, mulatta. But it was true that in that room of white faces they had developed a fierce, almost sibling bond, and the connection had held even as their lives had gone in such different directions.

When Brett shifted to television, his career leapt ahead. He specialized in supernatural phenomena, mostly zombies. It was as if the same blankness that had made his fiction writing fall flat became a superpower in television. He worked his way up in the bright, glittering industry that had hovered behind Jane for years while she stubbornly hunched over her novel, pretending not to notice it. By the time he was thirty-nine, he was a showrunner. Now he was beginning to direct.

Was Brett happy with his success? Did the money make up for what seemed to Jane rather mind-numbing work? She wasn't sure. Brett sometimes spoke about wanting to make a different sort of show, something more personal, a show, he said, about people like him and Jane—a show with two halfie leads. He'd said he wanted the fact of them being biracial to be not the subject of the show, exactly, but just something they happened to be—when race came up at all, it would be more an impetus for humor than something tortured and heavy. In other words, it would be a comedy, not a tragedy, something so punchy and funny that people wouldn't remember all those old-timey tragedies of yore—the Douglas Sirk of it all—and would only see the future of mulattos, the whole sunshiny vista that lay ahead. He called it his vanity project and usually ended his musings by saying he'd never get the time to do it, he had too much else on his plate. Jane always encouraged him to find the time if he really wanted to make it, but secretly she hoped he would never attempt his race comedy. For one thing, he'd make a mess of the subject. He lacked the invisible thing that she possessed, that thing nobody talked about anymore: Black consciousness. If you did not get it as a child, as she had, it would not come to you later, not really. You couldn't pick it up in a college AfAm seminar after the fact. She thought it best, given Brett's childhood, that he stick to zombies and Thor and giant arachnids.

Once, at a bar, Brett had told Jane, drunkenly, that the older he got the more he valued friends who had been his friends through all his life changes. People who were witnesses to the whole arc of it. He told her that night that he loved her. Not in a creepy way but in an intense way that surprised her, his eyes burning. She got the sense that she was a thread he was trying to hold on to, a tenuous tie to both the starving artist he'd never become and the Blackness that was always just out of his reach.

She'd been pleased to discover that Brett still had a copy of her first novel on his office bookshelves. She could not remember having written the inscription though. *Fuck these pale-faced motherfuckers*, it read. *Let's burn this house down. Love, Jane.*

For the past six months, Jane had been following the advice she gave her students. She woke each morning before dawn, when Lenny and the kids were still asleep, and walked barefoot across the yard to the studio, not pausing to make coffee or check email or brush her teeth. She wasn't even fully awake when she sat down at the desk in the semidarkness and began to write.

She worked through those early morning hours with energy and purpose, the kind she had never had before. Brett's office had been the key. She'd needed this space of her very own. On the walls she'd hung all her inspirations, all the faces of her characters, real and imagined. She taped up archival documents, including Thomas Jefferson's famous letter from Paris, where he came up with the mathematical equation showing how many generations it takes to make a mulatto white. *Let the 3^d crossing be of q. and C. their offspring will be $q/2 + C/2 = a/8 + A/8 + B/4 + C/2$. call this e. (eighth) who having less than 1/4 of a. or of pure negro blood, to wit 1/8 only, is no longer a mulatto.* She put up a picture of O. J. and Nicole with their children, Sydney and Justin, the interracial family in happier times. She put up a photograph of some free people of color she'd copied from a library book, a family of sepia-toned mountain mulattos from the turn of the century standing on the steps of a porch, the father holding a shotgun. They looked like she imagined the family in her book. She put up a picture of Carol Channing grinning like a Cheshire cat. She used Brett's whiteboard—where he'd no doubt storyboarded many a hit show—to draw a time line showing the progression of her novel. It moved from 1813, the first recorded mention of the mysterious Melungeon people in a church in Virginia (where a white parishioner had been accused of "harborin' them melungins") to the 1950s, the life of the actress, that sad, drifting quadroon girl wandering that big old house wondering how to get rid of the baby, that dreaded baby, growing inside of her, to the vague present-day story, a racially indeterminate family living in a Craftsman house in a beige dreamworld that could only be California.

Every morning for six months she had worked like a demon. She was like a mammal that is preparing to give birth, that hides under the porch, waiting for the litter to come. She worked until the voices of her family floated out to her, the children calling to her that they were hungry, so hungry. Then and only then would she shut her computer and head back across the courtyard to fix them breakfast. And the closer she came to finishing, the harder she found it to return to the main house, to her children's frenzied demands, to Lenny's grumbling about the news. Even as she went through the motions of frying eggs and pouring cereal, she would look back across the courtyard at the little studio and imagine that another her was still sitting there, working.

ONCE, YEARS AGO, Lenny and Jane had attended a party at Brett's house in celebration of one of his successes—a series that had gotten green-lit or a pilot he'd just sold, Jane couldn't remember which. She did remember Piper walking around the party in a silver dress serving drinks and how all the other guests had bronze skin and blazing white teeth. Lenny and Jane were the only nonindustry people in attendance. They had stood together in a corner feeling out of place, equal parts superior and ashamed. At one point, Jane had glimpsed their reflection in a gilded floor mirror and thought they looked like a pair of peasants who had wandered in off the street to beg for bread. On their way out, Lenny had grabbed a few cookies off a silver platter, wrapped them in a napkin, and put them in his pocket.

On the drive home, he had made his usual snide comments about Brett and Piper, the art on their walls. He called Brett a sellout, a tragic mulatto, though Jane argued he wasn't as interesting as all that. He was just another hack cranking out zombie shows.

She wondered aloud what it must be like to have such a white-looking child as Max. "I mean, does one even consider him mixed race? Hasn't all the Blackness been washed out?"

"It has, for certain," Lenny said, "but when it comes time to apply for college, you just know Brett's gonna tell him to claim he's some kind of

Black kid. He'll drag out the old bylaws—the one-drop rule—to make Max seem more interesting. That's how they do it. These wily mulattos be blending into the furniture until Blackness seems like it might get you something."

"God, are mulattos just awful people?" Jane said.

"Not you. You're the last good mulatto. Brett's from that Tiger Woods school of cluelessness."

Jane laughed. But silently, secretly, she had already been imagining what it would be like to live in a house like Brett's someday. She could see Lenny's art on the walls. She could see Lenny standing beside one of his paintings, discussing his work with a curator from Gagosian who wanted to give him a show. In her mind's eye, he was dressed in painter chic, an Oxford shirt and cargo pants like those he was wearing but of infinitely better quality. His artwork was the same as his artwork now, splashes of color overlaid on some image you couldn't quite make out but knew was there, the shape of a body lurking beneath a surface of color—but now the world understood what he was doing, they saw his brilliance, finally. Jane was there in the fantasy, standing before a table that held copies of her new novel. The book was an object, a real thing, alive, outside of her—born. And her children were in the vision too, up past their bedtime. Ruby flitted among the guests in a pink frock with another little girl—because in this dream she'd finally lived in one place long enough to have a real best friend. And Finn was there, standing on the steps in a camel-colored blazer, holding forth like a tiny professor, lecturing a charmed cluster of guests on the history of the solar system.

THERE WAS A framed photo of the family that Jane had brought with them to Brett's. She liked to hang it up in each new house they occupied, hoping its presence would make the children feel that wherever they were, no matter how unfamiliar, was home.

The portrait had been taken years ago when the kids were still babies. In it, Jane appeared heavier, softer, more maternal than she did now. Her breasts were round, her stomach still swollen from recent pregnancy. She was holding Finn in her arms and Lenny was holding Ruby, and none of them were smiling.

The man who took the picture was a friend of Lenny's, a Serbian war photographer he'd known back in art school. The photographer was passing through town on his way to some new war zone and had stopped by the apartment they were living in at the time, the one on Rossmore Avenue, where he'd sat for hours at their kitchen table drinking cup upon cup of coffee and laughing in a secret way with Lenny about their life before wives. Just before he headed out to the airport, he'd insisted on taking a photo of Lenny and Jane and the kids on the rooftop of the building.

Jane had forgotten about the photo until a print arrived in the mail several months later. The image was not what she'd expected. When she showed it to Lenny, he looked pleased by what he saw. He stared at the portrait for a long time, smiling, then said they looked like a family of Palestinians in the West Bank. Jane could see what he meant. In the picture, they didn't look as American as they did in real life. They looked like a family from some other place. And the city that stretched out behind them didn't look like Los Angeles. It looked grim, battered, ancient.

The sky appeared cloudy, low hanging, not wide and blue the way it really was. Finn, still an infant, stared out as if startled by something he'd seen or heard, a bomb exploding in the distance. Ruby, her head resting on Lenny's shoulder, wore an expression of deep melancholy, as if already, at three, she knew war and occupation. They looked like they'd witnessed something terrible, though they hadn't, not really. And if you looked closely, you could make out, in the distant hills behind them, the corner of the Hollywood sign.

2.

Jane had first met Lenny at a house party in Brooklyn. He'd come on the arm of another woman. Jane had come alone. She'd been just emerging from a bad breakup, the latest in a string of them. She was not usually the sort of woman to go after another woman's man, and she might not have done so had it not been for the psychic. Not that she believed in psychics, not now, not then. But the first session had been an early birthday gift from her sister, who had a long relationship with the occult. Jane found the psychic's soothing voice over the phone comforting.

His name was Wesley Brown. On his website, he had not actually used the word *psychic*. Instead, he'd called himself an "intuitive psychodynamic counselor with a specialty in racial alchemy." In their first session, he told Jane that her future husband was on his way, nearly there. The way he said it, with a kind of bemused certainty, made Jane understand why her sister liked him so much. He was more fun than a therapist.

Across the room at the party, a Black man was standing at the chip table alone, shoveling corn chips with salsa into his mouth. He was wearing Vans sneakers and a T-shirt that said PART OF THE PROBLEM. What was it that the psychic had predicted? He'd said Jane was about to meet a Black man who was funny—a Black man who would be wearing "West Coast shoes." The Vans were definitely West Coast. And the T-shirt was funny. Pretty funny.

She sidled over, drink in hand.

"Do you live around here?" she asked.

"Brooklyn? No. I hate Brooklyn. People here are pigs."

She asked him where he lived instead.

"Nowhere, really." He wiped the chip grease off his mouth with a cocktail napkin. "I'm staying in LA for now. I hate it there too. Different breed of pigs."

They introduced themselves. They got into a strange, joking discussion—she didn't remember how—about ice cream. Lenny said a person's choice in ice cream was influenced by their race. He said that Chinese people tended to like pistachio; white people liked sloppy flavors, like Rocky Road or anything with a lot of chunks in it; and Black people liked clean and tidy flavors, like mint chocolate chip. Were they flirting? She couldn't tell. His eyes roamed the room occasionally, as if he were looking for someone else.

Jane was trying to think what else to say to interest this man when a woman appeared beside him. She slid her arm through his, kissed his cheek territorially, gave Jane a cutting look, then whispered something in his ear. So—he was taken. Jane found herself surprised by the presence of the woman, who had not been in the psychic's prediction. She found herself scanning the room for a different Black man, a second funny Black man in West Coast shoes, but there was nobody—only miles of white writers and a few racially ambiguous mystery-meat types like herself. When she looked back at Lenny and the woman, they were speaking to each other in low lover tones, as if she weren't there, and she felt her throat catch. She felt as if she were already involved with this guy, as if she were already his mistress.

Jane had been in New York for ten years at that point. She'd moved there after college, still believing that her life would unfold in a certain order. First, she would launch her career, then, after a series of difficult but teachable-moment love affairs, she would meet The One—her future mate—and settle down somewhere outside the city where they would spawn beautiful, gifted children. Later, when said children grew up and went to college at a school that looked exceptionally good on a bumper sticker on her Audi, Jane would spend the rest of her days writing novels and tending to her yard in Eileen Fisher clothes, her face set in deep thought like a kind of Pema Chödrön for the biracial set. She would age gracefully as a rich Buddhist.

But it had not happened that way. The night she met Lenny, she'd already reached that Didionesque moment when her life in the city began to feel repetitive, stunted.

As her thirty-third birthday loomed, she found she'd lost interest in dating altogether. The parties all began to look alike. She was no longer able to remember why she'd broken up with her previous boyfriends. She'd gotten to the part of the story where she began to circle back, calling exes late at night to see if they wanted to get back together.

By then she had quite a number of ex-boyfriends, a spate of them—some boys, some men, relationships that had each lasted long enough for them to take off the condom. Her married sister always said serial monogamy was like being a slow-cooker ho. And Jane had the medical records to think maybe her sister was right. A few infections, nothing fatal or permanent. A malformed cell on her cervix that had needed to be burned off. Something else that required a tube of antibiotic cream squeezed inside of her. The perils of the journey. Many of the men had wanted to settle down with Jane, but she hadn't been ready. In her twenties, she had wanted nothing to do with domesticity. And this not-wanting had made her the target of several good men. Looking back, it seemed she'd spent the decade dodging engagement rings flung at her across taxi seats. She'd wanted to stay a precocious girl-woman, to tend to her own needs forever. She'd been satisfied with the performance of marriage without the ring, the rising action of discontent, the falling action of the breaking up, the escape to freedom before the story started all over again. For so long she'd found her own foibles interesting.

But now, on the cusp of thirty-three, everything had started to look different. The suitors had stopped throwing the rings at her for one thing. When she called them late at night, one by one over the course of the year, she'd learned that somebody else had caught those flying rings. Kamau told her, with delight, that he was expecting his first baby with a filmmaker named Shari. Chino told her that he was in love with an Irish girl and moving to Dublin. Farouk told her he was now happily living with somebody named Gavin. Benjamin told her that he was still in love with her but that his therapist had helped him to see all the ways she was a narcissist. He said he needed to "go no contact." She'd even called Colton, the last of the white boys, the one with the scratchy lumberjack beard, who told her he had moved upstate with someone named Susan.

Jane wished them all well. After she hung up, she stared at the dried-flower arrangement on her mantel that looked like kindling for a fire—a design trick she'd learned from *domino* magazine. She wanted what the exes had or were about to get: a child on the way, a mortgage to pay, a Volvo, a pile of laundry that needed washing.

That same year, a catalog showed up in her mailbox for Hanna Andersson, a Swedish-inspired clothing company out of Oregon she'd never heard of before. They mostly sold children's clothes, but there was sleepwear for adults too. The catalog was addressed to the roommate who had moved out a long time ago. Jane was about to throw it in the trash when the picture on the cover caught her eye. A family of four were wearing matching striped pajamas and laughing—a medium-brown-skinned Black man and a beautiful brown-skinned Black woman with high cheekbones, the two of them flanked by a perfectly adorable boy and girl of the same skin tone. Jane went to the couch and began flipping through the catalog. The same kids modeled the clothes inside. In a few images, they appeared with their quasi parents too. Jane's mouth watered as she stared at the shots of them lounging around a swimming pool in matching bathing suits. In another photo, the mother and daughter walked on the beach, holding hands in matching mother-daughter sundresses. They were all of them always smiling, perpetually on the verge of laughter. What was so funny? Jane wanted to know.

She kept the catalog beside her bed for months, and when she was not looking at it, she'd think of the family inside with a peculiarly intense longing. She thought of them when she was standing shivering on the subway platform in Brooklyn in her combat boots, or on her way to a party in her giant parka, or even while at a party, staring at the faces of her drunken, bellowing friends, or when she was out on a date with that white hedge fund guy who had Tourette's syndrome and between courses erupted with *dirty cunt*—words he didn't mean, of course. (She'd been prewarned about his tic by the friends who had set them up.) She perused the catalog at night, alone in bed, when she was tired, so tired, gazing unblinking at the Black family who were exploding together with joy.

She called her mother one night and confessed something shameful: she wanted to settle down, have a few kids, live in the suburbs. Her mother, the aging beatnik, perpetually single, said that she couldn't believe she'd raised a daughter who had such bourgeois Restoration Hardware fantasies. Wasn't it ironic, she said, how women spent their twenties trying to catch a man and have his babies, then spent the next decade wishing they could escape through a bathtub drain? Settling down was just a euphemism for inching toward death. Death was the ultimate form of settling down. She said Jane should pine to create great art instead because, in the end, men were letdowns and kids were disappointments who grew up—like Jane and her sister—to blame their mothers for everything. Only art and friendship remained.

Jane hung up and called her sister, who told her their mother was full of white feminist second-wave claptrap, that she'd always cared more about feeding her own ego than feeding her half-caste children. "Don't you remember how awful it was for us growing up, Jane? Don't you remember what we went through? Don't listen to her, Jane. She's toxic."

That was when her sister said that what Jane needed was a psychic. There was this guy—a friend of a friend from college—who had predicted her own husband in a roundabout way. Now he was a psychic to the stars. He'd set Jane straight.

THAT NIGHT OF the party in Brooklyn, Jane had wanted to expel her mother's voice, her sister's voice, even Wesley Brown's voice from her head. She wanted to be just Jane for once—Jane at a party, letting her life unfold. But *they* were all in there, a coven of witches, whispering to her as she stood across from this Black man and the white girlfriend she'd learned over the last fifteen minutes was an ecopoet named Lilith.

Jane reminded herself that Lenny was just some random guy she was standing across from, a random guy who was in a relationship. But when Lilith said she was going to get a drink and Lenny called out to her to get him a whiskey "on the rocks," the words had a funny echo, and Jane remembered something else Wesley had said. He'd described the guy she was going to meet as "tall, dark, handsome . . . funny, wearing West Coast shoes, on the rocks."

"Random question," Jane said to him now. "Have you ever seen a psychic?"

She wasn't sure where she was going with it. She just needed to keep him looking at her.

But he was looking at the snack table, searching for something. "I don't believe in that shit," he said.

"I do." It was Lilith, back with his drink. She handed it to him, then linked her arm in his. "I guess what I mean is I used to believe in them," Lilith said. "I used to go to psychics all the time. Palm readers. Tarot card readers. Reiki. Energy healers. You name it." She gave Jane a wincing smile full of pity. "The thing is," she said, "people only go to psychics while they're single. Have you noticed that?" She laughed and kissed Lenny. He kissed her back—stiffly. She thought she caught a glimpse of trappedness in his eyes. Jane wasn't letting up. She forged on with aggressive small talk.

"What do you do for a living?" Jane asked him.

"I'm a painter. And you?"

"I'm a writer. A fiction writer."

Lilith was still stroking him, pouting a little, trying to get him to look at her. But he kept his eyes on Jane. "What world do you write about?"

Jane liked his question. What world? He was clearly somebody who understood how this worked.

"Mulattos," she said. "I write about mulattos."

"Isn't that an offensive term?" Lilith said.

Lenny smirked at Jane. "I've always liked it. Better than biracial, right?"

"Definitely better," Jane said, feeling a real flicker between them now. "Biracial could be any old thing. Korean and Panamanian or Chinese and Egyptian. But a mulatto is always specifically a mulatto."

Lenny nodded, eyed her. "That's for sure."

Lilith was watching Jane now with interest, taking in her features one by one. "If we had a baby," she said to Lenny, "would she look like her? Sorry, what's your name again?"

"Jane."

"Would it look like Jane?" Jane was almost impressed by the subtle way the woman had neutered her, reducing her to a baby, and at the same time, in the same sentence, had conjured up her own interracial sex life and future family with Lenny.

Lenny didn't answer, just gave Jane an awkward, maybe apologetic, look.

Lilith whispered something in Lenny's ear then, and it was as if Jane disappeared. He smiled and nodded, and Lilith started kissing him slowly on the neck. Lenny tried to wriggle out of Lilith's grasp, but she pulled his face toward her. Then he submitted and they were kissing for real, tongues and all, and Jane was standing there before them, her face burning.

"If you'll excuse me," she said to nobody, and wandered off.

In the kitchen, she fixed herself a large icy glass of rum and Coke, then she stood in the doorway trying not to watch them but watching them. Lilith was the lover, and Lenny was the beloved. She could see it in the way she tilted into him, eyes fixed on his face, and in the way he leaned back slightly, his tense smile.

Now Lilith was stroking Lenny's face, saying something that made him shake his head no, laughing. Jane took another gulp of her drink, bilious thoughts crowding her brain. What did he see in her? Lilith was so thin, so frail, with pale, almost translucent skin and a giant mane of blonde hair. Was he necromantic? Did he have a thing for cadavers? Why would an educated, sane Black man choose to be with a woman like that, in this century? Did he not realize that once he married white he would never get to talk unremitting shit about white people again? He'd always have to worry about hurting Lilith's feelings. And he couldn't bring her out in public with his friends, could he? Unless all his friends were white, which she doubted. He wasn't giving off miscellaneous vibes.

Though, what did she really know about Lenny? He was a stranger—someone she'd just met. And, she reminded herself, Wesley Brown was just a charlatan with a fancy website. Maybe this couple she was watching tongue-wrestle across the room were actually a good match. Jane tried to think generous, postracial thoughts. Maybe Lilith was kind, or funny. Maybe Lenny loved her for her kindness. Jane could already tell that she was not kind.

Jane came from a union like the one that Lilith and Lenny were about to embark on—ebony and ivory, together in disharmony—and yet, perhaps because it was her origin story, she could not bear the sight of interracial love. Well, she could, but not when the man was Black and the woman was white. Of course she didn't express this opinion often, and not in mixed company. She knew it wasn't a good look. When you hated the same thing Strom Thurmond did—albeit for different reasons—you knew you were in problematic territory. She took comfort in the fact that it wasn't white womanhood she was trying to protect. It was Black manhood she wanted to save from the clutches of white womanhood. That was different, right?

"Why the long face?" It was Stu, their host. Stu shared an office with Jane at the college up in the Bronx where they were adjuncts. He was one of those goofy oversize white guys who somehow cobbled his middling novels into a career—that mediocre white guy they kept hiring year after year out of nostalgia. Stu was self-deprecating in the extreme. He knew he was living on borrowed time. He understood his own obsolescence, and that made him bearable, even lovable.

The party tonight was to celebrate Stu's engagement to Priya, an Indian social science professor who was writing a book about the caste system.

"Do you believe in psychics?" Jane asked Stu.

"Hell no." He threw an arm around her. "Okay, so listen, Priya has a cousin here tonight. He thinks you're cute. Will you let me play matchmaker?" He pointed to a guy standing in a circle of other guests. The guy was shyly smiling at Jane. He wasn't bad. Not bad at all.

Jane looked back at Lenny, who had Lilith's tongue in his mouth again.

"That's okay," she said. "I'm sort of involved with someone else already." Somewhere between the chip table and the kitchen, she realized, she had fully committed to Wesley's story.

"Damn," Stu said. "I was hoping we could be cousins. Or whatever it is we'd be if you married Vijay. Siblings?"

"I'm touched." She looked at him with a welling of drunken affection. "Stu, you're the last white man I can stand to be around. Have I ever told you that?"

"Thanks, Jane."

She looked again toward Lenny and Lilith. "What's with those two?"

"Ha. They're really going at it. That's the guy Lilith has been telling me about. You know Lilith, right? From the Moth?"

Jane glanced at Stu. "Sure, I know her. I thought old Lilith would never settle down." She rolled an ice cube around in her mouth.

"From everything Priya says, she's bonkers for him. She's planning to move to the West Coast to be with him. Can you imagine? Lilith with her Victorian skin walking around in the Los Angeles sun, baking?" He laughed a little. "Priya says Lilith is suddenly obsessed with having a baby with him. *Lilith*. A baby. Are you processing that?"

"I'm trying."

"I guess it makes sense. I mean, their kids would be cute, right? Like you."

"They might be monstrous."

"No, and seriously, nobody wants to have white babies anymore," Stu said. "Not even me—and I used to be one."

"Come on. Why not? White babies can be cute."

"But not like the babies I'm going to make with Priya. They're gonna be fucking insane."

LATER, close to midnight, Jane stood outside on the stoop of Stu's building, shivering, smoking a cigarette. She'd bummed one off Priya. She found Wesley's number in her contacts and called him. She'd figured it was okay since it was only nine in California, but he answered groggily, like he'd been asleep.

"What?"

She remembered now, too late, a list on Wesley's website—his rules for healthy living. One was to go to bed when the children go to bed—toddler hours were great for the complexion, he said.

"I'm sorry. Is this too late? Should I call another time?"

"I hate it when people do that. It's like, make the choice not to cold-call people late at night. But if you do it, don't ask if I'm awake. Obviously I am—now."

"Sorry, right."

"So, go on."

"Listen, I'm outside a party. There's this guy here—he's exactly like you described. But, the thing is, he's with another woman. Seriously with her. A poet. An anorexic poet. A white anorexic ecopoet."

A man and a woman came out of the party and walked past her, laughing. "Don Cheadle," the woman was saying. "I'm telling you. Don Cheadle."

Jane felt suddenly foolish. "Listen, I'm sorry to call like this. I should have made an appointment. I can try you another time."

"No, no, I'm awake now," he said. "I'm trying to find your file."

She heard fingers tapping on a keyboard. "Here it is. Right. Of course. The dude—are you sure he's the same one? Sometimes the universe sends a red herring. The universe is playful like that."

"Black. Creative. Funny T-shirt. Medium-brown-skinned. Vans. Tallish. He lives in Los Angeles."

"Los Angeles. Shit. That's him. Definitely him."

"My friend Stu thinks he's going to propose to the woman. The ecopoet."

Wesley sighed long and hard. "Can I ask you something? What is it with these overeducated Negroes? I mean, don't take this the wrong way because I know you're the product of one of these unions, but these guys. I mean, all the schooling in the world and they don't seem to realize that marrying a white woman is simply not going to benefit them. Now, it'll benefit the white woman; she'll thrive. She'll seem more *interesting* for having done it. She can dine off that shit for years. But the Black man, his life will go to hell in a handbasket. He'll get out of the marriage in a far worse place than when he entered it."

Jane could feel that some mask Wesley had been wearing before, in their other sessions, was falling away. Maybe he'd taken a hit or two before toddler bedtime.

"Honestly," he was saying now. "Somebody should make a sequel to *Guess Who's Coming to Dinner.* Let the world know the truth of what happened to Dr. John Prentice after his marriage to that blonde chick. That shit would be bleak."

Behind Wesley's voice, Jane thought she could hear waves crashing— or maybe it was a freeway—and distantly, a dog barking. She'd seen the picture of Wesley's dog on his website, a chocolate lab named Marilyn McCoo.

"Black women, on the other hand," Wesley was saying. "They actually do worse when they marry within the race. Like my sister Wanda— she could have married that Jewish boy who was so gaga over her in college, but she didn't. She had to be all righteous and marry that socially inept computer engineer instead, Herman, with his ashy skin and the fucking side part in his Afro. And now look at her."

Jane leaned against a brick wall behind her, feeling the cold seep through her jacket into her skin. "But wait, I thought you said I should marry a Black guy. This Black guy."

"I did!"

"But now you're saying Black guys are bad for Black women."

"I was talking about Wanda. A real Black woman. Wait, that came out wrong. I'm not saying you aren't really Black because, technically, of course, you are. But with you, Jane, when I look at your chart, I get a lot of confusing signals. I see zigzags and negations. It's like a census questionnaire. Hispanic, non-Hispanic. Other. That kind of chaos."

Jane reminded herself this was bullshit. Wesley's prophesizing was about as accurate as a Ouija board reading or the answer on a Magic 8 Ball. Still, her voice sounded small and scared as she asked Wesley what would happen to her now that the man the universe had intended for her was with somebody else.

"Well," Wesley said. "Let me see." He paused, and there was a loud sound of pages turning. Again, Marilyn McCoo barked into the California night. Wesley said, "Here it is, right. In about twenty-three years, Jane, no, wait, twenty-four, yes, twenty-four, Mars will enter Virgo again. At that point, and no sooner, you'll have another chance to meet someone. To change your life. But not before then."

"I'm going to be alone for twenty-four years?"

He sighed. "Only if you screw this up." Then he launched into his "six years ago" speech, an abbreviated version of the one she'd heard him give in the video link on his website. "Six years ago," he said, "I was almost homeless, trying to sell my self-published book out of the trunk of my car. Now I'm living in a six-point-five-million-dollar home in Montecito with a daughter named Tuesday and a claw-foot tub imported from England. Don't let life happen to you, girl. This is your one precious time on this planet. Work it."

"What are you suggesting?" Jane said.

"I'm not suggesting shit. I'm telling you. Go upstairs and claim your fate. And by fate, I mean Mr. Funnyman in the California kicks. Go back to the party. Flirt. You won't have to do much. He's miserable. He feels trapped in a *Sesame Street* episode. He's searching the room for you right now."

"Are you sure?"

"Sure I'm sure. Listen, our ancestors didn't survive the horrors of the Middle Passage so some Caucasoid poet could miscegenate us out of existence. He might think he's happy, but he's not. Make this brotherman see the truth, that he needs to marry a non-Hispanic quadroon like you if he values his life and longevity. This is bigger than you and your silly heteronormative daydreams, Jane. This is about the universe. And trust me, you don't want to fuck with the universe because that bitch has no mercy."

LILITH DIDN'T DIE. She didn't go mad and throw herself into the ocean like Virginia Woolf. She simply didn't get Lenny. And, according to Jane's occasional bouts of internet stalking, not only did Lilith survive the breakup but three years later she married a different Black man, an uglier Black man, proving one of Jane's father's favorite sayings: "A sucker is born every minute." The Black man she married was an art critic, short and stout, with a bushy white beard and wire-rimmed glasses, what Jane imagined was a nasal voice. Lilith looked happy in the pictures she posted of her and Clarence at poetry readings and art openings. Over the years, Lilith won some awards for her ecopoetry, though as far as Jane could tell from her Instagram page, she did not have any babies. Maybe Papa Smurf was shooting blanks. Still, Jane didn't think Lilith had done so badly in the game of life. Which meant that Jane's karma, if not quite clean, was drinkable.

And Jane, over the six months that followed the night of the party, got all that the Hanna Andersson catalog had promised. First came flirting, then came ice cream, then some tortured months of their long-distance, much-whispered-about affair. Then came love, then came marriage, then came big fat baby Ruby in the baby carriage. Followed by wiry and ethereal Finn, who, when he learned to talk, told them his real name and his provenance from another planet. They were varying shades of brown: honey-colored, nut-brown, café con leche, pick your food metaphor. If they were Crayola crayons, Jane had once figured out while coloring with the children, Lenny would be Fuzzy Wuzzy, the kids would be Blast Off Bronze, and Jane would be Tumbleweed.

Jane talked to Wesley several more times, and the sessions got stranger. Now that she'd found the guy he'd predicted, he used the sessions to spew his theories about race and love and the convergence of the two. One time he told her his theory about mulatto men. He said they were way more tragic than mulatto women. Straight mulatto men were almost doomed to stay alone forever. Mulatto men had commitment issues. Not the kind you usually think of with men. It was that they simply couldn't pick a race.

Mulatto men, he said, couldn't be more different from the women. The women, he said, came out predators and the men came out prey. The women were more decisive. Thanks to their fertility clocks, they would, after a certain age—"like yours, Jane"—rush to pick a color, any color, anybody with an active sperm count. Mulatto women at least had learned to bite the racial bullet—getting themselves impregnated by a Black cinematographer or a white editor or something more noncommittal, like a Lebanese lawyer or a Korean chef or maybe even a Puerto Rican playwright. But mulatto men didn't feel they were in a rush to have a baby—so they got to wallow in their racial ambivalence for years and years, not realizing until it was too late that they had only the leftover women to choose from, the damaged goods. Skinny women with scarred fallopian tubes. Skinny women with narcissistic tendencies. Skinny women with genital warts. New York—Brooklyn in particular—was a Kraków ghetto of mulatto spinsters. And that, Wesley told her, was what he was saving her from—mulatto spinsterhood. Wesley said gray hair looked good on some white people and good on some Black people but always was terrible on mulattos.

Jane knew she should stop calling Wesley. It was hundreds of dollars a session, and nothing he was telling her had any practical application to her life. She was already on her way to a real relationship with the person he'd predicted. But she kept calling anyway, addicted to his theories. Lenny would, much later, in fights, claim she had a profound characterological susceptibility to brainwashing. "Anybody with a theory, you're right there in the front row, taking notes." And maybe he was right.

She called Wesley weekly up until the day a woman answered and said in Spanish that Jane had the wrong number. And when Jane went to check Wesley's website, it was gone. "403—Forbidden—You don't have permission to access this resource." Her sister couldn't reach Wesley either. She said she thought he'd gone what she called "rarified"—when a person can only be reached through a private network of linked celebrities. What did it matter though, her sister said. Jane had already gotten her three hundred dollars' worth of Wesley. There was nothing more to say.

Jane liked to believe that Wesley was right. That it was not only pleasing to the universe that she'd ended up with Lenny but also that she'd saved him from that *Guess Who's Coming to Dinner* fate. She chose to believe that she'd been good for Lenny's health. That marrying a white person could raise your blood pressure, make you age before your time. And maybe that was true. When she and Lenny watched television and a Black comedian came on who was performing a particularly odious version of Blackness, Lenny could look at Jane and mutter, "Shuckin' and jiving." Or "Cooning it up."

Jane could say, shaking her head, "My people, my people."

Watching the news or a movie, they could glance at each other for a millisecond and understand everything that was wrong with this picture.

With Lilith, Lenny would have had to be righteous. With Lilith, he'd have been doomed to watch the footage of the march on Selma every MLK Day with tears in his eyes. With Lilith, he'd have to be angry or sad or downtrodden at all the right theatrical times.

With Jane, he could be silly and angry and quiet and loud and ironic and bitter or nothing at all. He didn't have to explain too much.

When she married Lenny, Jane had the feeling that they'd both extended their lives. It was a physical sensation, a slight loosening of some tension they'd each been holding for so long.

In the early days of their marriage, when the kids had finally gone down, Lenny and Jane would tiptoe out of their bedroom and meet in the kitchen in the evening to pour a celebratory glass of wine. They'd sit together drinking, discussing the details of their day, replaying the funny things the kids had done. They would revel in the particular satisfaction of parents who had survived another day of sublimating their basest, most selfish desires. The hours of educational videos and teachable moments were over. Finally, they could be their true selves. They would watch their favorite dirty pleasure: Trash. Black trash. Chitlin' Circuit stuff. What Lenny called "colored television." Tyler Perry, with his cartoonish poor-person-turned-rich-overnight version of success. All those marble floors and chandeliers and sweeping staircases. The button-nosed Black girl sitting at the end of a ghoulishly large dining-room table cutting beef with her cold, megalomaniac Buppie husband at the far end, a uniformed white butler carrying a silver gravy boat between them. It was always a recipe for murder. Insanity. Both.

Their favorite show to watch back then, after the babies were down, was a low-budget BET prank show called *Hell Date*, where the sadistic producers would set up some unwitting fool on a date with the perfect guy or the perfect girl. The perfect date was an actor, and it was all a setup to film the poor sap's reaction as the date went from good to horribly wrong. Sometimes the trigger was a juvenile prank, like an earthworm in the soup or a four-foot man dressed as Satan who emerged from under the table brandishing a chain saw. Other times it was crueler, like having a fake ex-wife show up at the bowling alley with a bazooka. Things always went too far on *Hell Date*, and in the final shots, there was usually real trauma on the dupe's face. Which was, Jane supposed, the point. People wanted to see real trauma on somebody's face. That's what they were paying for. That's what the producers were going through all this trouble to get a glimpse of—a moment of truth. The pranks on *Hell Date* were about as funny as the pig-guts scene in *Carrie*, but Jane could never turn her eyes away. And at the end of a day of parenting, what she and Lenny sat down to watch had to feel like the opposite of a teachable moment.

Hell Date had been killed off after two seasons. Once the population of Southern California aspirational Buppies had all heard of it, the producers couldn't find a target to trick anymore. It wasn't funny to watch some grinning guy in a restaurant searching for hidden cameras over his pretend date's head.

The family she made with Lenny was, of course, not the same as the family in the Hanna Andersson catalog. The real Lenny was ten pounds heavier than the model in the catalog. The real Lenny ordered his khakis in bulk from a camping website and liked to sleep naked. The real Lenny was a man who would never agree to wear matching striped Swedish pajamas. He hadn't even agreed to wear a red nose for Red Nose Day at Ruby's preschool—a charity event to end child poverty once and for all. All the dads were supposed to wear red clown noses. Lenny refused, saying, stone-faced, that as a Black man he would be sending the wrong message to the world.

And maybe he was on to something, because a few weeks later, Jane saw a billboard for Red Nose Day on La Cienega, and in the collage of movie star faces, only the two Black male actors were not wearing the clown noses but rather just holding them up, laughing, while all the white actors donned them.

3.

The campus was more active at night than Jane had expected. Clusters of students smoked and shrieked and whispered and huddled together in the darkness. She kept her head down as she walked from Lot C toward Chester Hall. She tried not to make eye contact with anyone in case she happened to run into a former student—someone she maybe still owed feedback on a story. She was already breaking a promise she'd made to herself when she left campus in the spring, that she would not step foot back there until she was done with the novel and had a publishing contract in hand. And most certainly she was not supposed to return until her sabbatical was over.

But she'd been seized by a burning need to find an article she knew she'd left in her office. It was an arcane report by a white sociologist from the 1950s, about the quixotic figure of the mulatto in history: "The Other Man." She'd attempted tracking it down online, but it was only available behind a paywall. She knew she had a photocopy somewhere in her office because she'd used it for a class she taught years ago. Now she felt certain it would play an essential role in her novel. Over the past few months, she'd gotten into making the novel multitextual—a collage. It was going to include actual historical documents and sociology texts that would reveal all the peculiar ways the figure of the mulatto had been treated in American consciousness throughout the ages. Even as the manuscript passed the four-hundred-page mark, she had been seized with a panic that she was leaving things out. She had the feeling that the book was her last word on something and she had to get it right. There would be no second chances.

She reached Chester Hall and pressed her identification card to the electronic keypad. The door clicked open and she pushed inside. A smell hit her—of young people, student minds, all those lithe, hopeful bodies who had come to her over the years seeking wisdom. All the youth she'd shepherded through that tender time in their lives, helping them find their voices, as if voices were lost objects hiding in the dark.

One of the strange parts of being a teacher was how it made time seem to stand still. If you didn't look in the mirror, you could almost trick yourself into thinking that time wasn't passing because your students kept staying the same young age year after year. You could fail to notice that you, nevertheless, were getting older.

One of the worst parts of teaching was how, like a series of mini strokes, it ruined you as a writer. A brain could handle only so many undergraduate stories about date rape and eating disorders, dead grandmothers and mystical dogs. A brain could take only so much purple prose and mechanical epiphany.

Professor Mischling had left a greeting card in her mailbox just before she went on sabbatical. On the front were side-by-side images from an old antidrug ad campaign. On the left, a hand holding an intact egg beneath the words THIS IS YOUR BRAIN. On the right, that same egg splattered in a frying pan beneath the words THIS IS YOUR BRAIN ON TEACHING.

Mischling had been right. Jane's sabbatical had made her see how much teaching had taken away from her work. Every idea she had imparted to her students about writing and craft had actually been drawn from a well inside her that was not replenishing itself. If she did this job long enough, one day she might look into the bag of ideas and find that everything—all those shiny silver objects—was gone or grossly deformed.

When she was carrying Finn, her obstetrician had dubbed it a "geriatric pregnancy." He'd explained to her that when a human female is born, she has as many eggs in her ovaries as she will ever have. But the eggs, he said, aged with you, and the ones you were left with by middle age were more prone to cellular abnormalities.

Now she wondered if maybe writing—language itself—was like the eggs she carried. Maybe the novel she was writing in the middle of her life was running the same risk. Maybe it too was a high-risk pregnancy.

She got off the elevator and headed down the carpeted hall to her office. Hers had a wooden plaque outside the door that said MAKE IT WORSE. It had been a gift from a student she'd taught years ago, a lovely kid named Rick who had been in several of her workshops. After he graduated, he kept in touch, and a few years ago, he'd sent her a note telling her he'd gotten a job as a television writer. Then one day he'd shown up in Jane's office to surprise her with this plaque. He told her it was in her workshop that he'd discovered he wanted to be a writer. With Jane, he'd found his voice. He said Jane's response to his first story was the single most important piece of advice he'd ever gotten about writing. *Make it worse*, Jane had apparently scrawled on the top of the first page. It made him realize that he'd been trying to protect his gay teenage protagonist from harm by having the kid's parents accept him so warmly when he came out. He'd made the guidance counselor only mildly creepy, giving off flirtatious vibes toward the kid but not actually doing anything. By policing his characters, he had failed a writer's first obligation to himself: to practice brave storytelling. The summer after he graduated, he'd gone back to the story with Jane's three magic words in mind and wrote a new version. His own liberal Santa Monica therapist parents were replaced by Orange County Christians. He made the guidance counselor a pastor instead, who no longer simply leered at the boy but groomed him. He forced the story to a new, uncomfortable place, in which his protagonist had to grapple with real, lived danger. The story turned out to be his ticket to getting a job in the writer's room of *Scandal*. He said Jane's words had guided him through three seasons on that hit show, and he'd come back with the plaque to thank her.

Jane had been touched by Rick's visit, of course, but also dismayed, the way she always was when she saw her students growing older, moving on to new adventures while she sat there growing older against the same backdrop. He'd asked after her novel, the one she'd told the class about when he'd been her student, and she was reminded that it was the same unfinished, untitled second novel she was still talking about to her classes.

At the time of Rick's visit, the novel had still been in its Sisyphus stage, a rock she'd labored at for so long that just kept rolling back down the hill. But now everything was different. Somehow in this sabbatical year, with this move to the magic house in the hills, through the strange alchemy of writing, that amorphous pile of paper had suddenly gelled into an almost realized thing, a creature with its own logic, its own rhythm, its own pulse.

She stepped inside the office. It had the still, dusty feeling of something embalmed. Everything was exactly where she'd left it last spring. The coffee mug featuring Sigmund Freud's face. The notepad in the middle of the desk with the beginning of a bucket list she hadn't finished. On the shelves, the stalwart anthologies of all those slightly banal stories she found so easy to teach. Genius, she'd learned, didn't teach as well as mere competence, where the mechanics were all visible on the surface. You couldn't teach a student how to write by assigning Toni Morrison, it would only create bad imitations. Next to the anthologies were the craft books, those reassuringly didactic writing guides she would drag out for an exercise or two to help fill the workshop time.

Jane had been teaching both graduate students and undergraduates for years. She preferred the lazy Gen Z undergraduates to the petulant and accusatory Millennial graduate students. Both groups were triggered easily and often by things she could not predict, such as the time she'd assigned a story that used the second person—that gimmicky "you" point of view. She thought the students would love it because it was so minimalist, but they said they felt oppressed by the second person. They had not been asked for their consent to be the protagonist of the story.

The Millennials' threats, Jane had learned, were to be taken seriously, whereas the Gen Zers you could ignore, ride it out. They were sleepier, more half-hearted in their outrage. Last year, when a white professor had stood in front of his class giving a lecture on the history of stand-up comedy and, trying to quote Richard Pryor, used the N-word in its full, uncut glory, three undergraduates had stormed out of the classroom and walked directly to the administration building to report him. It had seemed the professor was doomed in the moment, but the aggrieved trio apparently became overwhelmed by the paperwork required to file an official complaint, and after a few days, they settled for creating an Instagram page where they detailed their slights in blurb-size anonymous posts.

The Millennials didn't read anything Jane assigned unless she included a trigger warning. The trigger warning was what spurred them on to search the story for the upsetting passage. The Gen Zers, on the other hand, only bothered to read stories that used a lot of white space. They didn't like big, sprawling, old-fashioned novels. Their brains had not evolved for that kind of reading experience. She was reminded of how, when her own kids were toddlers, she'd had to cut their food into small pieces to guard against their choking. She had in recent years begun to assign only minimalist autofiction by queer POC authors to her undergraduates, and she had to admit it was a better classroom experience for all.

Teaching had made Jane think a lot about her own Gen X–ness. She'd decided it was the only indisputable identity she had. She checked all the boxes. She'd been a latchkey kid who had moved between the homes of her divorced parents. She'd had the de rigueur Gen X molestation at age ten and later lost her virginity in semiconsensual sex with a much older man. Like any Black Gen Xer, she hadn't had time to worry about microaggressions, what with all the good old-fashioned macroaggressions she'd experienced: white kids throwing rocks at her head, white kids calling her father "nigger" with impunity, white kids leaving bananas on her family's porch when they moved into the neighborhood.

Of course, what made her most Gen X of all was that she was part of the first baby boom of mulattos, whose parents were of the first generation of legalized interracial marriages. Jane felt she'd been lucky to be raised in the early days of mulatto militancy before you could check two or more racial boxes on school forms. She'd been raised knowing—in the immortal words of Tupac—that Black was the thing to be. She refused to use the cloying phrase that some of her cohort had adopted, the Loving Generation. Her parents had always, as far as she knew, despised each other, so she was more a part of the Hating Generation. But in either case, she was deeply, authentically Gen X.

Like most people, Jane considered her generation superior to those that came after. But sometimes, driving away from the college, she would remember herself at her students' age and think that she had not been so unlike them. Because her bratty students were, she knew, almost always right. And the point of young people was to be annoying about the truth they saw until it became evident to people like herself. Every generation must leave an impression. And it had to keep pressing into the group ahead of it until the impression was made permanent. Then a fresh generation would be born and look around, bewildered, at their elders and assert some newfangled idea that years from now would make perfect sense. Her job, she knew, was mainly to pretend to be in charge of her students while she capitulated to their demands. Still, it was exhausting.

There it was. In her desk drawer, the photocopy of the essay she'd been looking for—"The Other Man" by Hiram Cavendish—with her angry notes scribbled in purple ink in the margins. She shoved it in her bag and started out of her office, but the sound of voices stopped her in the doorway. A door down the hall was wide open, and light and voices were floating out. Who else could be here at this hour? Slowly, with dread, Jane made her way in the direction of the voices, wishing there was another way out. She needed to get to the elevator, but she didn't want to witness an indiscretion. The image of any of her colleagues having sex with each another made her want to gag, and the thought of any of them trying to seduce a student was not only disgusting but also would force her to become involved in some kind of disciplinary process just when she was so close to finishing her novel.

But as she neared the open door, she realized, with some relief, that the voices were coming from a radio inside Kay Franken's office. It was *Wait Wait . . . Don't Tell Me!* and Peter Sagal was in the middle of giving a clue, a limerick. *"When breath is too stinky, it's tough to get kinky. Still, doc says have sex and eat . . . "*

"Garlic."

It was Kay's voice.

Jane groaned, inwardly, silently. She didn't want to see Kay, of all people. Kay was such a bore. She pulled her hood over her head and began to walk swiftly, head down, past the door, hoping Kay would not spot her. But as she walked by, she glanced into Kay's office, then slowed her pace and stopped, confused. It was Kay, yes, but she was wearing the strangest costume. No, not a costume. She was wearing pajamas. Pink flannel pajamas. She stood with her back to the door, flossing her teeth as she looked out the window. Jane's eyes took in the rest of the evidence. The couch in Kay's office had been turned into a bed, with sheets and pillows and blankets. On the small coffee table were stacks of what looked like student papers. A skirt and blouse—and a bra— were slung over the desk chair. Kay turned her head to reach a back molar, and as she did so, she glimpsed Jane's reflection in the window behind her. She whipped around, her face reddening with embarrassment.

"Jane," she cried out. "I can explain."

Later, Jane would not be able to say why she took off like that. It was a childish instinct, to run, as if she were the one who had been caught in a compromising situation. She could hear Kay calling out behind her, "Jane! Jane?" But she kept going, past the elevators to the heavy stairwell door. She pushed through it and galloped down the four flights, not stopping even when she was outside. She ran past the huddles of vaping students, kept running even as she approached Lot C and could see her car in the distance, even as she fumbled for her key fob and pressed the button to unlock, unlock. She didn't stop until she was in the driver's seat, where she sat, catching her breath, for a long time before she started the engine.

Five years ago, Kay Franken had been just like Jane. She'd gone on leave, having been told she had to finish a book and get a contract to publish it or she would be demoted to teaching faculty when she returned. She had not finished the book.

Kay later confessed that she'd ended up using the time to get surgery on her bunions. She had decided to get both feet done at once and had spent the whole sabbatical in bed, which seemed in theory like a good place to finish a book. But books, it turned out, required the normal rhythms of life. They required walks and friends in the evening and quick snacks from the kitchen. Without that, Kay said, the loneliness and despair and boredom had been their own distraction.

After she returned, Kay showed off her feet to anybody who would look. Once, she cornered Jane in the ladies' room and made her look at them, and Jane made the appropriate comments about how straight they looked and how small the scars were. It was as if Kay needed to brag about her feet to excuse what she hadn't accomplished. Unfortunately, the dean and the department chair didn't care about Kay's feet. Her demotion was immediate. On the website, the secretary changed her title from "research" to "teaching faculty"—and her load changed with it. Instead of two classes, she was expected to teach four each semester, half of them freshman composition. She was placed on every committee possible and burdened with a staggering amount of what was called "service."

WHEN JANE GOT back to the house, she went straight to Brett's office and sat down to read the journal article she'd retrieved from her office. The author seemed to have accomplished very little else in his life beyond this exhaustive study of mulattos, which he'd apparently had plans to turn into a book but never completed. In the article, Cavendish argued that the mulatto in America would always remain poised between worlds, in psychological uncertainty—"an other even amongst others." The mulatto psyche, he said, would always reflect the discords and harmonies, the repulsions and attractions, of the disparate worlds he inhabited. Mulatto problems were, of course, not so unlike those faced by other marginal men—the Chinaman, as Cavendish put it, the Jew, even the wily Negro himself, with his Du Boisian double consciousness. But according to old Cavendish, the mulatto in America outdid all these groups in marginality. His double consciousness was not just a clever literary metaphor. It was literal.

Now Jane understood why she'd gone looking for this article. Cavendish was the character the novel had been missing. He could bring to the story the distanced, anthropological voice it needed—he was the one who would see the mulatto from the outside, coldly, as a scientist studies a specimen.

COLORED TELEVISION

Exhilarated, Jane spread her manuscript out on the floor like a carpet. She crept into the house to retrieve Finn's left-handed scissors and a glue stick from the living-room floor. She went back and cut up the article into its constituent ridiculous passages and found just the right places to paste pieces of it into the margins of the manuscript. Cavendish's voice would enter at key moments of hope to explain to the reader how and why the mulatto in America was doomed. His white gaze, his white imagination, disembodied, would act as a kind of relentlessly haunting specter. The physicality of cutting and gluing felt energizing after so many hours—months, years—in front of the computer screen. The hours flew.

"The mulatto in America never grows old," Cavendish declared at one point. "Like a debutante, the mulatto stands perched at the top of a marble staircase waiting to walk down, to announce his entrance into fashionable society. But somehow, he never gets past the third step. He remains perched there at the top, ready for an introduction that never happens.

"The mulatto," he went on, "will always be the first mulatto who ever lived. For you see, my dear reader, the mulatto in America is permanently on the cusp of discovery but never really found. He forever remains an unknowable creature, indescribable, doubtful, mysterious, and unclean." Jane understood that night, perhaps for the first time in all these years, that the book she was writing was larger than herself. She could see that it had needed to be this epic, this grand, this sweeping. She was attempting the impossible—to write a history for a people without a race. Without a race, one could not have a history—and without a history, one could not have a race. That night, crawling around Brett's floor weaving excerpts from Cavendish's essay into the margins of her essay, she felt fueled by an almost missionary zeal. She'd had to do this. She'd had to ruin her life for this project. It had been necessary and it would be worth it.

The sky was just beginning to turn light when Jane headed to bed. Lenny had fallen asleep with a new book open on his chest. *Hitler's Black Victims.* "There you are," he said groggily, as Jane climbed in beside him. "Were you on campus this whole time?"

"I got back hours ago," she said. "I was working in Brett's office."

On the way home, she'd imagined telling Lenny about Kay. They would laugh about it together, and laughing about it would assuage the terror she had felt at the sight of her colleague, living in her office, like a rodent. But now it seemed like it would take too much energy to explain, more than she could spare from the burning fever she felt for her book, this new dimension she had brought to it. It was all making perfect sense.

"Lenny, I think I'm almost there," she said, laying her head on his chest. "I can see the end in sight."

And Lenny stroked her hair and mumbled as he drifted off, "Keep this mulatto girl writing."

4.

Jane hadn't expected to finish her book so soon. But once she'd written the words *Years from now, that will be us*, she knew. She'd reached the end. It was March. She did the math. It had been nine years and six months since she'd started the thing. She had been young when it began and now she wasn't. She sat at Brett's desk, listening to the coyote pups yelping in the canyons, tears streaming down her cheeks. The actress was dead, washed out to sea, but Jane had looped back in the final paragraphs to something more hopeful—a scene from a hundred and fifty years earlier, on that mountaintop in post-Reconstruction Tennessee, all those free people of color, those Melungeons, cavorting, playing their banjos, and dancing beneath the pinkening sky in their newly formed triracial isolationist community. It was a scene of jubilation but also of dread, for the free people of color did not know what the reader knew, all that lay ahead.

Was this in fact the right ending? Should the actress—the great-great-great-granddaughter of that first Melungeon—really drown herself off the coast of Malibu? Or should Jane find a way to save her? Jane caught herself doing that thing where she second-guessed herself. She had to stop. She wiped away her tears. She needed to send the book out before she started to fuss with it again. The actress would die.

The novel was called *Nusu Nusu*. In Swahili, the phrase meant "partly-partly." Jane had learned it years before at a dinner party where she'd sat beside the son of a Kenyan diplomat. He'd explained to her that in his land it was the term for people who were mixed race, like Jane. She'd liked the redundancy, the slightly taunting repetition of the phrase.

She closed the file, which she was surprised to see had swelled to more than 150,000 words. She spent the next twenty minutes trying to draft an email to her agent to go along with it. Honor would be pleasantly surprised to get it—maybe even shocked. She'd known in theory that Jane was working on a second novel because Jane had mentioned it whenever they spoke and because Jane had published two excerpts from it over the years—a short chapter about the actress's early days in Hollywood in *Ploughshares* six years ago and, a year or so later, in another journal, a twenty-page story pulled from the chapter about Thomas Jefferson in Paris. She'd sent Honor links to each of the excerpts as they'd come out, explaining that they were part of the historical epic she was writing, reminding her she was still alive, still writing. And Honor had sent back vaguely encouraging words of praise. But that was years ago, and Honor must have doubted that an actual book would ever emerge. She probably thought Jane had floated off into the ether of middle-aged, middle-race, midlist women writers who used to have interesting things to say but now just drifted around their California gardens tending to succulents.

Yes, she would be pleasantly surprised to learn that old Jane Gibson had finally squeezed out a second novel—a real doorstop. Even, as Jane had fantasized in the heat of writing, an award winner.

"Dear Honor," she began. "I'm so sorry this has taken so long, but here, at long last, it is. As you'll see, it is a big novel—a major one, if I dare say so. It goes off on a lot of tangents, and there's a lot to keep track of in here, but I hope you will find that the chaos pays off . . ."

She stopped. She wasn't sorry for what she'd done here. She wasn't ashamed of having taken so long. Novelists took whatever time they needed to make immortal art. If you wanted something to last forever, sometimes you had to take forever.

She started again, trying to channel some of Lenny's firstborn-male arrogance. At last, she wrote simply, "Attached please find my second novel. Enjoy."

She attached the file and hit send. It was just after midnight. Then she went into the house and found Lenny asleep on the couch in the living room. His headphones had slipped off and she could hear the Berlitz Japanese teacher whispering into the quiet. Jane felt a surge of tenderness—a surge of possibility. One thing she'd realized over the years was that good things beget more good things. The converse was also true. It was why the rich got richer and the poor got poorer. One setback was never one setback. And one accomplishment usually led to more. She had finished something monumental. The tide was turning for her—for *them*. Lenny had always seen them as a pair of artists, which was the most feminist thing about him. He found her sexier the closer she came to reaching her full potential. He wanted them both to soar.

She went into the bedroom and changed into a muumuu of Piper's. It was not a real Hawaiian muumuu. It was something fancier, whiter, of the airiest and most elegant of cottons, an allusion to an ethnic garment, something that cost a lot of bucks to make you look like you didn't care. Piper had probably picked it up in a boutique in Silver Lake or Los Feliz.

She was surprised to find the wine cooler empty. She went to the wine pantry and stared at the wall of bottles in the dim light. She reached for one at random. Back in the brightness of the kitchen, she saw that it was a dust-covered Barolo, a 2006 Giacomo Conterno Monfortino. She hesitated for a moment, then opened it and poured two glasses. She carried them into the living room and nudged Lenny awake.

"I'm finished."

He sat up, blinking. "What?"

"The book. I sent it off to Honor. Just about ten minutes ago."

A slow smile crept across Lenny's face. It struck her that he had not believed she would ever finish. He'd thought her novel was this permanent albatross on their lives, a project they'd be dragging around forever, like a slacker son who never leaves your couch.

"Sweetie," he said, a term he hadn't used in what felt like years. "Congratulations—this is huge."

"Listen," she said. "Don't call me cheesy, but I want to say something. I'm so grateful to you and the kids for sticking by me through it. The first thing I thought when I pressed send was that I wanted to come look at you all. I've missed you. I've missed real life."

Lenny took her hand and kissed it. "All I've ever wanted was for you to do your art, babe. And you have. I'm proud of you."

He sat back and sipped his wine, staring at the fireplace.

"So what happens next?" he said. "Remind me how you book people do it."

She explained to him how she thought it would go. Honor would be surprised, so surprised by what Jane had pulled off—and she'd be amazed by the scope and ambition of her project. After reading it, she'd send it to Jane's old editor, Josiah, who would read it and be amazed and surprised too. He'd make his offer. Assuming he offered enough money—Josiah had not paid much for her first novel, but it had not been anywhere near as ambitious as this one—Jane would stay with him. He hadn't been a perfect editor, but she felt he'd been good enough, loyal and respectable, a respectable man at a respectable house: the devil she knew. Plus, Honor had told her once that it was best to keep her books under one roof. She imagined staying with Josiah would allow him to reissue her first book, its importance all the clearer in relation to this one.

And once she had a deal, Jane could go back to Mischling with proof that she was a writer who could fulfill her promise. And she'd get tenure. Which wasn't wealth but was something possibly better, a kind of stability she'd never had before.

"This Barolo is exquisite," Lenny said. "Brett really knows his way around a wine store." He looked at her. "You don't think he's going to make us replace all the bottles we drank, do you?"

"Come on. Brett's like a brother. He won't care." She leaned her head back, sighed. "Do you think our luck is changing?"

"I don't believe in luck. I believe in resilience. As an artist, you have to be resilient above all else." He lifted his glass. "Here's to your sticking with it."

Jane went to stand in front of the window. The garden glowed like a scene in a fairy tale, thanks to the automatic lights Piper had installed. They turned on every evening when the sun went down, little solar-powered jewels hidden in the flora, casting her reflection back to her. She wondered what a younger version of herself, Brooklyn Jane, would think if she could see them now—if she were transported here by some kind of Ghost of Christmas Future. What would she make of this scene? What did they seem like, from the outside looking in?

Brooklyn Jane would be happy to see this future house. She wouldn't have to know that it and almost everything in it belonged to someone else. She would be happy to see Lenny, rugged but still handsome. From a distance, in his horn-rimmed glasses, reading his serious book, he would look like an inspired choice. And alongside him, in Piper's muumuu, Jane would look like she was headed toward a Black bohemian version of the American dream, like she was going to be a rich hippie someday. Because who didn't want to be a rich hippie? Who didn't want to be what the French called gauche caviar? Brooklyn Jane would glimpse the children's toys lying in the courtyard, the ones Ruby and Finn had been playing with outside earlier—Max's wooden, toxin-free toys—and she would be delighted to know there were children living here in her future. She would know just from looking that she was going to give birth someday, that she was going to have a *dwell*-magazine house in the hills and an interesting husband with paint stains on his pants. She was going to spend evenings lounging barefoot in a muumuu talking to her husband about her accomplishments and career goals. She was going to triumph with her second book, a manspreading major American novel. She was going to become the voice of her people.

Jane could almost see Brooklyn Jane standing out there in the garden in her parka and her combat boots, her rain-tangled hair. She would know she was going to make it to this promised land, the sunshiny present.

Jane turned to Lenny, fixing her face in a coy smile. "Should we have book-completion sex or something?"

Lenny laughed. "If you want."

"If I want? What about you?"

He shrugged. "I mean, sure. Yes, let's."

She went over to him. Yanking up the muumuu, she straddled him like a femme fatale in a thriller and started kissing him. At first it felt strange. It was as if she'd changed or he'd changed, as if they were actors playing a couple in a movie and all this had been choreographed by an on-set intimacy coordinator and she was wearing nipple covers and a merkin. Maybe it was just that it had been so long since they'd made out before having sex. But then she felt it. The old ghost of desire. Kissing was the real intimacy. They stood and stumbled, mouths linked, into the bedroom. She fell back on Brett's bed. Lenny fell on top of her and began to pull off the muumuu. She closed her eyes and tried to imagine they were the couple in the Hanna Andersson catalog, the ones in the striped pajamas. Only they were naked now. And he was going down on her.

The sex that followed was long and complicated, with actual Kama Sutra positions, lesbian highlights. They hadn't done it like that in a while.

COLORED TELEVISION

And as they did, she imagined Brooklyn Jane outside in the garden, her face pressed against the glass, watching. Jane wanted her to believe that this was their real life. Permanent. Unimpeachable. She wanted to show her a vision that she could take back to Brooklyn, as if it were a magic pebble. A vision so good, it would get her through the interminable winters. Through all those bad dates and lonesome weekends and middling sales and strange men ogling her on the subway. Jane wanted to give her a glimpse of another world—a premonition that could keep her away from the platform edge, which, sometimes, in February—the Blackest month, the shortest month—beckoned her to step closer.

5.

Jane carried the sheet cake out into the garden as the eight girls and their mothers sang "Happy Birthday" to Ruby. The party had been Jane's idea. She'd conspired with Ruby's teacher to invite a selection of Ruby's new classmates over this Saturday afternoon in late March. Why not take advantage of the house while they still had it? Lenny had agreed even though he hated kids' parties, all those mothers standing around in intimacy bubbles.

Ruby hadn't had a real birthday party in years. They had always been on the verge of moving out or had just moved in, the apartments they were moving out of or into too small and grimly lit for entertaining anyway. And Jane had always been too stressed about teaching and her unfinished book to entertain children. The last party she could remember throwing for Ruby had been at a janky indoor ball pit that smelled of dirty diapers.

She watched Ruby sitting at the head of the table surrounded by girls her age.

The book Jane had read about orchid children—kids like Finn—had also talked about dandelion children. Ruby was one of those. Unlike orchids, dandelions were adaptable, resilient. They could take what life threw at them and still grow straight and tall. Ruby had attended four schools in four years and never complained. She was still a girl who believed in Jane and Lenny. She was still that child who could sit for hours making secret worlds out of stuffed animals. She could still throw her body across their laps like a cat and climb up her daddy's shoulders. She still sometimes crawled into bed with them at night to cuddle when she'd had a nightmare. But she was growing up into this beautiful, resilient girl, steady and strong.

The mothers were the demographic that peppered this mountaintop—formerly hot moms, formerly hip moms, formerly ambitious moms—white women now over forty, slightly diminished but still wanting more. Rapacious white women. They had moved on to their next chapters, their second careers—jobs Jane had not known were jobs. Already today she'd been introduced to a kitchen healer, a jewelry maker, and a sweet, mousy woman who called herself an abortion doula. These were women who had not made enough money to send their kids to private school but who made just enough to live in this neighborhood with the blue-ribbon public school.

She watched them ogling Brett's house now, flickers of envy and awe crossing their faces. They were an aesthetically sophisticated lot who appreciated this house and its ironic twist. "What a cool trick!" one of them had exclaimed as they came out into the courtyard and took in the garden and the floor-to-ceiling glass. Suddenly they were interested in Jane, the standoffish new mother they hadn't paid much attention to before. She could feel them trying to suss her out, suss Lenny out, suss Finn and Ruby out. What had appeared to them as a regular public-school family had transformed into something glittery, deracinated. This house made them seem like lucky, special Negroes.

Jane was wearing a low-cut yellow silk blouse of Piper's that she'd found in the closet. She'd already received several compliments on it, to which she'd smiled coolly and said she couldn't remember where she got it, she'd had it so long. Someone said they loved her couch. Where was it from? DWR, she said with a shrug, because she didn't know another place to name. Was DWR too down-market for this crowd? Apparently it wasn't, because they nodded, convinced. She did not bother to correct their assumption that all of this was hers. Because what did it matter? She and Lenny and the kids would be gone soon. They might as well leave a good impression.

Jane set the cake down on the table in front of Ruby just as the birthday song reached its warbling crescendo. It was a cheap cake from Baskin-Robbins, *Frozen*-themed. She worried it was a tell that this house, even this shirt, didn't belong to her. But maybe it was the opposite—maybe it made them seem more ensconced in this life, better, cooler—the kind of people who would buy a *Frozen* cake from Baskin-Robbins with an ironic shrug. The kind of people who were so rich and busy that they did not need to prove their worth with a high-end cake. After all, shitty sheet cakes from Baskin-Robbins were what kids liked to eat, even rich kids.

Ruby leaned over the eight flickering candles, her eyes closed, her lips moving in a silent wish. Jane wished too that this day would fulfill her little girl's dreams. She'd gone all out to make it so, splurging on a gift for which Ruby had been pining for years. In the past, Lenny had refused to let Jane buy it for her, not only because they couldn't afford it but also on the grounds that the doll was just another late-capitalist, faux-feminist trap.

It was an American Girl doll.

Both of Lenny's points still held, at least for now. But there had been such a lightness in the household as soon as the book was out the door. Jane could not believe how much air it had sucked out of her life, out of all their lives for all these years. Now they sat and watched trashy movies together like old times, making snide comments and passing a bowl of popcorn.

Honor had responded by return email the morning after Jane had sent her the manuscript just to say she'd received it and was thrilled to dig in, thrilled to have new pages from Jane at last. Then she had called only a week later, to say she'd read it with great interest and enthusiasm. That was the phrase she'd used—"great interest and enthusiasm."

"It's really wonderful, Jane," she'd continued. "Fascinating stuff! I think Josiah is going to be thrilled."

Jane had been surprised and impressed, then a little suspicious. Had Honor really read such a big complex book so fast? When she pressed for specifics about what exactly she liked about the book, Honor would only say, "I like the whole damn thing." Did the part about Thomas Jefferson—his mathematical calculation about what constituted a mulatto—go on too long? Jane asked. Should she leave it in or shorten it? Honor said they could leave it to Josiah to advise about that. In fact, Honor had already sent it on to him, so the option clock was ticking.

Jane couldn't believe how fast everything was moving. It was in the adrenaline rush of imagining the novel being read by actual eyes outside her own—by Josiah, who would, she was certain of it, be thrilled, *thrilled*!—that she had gone off to the Grove to buy Ruby's big gift.

She was so overwhelmed that she'd gotten lost in the American Girl store for more than an hour. She'd looked at all the dolls but only really seriously considered the Black options. There was one called Melody Ellison, a singer from the sixties, but she appeared to have straightened hair, and they were trying to heal Ruby's hair issues. She'd hoped to see one named Cécile Rey, who was from 1850s New Orleans. Jane had read about her on an American Girl fanpage. According to the site, Cécile was from a well-to-do family—they were free people of color. The doll's character was described as "quite mischievous" and "bold" and "good at keeping secrets." But when Jane got to the store, the salespeople informed her that the doll had been retired. Jane had somehow missed that on the website. The only other one they had in the store was Addy Walker. She had the same skin color as Ruby, a medium brown, though other than that, they didn't look alike. Addy had the same deracinated features as every other American Girl doll—the same plucky expression and slightly bucked teeth. She came with a book called *A Heart Full of Hope* that Jane had read inside the store, feeling oddly moved by the story. It told how Addy Walker had been born into slavery in the 1800s, how she and her mother had taken a chance and escaped to freedom in the North. Addy wasn't a slave anymore, the book said, but it was important for girls to remember she'd once been one.

A saleslady with dead doll eyes herself talked Jane into buying not only Addy Walker, but also a matching white pinafore for Ruby, identical to the one the doll was wearing. "Your daughter is going to love Addy so much she's going to want to dress like her!"

Lenny snorted when she told him what she'd done. "Here we go. Members of the sucker class." But he had not made her return it. Had not said it was too much. He too wanted to see their Ruby happy today, to see her getting something she really wanted for once.

Since she'd sent off the book—since the night they had drunk the Barolo and consummated their new chapter in Brett and Piper's big bed—she and Lenny had been different with each other. They joked again about all the things they used to joke about. They played Forensics. And just this morning they actually had morning sex. She didn't know how it had happened exactly. The sky was only just beginning to lighten, and one of them had rolled over and touched the other in just the right way before they'd fully emerged from their dreams. They'd made love just like old times, a sweet, somnolent love that built into a kind of fervor and coated the whole morning afterward in a kind of shimmer even during the grind of getting ready for the party.

Ruby blew out the candles on the first try, which Jane thought was good luck, a good sign about everything. Lenny moved forward then with a kitchen knife, and all the mothers laughed, exchanging uneasy glances, as he sliced right through the middle of Elsa's face. Jane searched the yard for Finn. She glimpsed him squatting in a corner by the door.

She had hoped he might play with the younger siblings who had come—that he might *engage*, as the doctor said—but he was more interested in what lay beneath the rock he was upending. Was his refusal to engage a symptom of the problem, as the doctor had implied, or a sign of genius, as Lenny claimed? Jane made the decision not to worry about it today. For now, everything was different.

RUBY HAD MOVED on to opening presents. All around her were piles of wrapping paper. Her classmates sat primly, watching her open her spoils, perhaps remembering fondly their own birthday parties of yore or imagining their birthday parties yet to come. Ruby was opening Jane and Lenny's gift now, an excited look on her face as she tore into the wrapping paper. Jane stepped forward to watch her reaction. The thing had cost, with the matching dress, close to one hundred and fifty dollars.

Ruby had gotten past the first layer of wrapping, and some of the other girls squealed with delight as the words AMERICAN GIRL came into view.

"Oh my God, which one did you get?" one said.

"I have five," another said.

Ruby lifted the lid. Addy Walker, child of hope. Child of resilience. The other girls cooed. But was it Jane's imagination or did Ruby's smile falter slightly—flicker—at the sight of the doll?

"I have Addy too," said a girl.

"Me too," said another.

"We can have an Addy party!" said a third.

Lenny snickered into Jane's ear. "Three Addies. Sounds like a horror movie." Then he called to Ruby, "Aren't you going to say thank you to your mom? This was her idea."

Ruby looked up at Jane, dull-eyed, as if she'd forgotten who she was for a moment. "Thank you, Mama," she said in a mechanical voice. Then she pushed Addy aside and began to rip open the other presents Jane had wrapped, the ones that were supposed to go with the doll—the book about Addy's life and the matching pinafore.

Again, that look. That stiffening in her smile.

Someone touched Jane's arm. Another mother. "There's a guy here. He says he's the magician."

The magician. She'd almost forgotten she'd hired a magician. Another thing they could not afford. He'd gotten good reviews on Yelp. There he was, a paunchy white man with an alcohol-swollen nose, setting up a folding table by the yucca tree. The girls went to gather into a circle around him, and Lenny began to pick up the wrapping paper that was scattered around the yard and put it in a trash bag. Finn was still off in the distance. He was pacing in circles, squeezing his hands, the way he did when his mind was fully someplace else.

Jane searched for Ruby in the circle of girls around the magician, but she didn't see her, and when she glanced into the house, she saw that her daughter was heading up the stairs alone. Jane followed and found her in her bedroom, face down on the mattress, crying softly.

Jane felt a slamming terror in her chest. This wasn't right. This wasn't how it was supposed to go. The shirt on her back wasn't hers. The house she was standing inside wasn't hers. Her child was crying on her own birthday and everything was wrong, wrong. The feeling Jane carried around always—that everything good was about to evaporate, that she was about to be exposed—came rushing back. It had never left her.

"What is it? Ruby, tell me."

Ruby lifted her tear-stained face. "The doll. I don't—I don't want her. And I feel badly I don't want her. You bought her for me, and I don't want her."

Jane wanted to cry herself. She wished, silently, that they'd kept to their original parenting plan—the no-media, no-white-princess-movies plan. But here they were.

"What don't you like about her?" Jane tried to keep her voice neutral, like a mother in an after-school special.

"I know what you're thinking," Ruby said into the pillow, her voice muffled. "But it's not because she's Black."

"Oh." Jane was mildly relieved. But she didn't believe Ruby. Of course it was because the doll was Black. "What is it then?"

Ruby began to cry all over again. "It's because . . ." She hesitated.

"You can tell me."

"Because she's the only American Girl doll I'll ever get. This was my chance, and that's the one you picked for me. And I'll never be able to afford any of the accessories for her. Or the clothes. The different outfits. She'll have to wear that nightgown forever. And I'll never be able to afford to buy another. I can't have Kaya or Samantha, who I really wanted. She's the only American Girl doll I'll ever be able to get, and you're not supposed to buy just one, Mama. The whole point is you collect them. All the different American Girls. But I won't be able to do it. I'll only have Addy. For the rest of my life."

Jane saw them, the floaters in her vision that came sometimes, unbidden, and could not be blinked away. Shadowy shapes the doctor had assured her were due to her retina shape, protein deposits, nothing serious.

"Maybe we can afford another outfit for her," she said.

Ruby began to cry even harder.

Jane tried again. "Listen, does she have to play with only other American Girl dolls? You have so many dolls! She could play with one of your Sasha dolls. They'd love to meet her."

The Sasha dolls were hand-me-downs that had been Jane's as a child, racially ambiguous dolls from Europe that her mother had found somehow somewhere. They were collector's items now. Ruby had taken to them and used to play with them for hours, loving even their imperfections—the places where they'd been broken and put back together with rubber bands by Jane's mother in her doll hospital, the permanent marker lines on their faces where Jane had tried to apply makeup. Ruby had found those war wounds magical, signs that her mother had once been a child. But she had stopped playing with them this past year, seeing their marks and scars as evidence of everything that was deficient in her life. Jane should have known better than to risk an American Girl doll.

"You don't understand, you don't understand anything," Ruby said accusingly, sounding suddenly like a tween, as if this birthday had somehow fast-forwarded their lives to a whole new level of complication Jane was not ready to face.

"Everything's about to change," she said, stroking her daughter's back. "I've finished the book and it's all about to change."

Jane did understand. She'd had her own childhood of moments just like this. She too had parents who were overeducated and underpaid—it was the worst combination. They had raised her and her sister in a ghetto of artists and poets, guaranteeing that they would be alienated from rich children and poor children alike, thanks to a cultural and political vocabulary that suggested class and privilege without actual class and privilege—gauche caviar without the actual caviar. Jane remembered wishing at a certain point, Ruby's age maybe, that she came from a dignified working-class immigrant family. Her kind of poverty was the loneliest kind, the least dignified kind, because her parents had chosen it. They had picked poetry over profit.

Now Ruby, this dandelion child, gathered herself. She pulled herself up. She fixed her hair and went to the window, through which came the sounds of the party, children squealing at something the magician had pulled out of a hat.

"Don't you want to go out and join your friends?" Jane asked from her spot on the bed.

"Those aren't my friends," Ruby said. "Those are just girls you invited. I don't know any of them."

6.

Los Angeles looked different to Jane. Now that the book was in Josiah's hands with Honor's blessing, the city looked less apocalyptic, more effervescent. Things were happening or about to happen. Everything was about to change.

She pointed at the intersection ahead. "Take a left up there."

"Why are we doing this again?" Lenny said. "You've seen our bank account, right?"

"Left, there. Yes, it's just a few blocks up and take a right on Oak."

"So we're just going to pretend we have money," he said. "Play make-believe, like some kind of folie à deux."

"I hate it when you speak French. It's pretentious."

"What's a foley-aw-doo?" Ruby, in the back seat.

"It's a shared madness," Lenny called back to her.

"Listen," Jane said. "Can you just indulge me for a minute? There's no harm in looking."

"That's what I'm doing," he said. "Indulging you."

The kids had been confused that morning when she told them they were going to look at a house.

"But we already have a house," Ruby had said, over breakfast.

"Yeah, why are we going?" Finn said. "We live somewhere already."

Jane had to remind them, not for the first time, that this house did not belong to them. It belonged to Brett. The pictures of people they saw on the walls, those weren't their family, those weren't their people. Those were Brett's family members.

She understood their confusion. Brett's relatives could plausibly be her own, if you squinted your eyes right. And anyway, the kids lived in the moment. Finn had been playing in Max's room for months, dressing in Max's clothes, tending to his wizened bearded dragon as if it were his own. Ruby was starting to adjust to the life they would soon be leaving. She had been growing closer to one of the girls who had attended her party, a little white girl named, curiously, Ever. Although her parents were failed actors, they had managed to get Ever an agent, and at eight she had already appeared in a GEICO commercial.

The reality was that they had only two months before they were homeless again. Two months before they had to go somewhere new and retrieve all their boxes of stained sheets and IKEA furnishings from storage.

As if to remind them, Brett had texted Jane the week before. He said he hoped they were all well and that they were excited about their next housing chapter. He wanted to give Jane a heads-up about some packages that would be coming their way, as he and Piper had begun to cull their life in Sydney. They should just stick the boxes in the garage. He couldn't wait to tell Jane about Australia.

Today they were going to an open house in the neighborhood Jane had nicknamed Multicultural Mayberry, the neighborhood where she'd always wanted them to live. The house was way out of their price range, given that their price range was zero. But who really knew what their price range might be soon? It couldn't hurt to look. If Josiah offered a lot of money and Lenny sold some paintings, on top of Jane's getting tenure and a raise, who knew? They might become members of the functioning middle class sooner than they thought.

Multicultural Mayberry was only about fifteen minutes from downtown Los Angeles, but it felt like a different world altogether. Gone was the *Mad Max Beyond Thunderdome* energy of downtown. Gone was the Manson Family Helter Skelter vibe of the hills. Gone was the suburban wasteland of Glendale and the trashy mini-mall sprawl of Mid-City. Gone was the relentless existential hum of the freeway, the racial blight of the LAPD, the handsome lying face of O. J. Simpson and the blank, bewildered face of his murdered wife, Nicole. Gone was the banally evil face of Mark Fuhrman and the nihilistic cokehead teens of *Less than Zero*. Gone were the Menéndez brothers and the white vigilante Michael Douglas played in *Falling Down*.

Movies over the years had depicted Los Angeles and its outskirts as a kind of dystopian futuristic hellscape—a clarion warning for the rest of the world about where we were all headed. But Multicultural Mayberry made it feel as if none of that existed. The most charming aspects of America's past had made love to its most hopeful Obamaesque future, creating this love child of a town.

The sunlight in Multicultural Mayberry was dappled because there were real trees here. Instead of chain stores and mini malls, its main street was home to businesses you didn't know still existed: A ye olde frame shop. A hundred-year-old soda shop. A barbershop with a candy-cane pole out front. There were only three schools in the district, all of them blue ribbon, and the middle-class residents all sent their children to these schools, so you saw kids walking around in clusters, going to visit their friends, who all lived here too. And yet, this fifties-era set piece was not some blizzard of white supremacy as you might expect. It was famously multicultural. Hence the nickname.

She could see why the filmmakers loved it here. And boy did they love it. Every time Jane came, she saw some street blocked by a craft food-service truck or a phalanx of film equipment. The films that had been shot here were too long a list to remember. She did know the town had been a stand-in for Philadelphia in *Thirtysomething*. And it was most famous for being Illinois in *Halloween*. Every Halloween, the town was filled with tourists walking around in Michael Myers costumes, past the actual house where young Michael had slashed his big sister to death.

And yet, for a town that was so perfectly perfect for a horror movie set in Illinois, there was something distinctly Los Angeles about it. LA could be such a chameleon. It could be anything you wanted it to be. And here it was every small American town or treelined suburban street you'd ever seen in a television show or movie.

Jane had done her research. Apparently, when you owned the right kind of house in Multicultural Mayberry you could make money renting it out for film and commercial shoots. The local government had its own film office. You could register your house on a website called HomeShoot-Home, where location scouts trawled the photos like porn. She'd trawled the website too. According to its FAQ page, homeowners stood to make the most money if their house had no palm trees visible from the street and no swimming pool visible from the backyard. Apparently, it was best to go easy on the stainless-steel appliances. You didn't want the home to look too obviously California. You didn't want to alienate the middle class in Middle America with your Wolf stove. You got the most requests if your decor was firmly Pottery Barn rather than Design Within Reach. You wanted your house and street to be able to pass as "Anywhere, USA."

Now, Jane actually felt her blood pressure dropping, her body humming, as they cruised down the street, searching for the turn.

"Why are we going to look at a new house again?" Ruby said from the back seat.

"Yeah, why are we looking?" Finn said. "We already have a house."

"I don't want to move again," Ruby said. "I like it on the mountain."

"I know, sweetie," Jane said. "But that house belongs to Brett. That's why we're here. We're trying to find our forever home."

"Who's Brett again?"

"My friend," she said. "The owner of our house."

Lenny sighed. He hadn't thought it wise to confuse the kids more by looking at an open house they could not afford. He thought they should spend the time looking for a rental in Burbank. He'd shown Jane a few he had found online. They were hideous. Jane argued that if they moved to a rental in Burbank they would only be yanking the kids up again in a few months when she sold her novel and got her promotion and raise. They would never want to settle down in Burbank.

So Lenny had agreed to come along, and he'd agreed to wear the yellow polo shirt she'd bought him last week.

"I feel like a fool," he said now, irritable behind the steering wheel. "This shirt."

"You look great," Jane said. And he did. They all looked perfect. "Dignified and articulate," she added.

Lenny snorted a laugh. "That's the most racist thing you've ever said to me."

"Okay. Eloquent and Du Boisian. Is that better?"

"Now you're scaring me." But he was smiling a little bit.

"Did you know that on the Finn planet," Finn said, "we speak our own language?"

"There's no such place as the Finn planet," Ruby muttered, rolling her eyes.

"It's called Satama. Kuka is the word for hello. Can you say kuka-jawani, Mama?"

"Kukajawani," Jane said. "Kukajawani."

"The longer We lives here, the less he remembers about the Finn planet," Finn said. "Soon it'll be all gone."

"Mom, will you tell him to stop talking about the Finn planet?"

The therapist at the clinic had explained to her and Finn that a conversation was like a tree. It grew in branches that flowed out from the trunk. Which meant you couldn't just enter a conversation talking about something random or you would break away from the tree.

"Remember," Jane said now, imitating the therapist's sanguine tone of voice. "A conversation is like a tree"—she looked up—"This is the street," she said. "The house should be right up ahead."

"Is that it?" Lenny said, nodding ahead to a cluster of neighbors standing on a lawn.

"No," Jane said, peering out. "That's just a lemonade stand."

"Ooh, can we get some?" Ruby said.

Lenny slowed down as they passed the lemonade stand, which was staffed by two little boys about Ruby's age. Both the boys were Black. Their mothers—at least the women Jane assumed to be their mothers—were also Black, one with a short natural, the other with long, straight hair. They were talking to a white hippie couple with a Labradoodle puppy. The hippie mother was a blonde beach babe type, and beside her was a handsome, shirtless dad wearing board shorts. Their towheaded child in a princess dress, short-haired, genderless, ran in circles waving a wand while the two families laughed together.

"Look, it's your new best friends," Lenny said, as they rolled past, reading her mind.

Across the street from the lemonade stand and the gathering of neighbors was the house they'd come to see. There was a realtor's sign out front. It looked even better to Jane than it had in the photos on the website. It was a rich shade of Craftsman brown, and the porch was a wraparound, with wicker furniture and lush potted plants. The agent was standing on the porch, adjusting pillows on a chair, when they walked up. Jane thought he looked pleased by the sight of them. Maybe because Lenny was a Black man wearing a yellow polo shirt. Jane had noticed over the years that everybody loved a Black man in a yellow polo. She watched the agent take in Finn, whom she had dressed in Max's slacks and red T-shirt and Converse sneakers. She'd found a new product for his hair that held the curls in place, so Black women wouldn't give her the side-eye at the park anymore. Jane had done Ruby's hair in tight braids on either side of her face, using plenty of conditioner to smooth the frizz away, and she wore a new outfit Jane had charged at the mall, white leggings and pink T-shirt over a light-green undershirt, sparkly pink sneakers—a little girl from a Hanna Andersson catalog.

The agent introduced himself as Steve. Lenny said he thought they'd met before. Had they met before? Steve said he was an actor and that he'd been in a few episodes of *Two and a Half Men*. He said this was a fun showing for him today since he and his husband lived only a few blocks away.

"You're gonna love it here. This neighborhood is Los Angeles's best-kept secret."

"You don't have to convince her," Lenny said. "She's obsessed with this area."

Steve asked what they did for a living, and when Lenny told him he was a painter and Jane was a novelist, the man's eyes went wide.

"Perfect. I could totally see you all living on this street. You'd fit right in."

Jane knew he was trying to signal to them what they already knew, that they wouldn't be the only Black people on the block and that the Black people on the block were also special creative Black people like them. Lenny asked Steve if he played tennis, and Steve said he did, and they began to talk about tennis. Jane watched them, pleased to see Lenny relaxing. He tended to enjoy the company of a certain kind of snarky but cheerful gay man. And men like that tended to like him back. Lenny got along well with sardonic lesbians too.

It was all part of a side of Lenny that Jane knew was there but usually remained hidden. It was the side of him Jane considered the real Lenny—the side of him that played tennis twice a week at a court in Pasadena with a white anesthesiologist he had met at a coffee shop. The side of him that still cut his food with his elbows off the table and who signed official documents with a weird dandyish flourish. The side of him who, when Jane returned from the ladies' room in restaurants, still rose from his seat with the gentlemanly bow of a man who once upon a time attended the Links ball on the arm of a willowy butterscotch girl named Sherline. Lenny was the son of Margaret Hope Gibson and Doctor Charles Jessup Thompson, younger brother of Sheila Dubois Gibson Thibodeaux, Esq. Lenny generally kept that self well hidden beneath his assertively ashy hands, his paint-splattered cargo pants, his overgrown Afro. He hid it behind a glowering passport photo—inside a passport filled with stamps of war-torn countries. He hid it beneath the guise of the simmering, iconoclastic, neosocialist outsider artist.

"Come on, let's go see the backyard," Ruby said to Finn, and hand in hand, the children ran off down a long hall, their feet slapping on the wood floors.

Lenny called after them, "Don't run, kids, this isn't your house." Then he and Steve shook their heads, laughing.

Jane could hear his gruff facade melting away as he and Steve laughed at the children—bonded over being beleaguered dads.

Jane wandered around the front room, eavesdropping on Lenny and Steve. Steve was giving the official spiel, telling Lenny all the things he had to tell a potential homebuyer—how the house was built in 1908 but had been gutted and renovated by a firm that specialized in turn-of-the-century homes. They'd kept many of the original details, he pointed out, but had made everything functional for a new era. That was the name of the firm, he said. Functional Classics.

Whoever had staged the house had gone for California casual meets world traveler meets Nantucket preppy. Jane found she liked the style. She wandered around, touching objects, imagining her and Lenny and the kids moving right into this staged life.

Just then, another family appeared at the door. It was a couple with a baby. They were several years younger than Jane and Lenny—attractive, well-dressed, slightly hip. Both Asian. The man wore black arty glasses and expensive sneakers. The woman held the plump child in a Baby-Björn strapped to her chest.

"You must be Ken and Emi," Steve said, walking to shake the man's hand. After cooing over the baby, Steve gave them the same spiel he'd given Jane and Lenny.

The man, Ken, spoke with a strong Japanese accent. Jane could hear him saying that he and his family had just moved here from Osaka. He was a musician who had been hired by the LA Philharmonic. Jane saw Lenny watching him from the kitchen door.

"Perfect," Steve was saying. "I could totally see you all living on this street. You'd fit right in."

The couple moved around, examining the front room and speaking in hushed Japanese. When they got to the kitchen, Lenny said something in Japanese.

The man looked startled, then broke into a smile. He said something in Japanese back to Lenny. And the next thing Jane knew, they were having an actual conversation.

Jane listened, surprised. She knew Lenny had been practicing but had not realized he'd gotten to the point where he could converse. Now Lenny was holding his hands around his face like a picture frame, tilting his head from side to side. Whatever he was saying made the man laugh, point a finger at him, and start to do his own routine. He made his arms flap like a bird, saying, "Herupu! Herupu!" Then he shook Lenny's hand, still laughing.

Lenny called out to Jane, "Ken's from Osaka, from one of my favorite neighborhoods. Isn't that funny?"

Jane fixed her face into what she hoped looked like a smile, nodded, then wandered down the hallway away from the sound of Lenny's voice, his strangely fluid Japanese, feeling a tightness in her chest, a dread that something terrible was happening or about to happen, though she couldn't say what. She went toward the sound of the children's voices.

She found them in the kids' bedrooms, which were connected by a large bathroom, Jack and Jill style. The stager had arranged the rooms to look like a real little boy and little girl lived there. On the wall in the boy's room, letter blocks spelled out BECKETT, and in the girl's room they read STELLA. Ruby sat on the floor of STELLA's pink and purple girl's room, playing with the dollhouse. Finn had flopped down on a giant beanbag chair and was looking at a book he'd pulled off BECKETT's shelf, a real book in this fake child's room. A book about insects.

As children, Jane and her sister had been part of a program called METCO that bused a select group of Black children—a talented two percent as it were—from the inner city of Boston to the suburbs. Not too many, just enough to sprinkle those suburban white schools with seasoning. Jane had been sent to a school in Brookline, where she made a friend, a wan white girl with a funny laugh named Emma. The girl lived in a neighborhood not unlike this one—an East Coast version. Apparently, it was heavy on doctors because it was nicknamed Pill Hill. The big old houses on those ancient, oak-lined streets were filled with stolid, professional, upper-middle-class liberal families. Emma's father was a doctor and her mother some kind of lawyer, and Jane had been aware, even at eleven, that they liked having her around, what it said about them and their daughter, who had befriended her. She could see it in Emma's mother's smile. Emma had a dollhouse like the one Ruby was playing with now. Jane had loved to play with it when she was visiting. Once Emma had told her that the dollhouse was made in Walpole prison, in a special program her mother had organized that taught the incarcerated men how to do woodwork. That dollhouse, Emma told Jane, had been made by a man who had been sentenced to die for murder. Wasn't that creepy?

Jane had spent many nights at Emma's house, but she'd never taken Emma back to her own house. That was an unstated understanding. And on those sleepovers, she would lie on the trundle bed in Emma's room long after Emma had fallen asleep, imagining that Emma's house was her own, that Emma was the guest sleeping over at her house. She would reverse everything in her mind.

Jane's father once told her that white people believed, deep in their hearts, that Black people would all choose to become white if they could. But Black people didn't want to be white, he had told her. They only wanted to have what white people had. He had said race was always about money, and money was always about race. That's what white people didn't understand. Black people wanted only a big yellow Victorian on the hill, not to be the white people who lived there.

And it was true that Jane never once wanted to be Emma, with her flaxen hair and her freckled nose. She did not want to have parents like Emma's. She wanted only their house.

Jane watched Ruby play now, her mouth filled with the bitter taste of want. She hungered for this house, but it was bigger than that, this want. Mulatto children of peripatetic artistic hippies did not want to age into being peripatetic mulatto adults with children. It was an endless loop. She wanted a real middle-class home the way only a half-caste child of seventies-era artistic squalor wants a home. She wanted her children to know what it felt like to be bored and listless in a house whose corners they knew as well as their own faces.

Ruby was roughly handling one of the dolls—a kind of knockoff American Girl—as she pulled off its clothes.

"Be careful with her, Ruby," Jane said. "This isn't our house. She isn't your doll. She's just there to show you what an actual house could look like."

Her voice sounded thin, reedy, empty. She could hear out in the front of the house the sound of voices speaking Japanese, Lenny's and the man's, laughing together at some inside joke. And, through some trick of angles, when she craned her neck to look in the mirror on the bedroom wall, she couldn't see herself. She wasn't there. She could only see the art in the hallway behind her. For a moment, she was overwhelmed with a fear that she didn't exist. She eyed the empty mirror, lightheaded now, not quite breathing. But then she forced herself to step forward, to look from another angle, and sure enough, her reflection appeared, clear and ordinary, and the feeling dissipated. There was nothing to be afraid of, not yet.

7.

Her agent called that afternoon while Lenny was at the park with the kids. It had been three weeks since they'd last spoken—three weeks since Honor had said all the empty, effusive things she'd said about Jane's book, three weeks since she'd sent the book out to Josiah.

"Jane." Honor's voice sounded far away. "I'm calling from Germany. Düsseldorf."

"What time is it there?" Jane asked. "Tomorrow—or yesterday?"

"Good one." Honor laughed. "I have no idea. How are you?"

"I'm fine," Jane said, feeling fine, really, though eager to hear what Josiah thought about the book.

"How are the kids?"

"They're doing well."

"You know," Honor said. "You and Lenny should take the kids to Germany sometime. It's dreamy for children, all these big squares."

"Yes, we should."

"How old are they now?"

"Eight and six."

"Wow, time flies. And Lenny? How's Lenny?"

"He's good."

"His paintings are so amazing," Honor said. "The last ones I saw were years ago—but they were outstanding. What's he doing now?"

"He's teaching himself Japanese. He has a show in Tokyo in the fall he's preparing for."

"Nice! I love Tokyo. I thought you were planning to relocate there at some point or am I misremembering?"

"It's a discussion," Jane said, irritated by the small talk. She could wait no longer. "Have you heard from Josiah?"

Honor went silent for a beat. And in that beat, Jane felt dread creep in.

"Honor?"

"Jane, listen, I know how long you were working on this book in isolation, but sometimes, well, sometimes we lose our way when we work alone like that for too long. We don't have any feedback—we can go down a rabbit hole and—just start to lose our bearings. Our instincts. I just wish you'd shared this with me sooner. Like, two years ago."

"I don't understand."

"I'm trying to say it isn't working. Josiah and I feel it isn't working."

"As in you have edits? I knew there would be edits."

"No. Not as in we have edits."

Jane touched her face, felt the outline of her features. She saw them again, floaters, those imaginary shadows hovering in her field of vision. Blinked twice. Found words. Spoke. "I thought you liked it. The last time we spoke you said you'd read it with 'great interest and enthusiasm.' You called it 'fascinating stuff.'"

"I thought some parts of it were, but—listen, after talking to Josiah and getting his feedback, I took another look and I really see his points."

Jane tried to remember any specific things Honor had said she liked about the book, but she couldn't think of any. And now she understood with a flash of shame that Honor had not read it at all or that she'd only skimmed it.

"I really think Josiah puts it best. Should I just read you the letter he sent me?"

Later, Jane would only remember certain phrases. Josiah felt the book was "Frankensteinian." Like the monster, he said, her book was an ungainly mishmash—and like the monster, it felt sloppily constructed, the stitches and scars showing. He said it was sarcastic, bracing and cruel at times, mawkish and purple at others. It bewildered him. He had no idea why she was cramming all these figures together. What did Zoë Kravitz have to do with the Melungeon people in nineteenth-century Tennessee? How did any of it connect to Sydney and Justin, O. J. and Nicole's kids, or to Jane's own creature—this fragile, trembling 1950s film actress who roamed the book in her negligee, barefoot and suicidal, worrying about the color of the baby growing inside of her. Josiah didn't understand what Jane was attempting to do here, but he cared about Jane and felt that publishing this novel would be a kind of career suicide.

Listening to the words, Jane had that odd sense again that she was not a real person—that if she were to walk over to the mirror, the floor-length one in Brett's hallway, she'd find nothing staring back, only the wall behind her. She felt airy, as if she were made not of flesh but of light and shadows, and she touched her face as she listened to Honor's voice, pressing into her skin, patting down on her hair.

"We both feel you're doing yourself a disfavor by writing about race again—by writing about, you know, the whole mixed-race thing. We'd love to see you expand your territory, Jane. I'm only sorry I didn't insist that you show me pages earlier so I could see what you were up to. I'm just sorry you've wasted so much time." Honor paused. "I realize this is a lot to process."

"Yes."

"Listen," Honor said, and her voice was softer. "This isn't the worst rejection letter I've ever read. And it's certainly not the worst attempt at a second novel that's ever landed on my desk. It's just—some works are not meant to see the light. Some books are meant to be left in a drawer. And honestly, Jane, if you want to know what I think as a friend—woman to woman—I think you should take a break from this novel. Maybe try your hand at a short story. I know *Ploughshares* would love to publish you again. And just—I don't know—be inside your life for a change. Novels are so all-consuming. They keep you from your real life in ways that are hard, especially when you're raising kids. Just try to be inside your life. It's a real life you've got there. A full life. And maybe some other time you can try your hand at a novel again—when your head is in a better place."

Later, Jane would not remember how the conversation with Honor ended. She was sitting at the dining-room table, on her second glass of red wine, Brett's wine, staring out into the dusky light, when the kids came in smelling of sunshine and pollution, wanting to show her their treasures—crappy, filthy toys they'd found buried deep in the sand at Cleland Park. Ruby held a Minnie Mouse figurine up to Jane's face and Finn held out an encrusted Mater toy he'd found there too.

"Papa says they might have been buried in the sand for fifty years," Ruby said, dreamily.

"The kids who left them there might be grown-ups now," Finn said.

"Amazing," Jane said. "They look ancient."

They ran upstairs to wash off their toys, and Lenny came in moments later, carrying Ruby's *Frozen* backpack.

He eyed her. "You started without me," he said, and went to the kitchen counter to pour himself a glass. "What's for dinner?"

She'd forgotten about dinner. She watched Lenny, unmoving. "How does it end, *Frankenstein*?" she said. "Does the monster live? I don't remember."

Lenny said he only remembered the Mel Brooks version. *Young Frankenstein*. The one where Gene Wilder tap dances with the monster and the monster freaks out and attacks the audience.

"Dressed up like a million-dollar trouper," Lenny sang, as he shimmied over to the table. "Trying hard to look like Gary Cooper, super duper." He sat down across from her, still laughing a little. "Did you know," he said, "that in the original *Frankenstein* the doctor never screams 'It's alive!' like he does in the movie? That was just cinematic idiocy. In the book, the moment the creature opens its eyes, the doctor, his creator, runs away. He can't look at what he's made. He's a coward and it terrifies him, which of course—"

He stopped talking, seeing something on her face.

"What happened?"

"Do I look different?"

"Your face looks swollen. Did you bang it on something?"

She touched her cheek. It felt hot, as if there were something beneath it, growing, trying to come out.

"Honor called," she said. "She heard back from Josiah. He read my book."

"Oh, wow. That didn't take too long. What did he say?"

"He hated it. And Honor hated it too. They both hated it. Together they despised it."

"You're kidding, right?"

"No."

"You're exaggerating."

"She suggested I put it away and take some years off from novel writing. Like, can you be fired from being a writer? I think that's what just happened."

Lenny rubbed his face. Hard. When he pulled his hands away, he looked wearier, older. "I thought she loved it. Three weeks ago she said she loved it."

"Well, that was three weeks ago. Now she's agreeing with all the terrible things Josiah said to me. They both think I should put it in a drawer and never look at it again and move on with my life. Become a woman who dabbles in short stories, occasionally publishes in *Ploughshares*. They want me to drift away into the purgatory of the midlist author. They're firing me."

"Firing you?" Lenny scoffed. "You need to fire them."

She could see Lenny adjusting to the new information, forming a theory. Lenny was a person who did not roll over. With each disappointment, he grew more assured of his own position. When America didn't love him, he declared America the problem. When he got a bad review, he declared the reviewer an idiot. When they'd discovered he was allergic to garlic, he declared garlic to be disgusting—something that covered up the real taste of food.

Now she heard him speaking to her as if from a great distance—from deep down the Black bourgeois well of confidence he kept hidden from view most of the time.

"Josiah is an asshole. A racist archaic asshole who wouldn't know Buckwheat from Cream of Wheat. I never liked him. And Honor—well, she's got water on her brain. You need a new agent, a half-intelligent agent who can actually make sense of what you've written and send the book out again."

"Maybe," Jane said. She glimpsed her reflection in the dark glass and saw she was sitting hunched over like an old woman—or a question mark.

Lenny went to the counter and refilled his glass of wine. "Now do you see why I've been wanting us to leave the country? Do you see it now? We don't belong here. This is an illiterate country. Dumb as fuck. It's a country that turns a blind eye to Black genius. It's always been that way and it will always be that way and I don't want to see it happen to you and I don't want to see it happen to Ruby and Finn either. This is why I keep on you about Tokyo. Us, there. Now do you get it?"

Jane closed her eyes and rubbed her temples. Tokyo. She should have seen this coming. He now had the evidence he'd been looking for—

something that would prove to Jane once and for all that there was nothing left for them in this sinking ship of a country.

It was sweet, she knew, his confidence in her. Sweet that he still believed in her as a writer despite all evidence of her failures. He was certain that the problem was what sociologists called "category confusion." Nobody knew—nobody had ever known—what category to place her in. And maybe he was right. After all, in America, the land of sorting, that was a kind of death.

Lenny was still in the kitchen, pulling a package of macaroni and cheese out of the freezer, unwrapping it, placing it in the microwave. Sweet, too, how he thought of the children. He was making the children supper after taking them to the park.

Ruby came downstairs just then in her *Frozen* dress and blonde wig, and began singing "Let It Go" in front of the floor-length mirror. Finn came down after her, carrying an armful of trucks. He squatted in the corner of the living room and began lining them up in a row on the floor, from small to large. That was supposed to be one of the symptoms, she thought, watching him—his interest in order and sequencing. Ruby spun in circles. "The snow glows white on the mountain tonight," she was singing. "Not a footprint to be seen."

The microwave beeped. Lenny took out the macaroni and cheese, stirred it, and then carried it past the children to the sofa. He sat down, turned on the TV, and began to shovel the food straight into his mouth from the container.

"I thought that was for the kids," Jane said, but he didn't seem to hear her. He'd found a station playing *Jaws*, turned up the volume, and continued to eat as he watched. Jane watched him spooning more food into his mouth. Watched his lips move, overcome by a feeling she didn't like. It wasn't quite hatred, but it wasn't nice. Unwanted thoughts tumbled through her brain—not just about the mac and cheese, but about Lenny himself, his poverty and his failure. If she'd had a better husband, she'd have written a better novel. If she'd married a better husband, she'd have written so many better novels by now.

She rose and headed across the lawn to Brett's writing studio, the scene of the crime. As she stepped inside, she remembered that first day working in this office, eight months ago, when she'd leaned back and swiveled in Brett's chair, so excited to have a space of her own at last. The office had looked so clean and orderly then, a space where you could really finish something.

Now she looked at the mess she'd made. When was the moment she'd allowed this horror of a book to take over? The pages were everywhere, spread across the floor, strewn across the desk. The charts and time lines on the wall, the photos she'd taken the liberty of printing on Brett's color printer, a panoply of mulattos and the people who had made them. There was a photo of Carol Channing at the center, with her hair in a platinum blonde mushroom cut. She appeared to be laughing at Jane, her eyes twinkling with amused contempt.

Jane felt unsteady on her feet. She went to sit at Brett's desk. There was a window open above her head. Sound traveled across the courtyard from the main house. She'd never felt so far away—and yet somehow not far enough. She could hear the movie Lenny was still watching. *Jaws*. Chief Brody was saying, "He's eating his way right through that line!" She could hear Finn asking Lenny if they had sharks like that in Santa Monica. Then Ruby saying, "I'm scared." Jane considered going in to tell Lenny to turn it off, but she didn't move.

Was the fact that she'd written this book a symptom of a fundamental brokenness in her brain? Jane thought back to an accident she'd been in many years earlier—before she met Lenny, before she had kids. She'd been going to catch an Amtrak from Penn Station to Boston for a weekend visit to her mother. She arrived at the station early and went into a bookshop in search of something fun to read on her trip. Somehow she lost track of time. When she came out, she saw people rushing to the escalators to catch their trains, and she saw on the board that her own train was only two minutes from departing. She raced down the escalator and jumped on board just as the train lurched forward. A moment later she heard the announcement. She'd gotten on the wrong train—this one wasn't heading to Boston. It was heading to Washington, DC—first stop not until Philadelphia. Jane panicked. She went to the door of the train, which was still open. The ground seemed to be passing very slowly—and in that instant, she thought she could just step out gently and walk away. But as soon as she stepped off, she went flying across the platform, rolling like a stunt double over and over again until she stopped at the edge of the opposite track. One more inch and she'd have been on the rails. When she sat up, she saw that her jeans were torn and bloody, and her head was wet with blood too, and her suitcase had split open, and her clothes and tampons and underwear and face creams were strewn all over the platform. In the tracks lay the book she'd spent all that time picking out, *Smilla's Sense of Snow*. Jane managed to get up and gather herself and limp out of the station, and somehow went back to her little apartment in Brooklyn, where she'd vomited for hours then fallen into a dreamless thirteen-hour sleep. She had never gone to get an MRI. Had never gotten any of her injuries checked out. She'd just limped around the rest of the weekend then forgot about it.

Had she had an untreated brain injury all these years? Was that why she'd written this monstrosity that surrounded her now?

Now she rose from Brett's chair and went to find a roll of small trash bags with the cleaning supplies beneath the sink in Brett's bathroom. She took one out, then went about the office ripping down the photos and quotes and time lines she'd taped to the walls and shoving them all in the trash bag. She crushed the pages down far, with real muscle, so they would fit. Afterward, sweating, out of breath, she carried the bag out to the trash can in the driveway and shoved it inside. When she returned to the office, it looked almost normal, almost like it had the first day—except for one thing. The neatly stacked, finished manuscript still sat there on the corner of the desk. How had she forgotten to include that in her cleaning frenzy? She stared down at the title. *Nusu Nusu.* Partly-partly. She picked it up and felt its weight in her hands. Ten years. Ten years of useless labor. She considered bringing it outside to join the photos and time lines in the trash, but she was suddenly too weary even for that. So instead she opened the bottom drawer of Brett's desk and shoved the draft inside. Then she sat down and put her head on her arms on the desk and closed her eyes.

God, that novel. She could almost hear it whimpering and thrashing, like a body she'd bound and gagged in the trunk of a car. It had been such a blight on her life. Ten years. What masochistic urge had made her think she needed to take on the entirety of American history? It was as if she'd thought she was the only mulatto writer who had ever lived or was going to live. As if she couldn't bear to leave a single mulatto era for anyone else to take on, for God's sake.

She'd seen a meme the other day showing a Real Housewife of Atlanta, NeNe Leakes, shaking her head and saying, "Girl, you're doing too much!" Jane heard NeNe's voice in her head now, because it was true, she had spent the past decade doing too much.

She opened her eyes and saw what was left on the desk. A framed photo lying face down. She had turned it over that first day, then the desk had gotten so cluttered with her work that she had forgotten it was even there. She sat up and picked it up now and propped it up again. It was a wedding photo of Brett and Piper, a generic shot of them on the beach in Los Cabos, staring into each other's eyes.

Behind them was the cluster of wedding guests. When she looked closely, she could spot her own face in the smiling crowd. She looked happy in the photo, though she recalled that her feelings that weekend had been more complicated. In reality, she'd been disgusted by Brett's choice of a bride as well as by his choice of friends, who reeked of Hollywood. Jane had attended the wedding alone. She'd been the only friend Brett still had left from their writing program. He was starting his new life, going to be an industry man, a scribe of screens big and small. It seemed to her at the time a tragedy of epic proportions that he was not going to stick it out with her in the literary trenches—that he'd given up on real writing.

Now, she sent Brett a text.

> You awake?
>
> Jane! What's up?
>
> How's the Outback treating you?
>
> In-fucking-credible. Check this out . . .

A photo came through an instant later—Brett and Max and Piper standing in a dusty clearing, all of them pointing in mock fright at a muscular kangaroo who stood only feet away.

> Yo, dude, that roo looks like a creepy buff Chad.
> WTF?

Even as she wrote the words, Jane could feel herself doing that thing Lenny teased her for, the "mulatto mirroring thing," where she started to talk like whomever she was speaking to, adopting their accent and manner of speech. He claimed that whenever she spoke to Brett she turned into a sorority girl at UC Santa Barbara.

> It's AMAZING here! Words cannot describe.
>
> I'm so glad, yay! Total awesomeness. How's the zombie show coming along?
>
> Finished. I mean, as much as I can do here, anyway. There'll be a shitload to deal with when we're back in LA. But I have a month of temporary freedom.
>
> So cool you're getting a real holiday!

> Well, you know me. I'm still working. I started writing the biracial thing I've been talking about for years.
>
> Biracial thing?
>
> LOLOL. Remember? The show I told you I wanted to make last year. The mulatto comedy. Where everything sad about us is played for laughs. Comic mulattos.
>
> OMG right. That one. I didn't know you were actually going to do it.
>
> Maybe I will, maybe I won't! I have some free time to mess around, so why not?
>
> Yeah, why not?
>
> Maybe I can make Jane Gibson laugh. That's my goal.

She sent back an emoji of a blushing smiley face, but it was the opposite of what she was feeling. He was seriously doing it? Making this bad idea a reality? It wasn't fair. He'd been the ultimate race-avoidant mulatto all these years, squinting at her when she talked about her epic novel like he was studying an ant under glass, as if he thought she was strange and silly to be so obsessed, so fixated on identity politics. He'd acted above it all, and he *had* been above it all, with his goddamn seven-figure zombie deals. But now he wanted to go toy around in Jane's territory simply because he was done making his most recent millions and had a month off and was bored. Only his version of such a story would be so neutered and banal, so without claws, that it would probably sell for a jillion dollars.

> Anyway, I'm still trying to see if it has legs.

She was glad he couldn't see her face.

> I bet it does! Long legs! Seasons and seasons . . .
>
> LOL. I'm glad you have faith, babe. Sooo . . . Should I ask about your novel?

He followed the question with a scared face.

Jane stared at the grimacing emoji. Something was dawning on her. Her second novel—Brett's endless questions about its progress. It had become a sick joke to him, something he'd known all along wasn't going well. He'd been having fun asking her about it.

She felt a surge of anger, an anger she hadn't expected. It felt better than the sadness she'd been feeling before. More alive.

> Novel is GREAT. I finished it just last month. Your office must be magic 🍾🍾🍾
>
> JANE GIBSON. YOU ARE MY FUCKING HERO . . . YOU FINISHED THE NOVEL!?
>
> Sure did.

Jane stared at the lie. That was not truly a lie. Because she had finished it. Finished it off.

> REMEMBER WHAT DENNIS TOLD US? THOSE WHO SUCCEED AS WRITERS ARE SIMPLY THOSE WHO CONTINUE TO DO IT.
>
> SO HATS OFF—HATS FUCKING OFF TO YOU, YOU FUCKING GENIUS. OMG. OMG. OMG. I CAN'T WAIT TO READ IT!

There was a long pause, then a moment later, he wrote again.

> WHEN DOES IT COME OUT?

Jane stared at his question for a moment. When was it coming out?

> Pub date TBD. Gotta run. Just wanted to say thanks for the house! It's been a game changer. ♥♥♥

Then it was over, their little convo, and she was sitting at the desk in his office—the site of her failure—with nothing to fix her gaze on except Brett's wedding photo. Strange how the sight of it still irked her. She hadn't wanted to go to the wedding, but she couldn't get out of it.

She'd searched for weeks for the perfect dress. She had been going for striking and cool, ironic, and sophisticated, the girl you want but never will have. She'd finally found the perfect dress at Barneys—a Miu Miu frock that recalled an ingenue in a French New Wave film. It was way over her budget, so she'd done this thing she had done a lot in those days, charged it to her credit card and kept the tags on so she could return it after the wedding. She'd worn it the night of the ceremony and reception in Los Cabos with the price tag tucked into her bra strap. It was a kind of stealing but not actual stealing. If she didn't spill any wine, she could tell the salesclerk on day six that the dress didn't fit her. She wouldn't be caught.

Jane was still single that night of Brett's wedding. She hadn't yet had her session with Wesley. She hadn't gone to Stu's engagement party, and she hadn't yet seen Lenny by the chip bowl. A lot of things hadn't happened, including her second novel, which she'd just begun. That night she'd been happy in a way, the stormy, uneven happiness of the early thirties set when the whole story has not yet unfolded. She'd had the feeling that she was on the precipice of something major. The new book was still a manageable story about a sad yellow actress. In her mind, it could be all the things she hoped it would be. She felt superior to Brett and all his industry friends. She felt superior to anyone who was not doing the work of high art, of elevating the culture. She'd felt sorry for Brett that he had given up on literary fiction after just the one slender story collection—sorry for him that he had allowed himself to be dragged down into the lower depths. He'd given up this promise of glory and immortality to spout drivel in that land where original ideas go to die.

"The mulatto in America," Cavendish wrote, "remains a ghostly apparition in most history books. He does not easily fit into any of the stories we've told ourselves about America. And indeed, he does not easily fit into his own mind. What a tortured figure we find in the American mulatto! His proximity to whiteness, you see, sparks ambition in him—an insatiable desire to have all that the white man possesses. But his proximity to blackness makes him despise his own ambition. Pride and shame, love and hatred, vanity and self-loathing mingle together uneasily in the mulatto's psyche, leading to a state of perpetual ambivalence, an indefinable malaise."

Through the window over her head, Jane could hear Ruby's voice saying again, "I'm scared." Lenny still hadn't turned off *Jaws*. There was a sound of yelling from the television. Jane knew the scene—when Chief Brody tells Quint, "You're gonna need a bigger boat." She again considered going in to tell Lenny to turn it off—that it was inappropriate for children. That's what a real mother would do, she thought vaguely, but still she did not move.

Instead, she picked up the business card Brett kept propped on his lamp and stared at the name on it. MARIANNE BERKOWITZ. She recognized the name—Brett's television agent. Jane knew they'd worked together for many years. She wondered if Marianne Berkowitz had been at the wedding in Los Cabos so many years ago. Jane didn't remember meeting her there. But it was possible that she was one of the skinny, brittle women who did the conga line past Jane where she stood, arms crossed, smirking in her stolen Miu Miu dress.

IN THE EMAIL she wrote to Marianne Berkowitz that evening, in the waning light of Brett's office, Jane told three lies. The first was that Brett had told her to be in touch. The second was that Jane had a television show idea she couldn't wait to share with Marianne—a pitch for a show that was "particularly relevant at this historical juncture." Whatever the hell that meant. She hoped the agent would google Jane and see that all she wrote about—all she'd ever written about—was mulattos. The third lie was that she'd just finished a *major* novel—"many years in the making"—and that she was ready to plunge into something new.

Okay, so this was true. She had just finished a major novel that had indeed been years in the making. Major could mean many things. Hers had been a major failure.

After she sent it, she stood up and wandered over to the bookshelf, where there were multiple copies of Brett's first book. *Lemon Rock: Stories*. She hadn't disliked the collection when it came out—because there was nothing to dislike. The stories were perfectly constructed nothingness. She took down a copy and flipped through the pages, searching for passages where he'd even begun to address being a half-Black boy in the white suburbs of Claremont. There were brief moments when he touched on it—*Enzo didn't have to wear sunblock like his friends. His natural tan was the only gift his missing father had ever bequeathed him.*—but each time a character's Blackness was mentioned, Brett backed away as if he'd touched a flame. How was Brett of all people going to have the chutzpah and the derring-do to turn the mulatto trope into comedy? He wasn't even a funny guy. He was too earnest. He should stick to deracinated zombies.

She wondered briefly, as she put his book back, if it was bad form that she had written to Brett's agent without asking him if it was okay. Certainly, she shouldn't have said he'd suggested it. She decided it didn't matter because she wouldn't hear back. A bigwig like Marianne Berkowitz would not have time to answer a query from a nobody like Jane.

8.

Marianne—an ageless slender brunette in heels—was waiting for Jane at the elevator. Jane did not remember meeting her at Brett's wedding. But that had been so many years ago, and Marianne looked like a thousand other white women.

"Jane," she said, holding out a hand. "We're so thrilled you could come. This is Carrie, my assistant." She nodded to the slight bespectacled girl who stood beside her holding a clipboard. "Jane's a friend of Brett's." She winked at Jane. "Isn't Brett just the greatest? We love Brett."

Jane nodded, smiling, and followed the women down a plush hallway to a corner office, where she took a seat on a white sofa. Carrie brought her coffee with cream.

"It's amazing how many of you I've been meeting, Jane," Marianne said. "Novelists, every week another one, looking to break into the industry. Isn't that right, Carrie?"

Carrie nodded. "And playwrights too."

"God, yes," Marianne said. "Hordes of New Yorkers migrating west. Bad for the world of arts and letters, great for us."

"I guess word finally got out that the novel is dead," Jane said.

"Oh, hooey," Marianne said. "Books are still alive, hugely important. Where do you think we get our IP? Lit is vital to what we do. We need each other." She webbed her hands together to show the relationship between novels and television, smiling reassuringly.

Jane wondered if the week she'd had showed on her face—the week she'd spent weeping, and in the brief intervals when she wasn't weeping, moving around doing tasks for the children as if she were underwater, her limbs heavy. It wasn't novels she was grieving, it was *her* novel.

Across from her, Marianne was talking about a novelist she'd helped transition, someone named Laurel. She'd gotten Laurel a job on a show called *Barefoot Dreams*. Laurel had claimed it was all for research on a novel she wanted to write, but after the show got canceled, she called Marianne asking to be put on another show, saying she had totally lost interest in writing novels. She had never realized how miserable it was until she'd glimpsed this other way of being a writer. She'd never felt as alive as she did in the writers' room; the depression she'd suffered from for all those years had dissipated immediately.

"So, Jane, tell us about yourself. Besides being an FOB"—Marianne winked again—"a friend of Brett, who are you?"

Jane recited the bare facts of her life. She'd just finished her long-awaited second novel; she taught writing at a college; she had a husband who was a visual artist and two children, Finn and Ruby, ages six and eight. As she listened to herself, her life sounded lovely, charmed, full. The details, spoken like this, in a breezy rush, made her sound like a woman who had pulled off the impossible "all" that women rarely got. She didn't have to fill in the rest, about her adjunct status or Finn's fledgling diagnosis and Ruby's raggedy blonde wig, or the fact that Lenny made not a dime from his art. She didn't have to tell Marianne that she was living on borrowed time in a borrowed house, Brett's borrowed house, and that in the fall she would be going back to a demotion and an assaultive load of undergraduate writing seminars, to the ranks of Kay Franken. By fall, maybe she and her whole family—if Lenny didn't abduct them to Tokyo—would be living full-time in Jane's office.

Most of all, she didn't have to tell Marianne what had happened with her second novel, that she'd wasted almost a decade on a monstrous creation that her agent and editor had decided was career suicide.

"I just find novels are not where the fire is these days," Jane said. "I want to influence the culture more directly. And trust me, English professors, the people who study literature for a living, they don't even talk about novels anymore unless they have to—they just stand around the water cooler talking about what they watched last night."

Marianne laughed with delight. "Isn't that something!" She shook her head and tapped a pencil on her lips, staring out the window at Culver City. "Do you know, Brett came to me ten years ago," Marianne said. "He'd just published *Lemon Rock*. I'll never forget it. It was the beginning of a beautiful partnership. He's never looked back."

Jane smiled tightly. Somehow Brett had known to come here after the first book. He'd known the whole enterprise was doomed. Whereas she had wasted a decade wading deeper and deeper into the monstrosity that was *Nusu Nusu* in the quest for literary stardom. Such an absurd phrase—*literary stardom*—an oxymoron, really, like *poetry groupie*. The scales were falling from her eyes now, but was it too late? Jane tried to quell the panic and remorse in her chest. She reminded herself that she was here now, on the tenth floor of the biggest agency in Hollywood. Carpe diem. She wouldn't waste another decade of her life on books.

Jane sipped the coffee and said that she loved being a novelist, but over the years, it had started to feel like an exercise in masochism. "I want to create art people want to consume," she said. "Not consume because it's wholesome or so they can brag about it, but because they can't stop consuming it, you know?"

The other two women were wide-eyed, grinning, and she felt energized by their faces. She kept talking. She said recently she'd realized that being a novelist in Los Angeles was not unlike being an Amish person. "I mean, it's quaint, a little bizarre, an extreme lifestyle choice. Like wearing a bonnet and churning your own butter. I just want to get out of this corset and join the modern world. I mean, what's the point of a horse-drawn wagon when you can drive?"

Marianne pointed a finger at Jane. "You're funny. Please tell me you want to write comedy."

Jane paused. "Oh, I do," she said. "I want to write a comedy about"—she paused, letting the suspense hang in the air—"about mulattos."

She waited for them to say it. To tell her that Brett was already trying to write a comedy about mulattos. She had a cool response waiting: "Mine is an entirely different beast. More feminine and a lot darker."

Instead, Marianne said, "Wait, isn't Brett mixed too? Or is he just"—she touched her cheek as if to suggest some other source of his swarthiness but didn't finish the thought.

Ordinarily, Jane would have been repulsed, but it was good news that they barely had thought about the fact that Brett was Black. They barely knew it.

Jane muttered a vague, "Yes, he is," then waited again for them to mention his new project.

But Marianne only said, "Funny, with Brett, I never think about skin color. I mean, Brett is just—Brett. Right, Carrie?"

"So true," Carrie said. "He's just, like, a guy. A really hot guy."

They all laughed, including Jane, who said, "You can say that again."

It seemed Brett had not yet told anybody besides Jane about his own percolating television concept, which, she assured herself, wasn't even a concept. A "mulatto comedy" was so vague as to be meaningless.

"I'm sorry to cut this short," Marianne said, glancing at her watch. "I have to get to a meeting, but Carrie and I will be putting together some generals for you. How does that sound?"

"Generals?"

"General meetings. They're like blind dates between writers and producers. They're fun. Nobody's there to commit or even pitch. Everybody's just exploring. You'll enjoy them."

"That sounds perfect."

Marianne walked Jane to the elevator. "So what's the timing on your new book?"

"New book?"

"The one you just finished."

"Oh, right! Hard to think of it as new—I've been working on it so long. But, yes, my publisher is still deciding on timing. You know the book world—everything takes forever."

"So true."

They were at the elevators. Marianne hugged Jane. "This has been such a pleasure, Jane." Then, as she turned to go, added, "I've got to write Brett and thank him for sending you in."

"No need," Jane cried out, louder than she'd intended. "I mean, I've already thanked him—"

But Marianne was down the hall and rounding the corner to her next meeting, and it wasn't clear if she'd heard her. Jane stepped onto the elevator and watched as the numbers began to descend, wondering how she'd eventually explain herself to Brett. The truth was, she'd written to Marianne in a moment of mindless panic not really expecting anything to come of it. After she'd sent the email, she'd returned to the main house and moved through the rest of the evening in a kind of torpor, only pretending to be there with her family, to listen to the children's chirpy voices. Sitting at the edge of Finn's bath, watching him play with his *Moana* figurines in the soapy water, she'd gotten lost in a fantasy of walking into Josiah's office and beating him over the head with her laptop, his brains all over the carpeted floor. When Jane came to bed, Lenny had tried to cheer her up with the wrong kind of pep talk about all the great Black writers who littered the dustbins of American history, Nella and Chester and Zora, destroyed not by literal censorship but by the lateral violence, he said, of sheer white bewilderment—a bewilderment born of privilege, a Caucasian befuddlement that had been honed like a knife. She knew where he was heading, to a renewed pitch for Tokyo, so she murmured her assent but begged off further discussion, saying she was too tired to talk and just needed an episode of *Intervention* to take her mind off her troubles. And then, as she opened her laptop beside him, she saw it, a return message from Marianne Berkowitz, and when she clicked on it, there were all those ecstatic exclamation marks emphasizing how thrilled she'd be to meet Jane, how any friend of Brett's was a friend of hers. And it had worked like a dose of Narcan. She'd felt herself coming back to life.

The elevator doors opened onto the lobby, and she headed across the marble floor to the glass doors and went out into the bright blast of Culver City sunlight. As she waited for the valet to bring her Subaru, she saw a man who she swore was Rob Lowe getting into a Range Rover, but when he drove past, she saw it was only someone who looked like Rob Lowe.

Surely Brett would understand once she explained the situation. She'd stress that she'd been having a nervous breakdown when she reached out to Marianne. She'd emphasize how surprised she'd been when Marianne wrote back, when things started rolling forward so quickly, how things had been so hectic with the children that it had simply slipped her mind to bring him up to speed.

And now, climbing into her filthy Subaru, which the valet handed over to her with a look of disgust, she thought maybe she was silly to worry. Probably it wouldn't matter to Brett at all. What did he care? He was a wealthy screenwriter. Film and television people had more generosity in their hearts than novelists, especially more than poets. She'd been raised by a poet. Poets were like red pandas; from afar they seemed cute and gentle, but if they sensed a threat or competition, they would rip your hand off. Novelists were like bearded dragons. They had to be raised alone in terrariums, away from other bearded dragons, or they would eat one another. Screenwriters, though, were like gorillas. They looked dangerous, and they had a bad reputation, but they were gentle, sociable creatures who understood they needed one another to survive.

ON THE DRIVE back across town, she thought about Dennis Mulholland, the guy who'd run her and Brett's writing program. He was a literary dinosaur, one of those midsixties white men who had never reached the heights of his heroes Carver and Cheever or any number of Richards and Jonathans, but who had been a good, sturdy, reliable MFA program director for forty years. Jane and Brett, in the meanness of youth, used to mock Dennis after each workshop. They thought he was hokey, a hack, the way he liked to quote from John Gardner's *The Art of Fiction*.

"There's a difference," Dennis used to say, "between a story and a situation. And what you have is a situation. It still needs a story."

Or "Without an inciting incident, there is no story."

Or "A novel begins with a character in a stable but flawed life—an unhappy marriage, a dead-end job. The novel hinges on the inciting incident—something to destabilize your character's life in the first thirty pages."

Jane had once tried to read Dennis's long out of print first novel but had found it mawkish, a bad imitation of one of those men he worshiped from the heyday of white male writers. The novel had not inspired in her much faith about his writing rules. Still, those chestnuts he'd repeated had lodged in Jane's head like a song she couldn't shake. They came to her at odd moments, especially when teaching, and she'd find herself spouting one of his aphorisms about craft to her blank-faced undergraduates. She'd noticed over her years of teaching that the more she parroted Dennis Mulholland, the better her student evaluations. Students liked to believe writing could be a paint-by-numbers exercise.

She had worked hard not to think of Dennis when she sat down to write her novel, worked hard to shake those dusty, crusty ideas about narrative so she could make something truly original, something that would smash structures rather than uphold them. She'd tried hard to fend off Dennis's dulling influence, but look where it had gotten her.

His voice came to her once again as she pulled out of the agency lot into traffic. If every story needed an inciting incident, when the character's flawed but stable reality was destabilized and they were forced on the journey that would teach them who they really needed to be, maybe the call from Honor was that inciting incident. Maybe it marked the end of her flawed, delusional life as a novelist. And here was the day her story could finally include those six words Dennis said every narrative needed: "And then one day everything changed."

AT THE HOUSE, she found Lenny working in his studio; the kids were still in school. He was playing music loudly, one of the rare songs they loved together—Switch, featuring Bobby DeBarge, singing "There'll Never Be"—and he didn't hear her enter. She watched him from the door, admiring his focus, the way he threw himself physically into the work. The painting he was making was enormous, almost half the size of the studio wall. She hadn't seen it in a month or so. It was one of his signature paintings on top of a painting. In this one, he'd first created some elaborate and intricate scene—a family seated at a table—then painted over them so you couldn't make out their expressions, only that they were four figures hidden beneath a layer of swirling gray paint.

Jane watched him work for a while before she came toward him and touched him on the shoulder. He startled.

"You scared me," he said. "When did you get back?"

"Just now."

"How'd it go?"

He was smirking, sarcastic. He thought it was a joke, a prolonged, not-very-funny joke, her encounter with a Hollywood agent. She'd floated the idea of going for the meeting as a lark, just the sort of diversion she needed before she turned back to the novel in earnest, maybe even fodder for it.

"It was sort of fun." She paused, and he turned back to look at his painting. She stared at it too, remembering what she'd felt for him when they first met, when she first saw his work. Its confidence and mystery had been so sexy to her. She recalled how the early months of their relationship had been so much about their working on their art together, the two of them hunkered down in his big loft on Spring Street in downtown LA, Jane at the kitchen table at one end of the space, scribbling and typing, Lenny at the other end, with the paint and canvases. Other than to eat and sleep, they took breaks only to grope each other, take each other. She wanted to feel that way again.

"Len?"

He turned back to look at her.

"Yeah?"

She pulled him toward her and started to kiss him.

He hesitated at first, then relented. They stripped down, there in the studio, and he pushed her onto the pile of tarps on the floor and they fucked there, as if they were new to each other.

Afterward, Lenny held her head on his chest and stroked her hair and said sleepily, "We've still got it."

She was thinking about her novel, the character at the heart of it, the actress she kept returning to through all those centuries, that sad, high-yellow beauty who drifted around Hollywood, trying and failing to get cast in a movie, until Jane had killed her off in the penultimate chapter. Now, lying on the floor of the studio, Lenny in a postcoital coma beneath her, the sound of the wall clock ticking, the smell of paint in the air, Jane missed that actress with an ache that surprised her, missed her like a childhood friend. But she was also, in a new, real way, glad she was dead.

9.

The assistant who came to find Jane in the lobby had a perfect face: full lips, a pert round nose, high cheekbones, sloping eyes. Everything sat in balance on the canvas of her face, each feature at the right distance from the other.

"You must be Jane!" she said. "I'm Layla. We're so excited you could come today. Can I get you a water? A coffee?"

"Water is fine."

Jane recalled a lecture she'd attended in college. The professor told the class that faces were beautiful not because they possessed features of any particular shape or mold; faces, he said, were universally considered beautiful when they were symmetrical.

After the class, Jane had gone to look at her own face in a compact mirror in the bathroom stall and saw that it was deeply asymmetrical, some kind of Picassoesque pairing.

Jane wondered if Layla was the assistant's real name. She guessed she was the child of immigrants. It wasn't just her skin color, which carried a depth and richness you didn't see in America every day. It was her smile too, so eager and hopeful, and her voice, with a hint of the Valley.

As she followed Layla down a long hallway, Jane played a round of Forensics in her head: Nigerian American Princess—daughter of rich doctors who'd moved from Lagos to La Jolla for grad school and decided to stay. Mother became a cosmetic dermatologist. Father the premier cardiologist on the West Coast. They sent Layla to prep school in La Jolla, Torrey Pines, where, despite her perfect face, she was not noticed as pretty by the phalanx of blue-eyed stoners who were her classmates.

They'd reached the conference room at the end of the hall.

"Sorry for the state of things," Layla said, leading Jane inside. "We moved in last week. Everything's just beginning."

Boxes were piled in corners of the room, and the smell of fresh paint hung in the air. Nothing on the walls. Layla handed Jane a bottle—glass, blue, no label—and said Mr. Ford was on a call but would be there soon. Then she left Jane to wait alone in the conference room.

Through the large window behind her was a view of the freeway in the distance. She stared out at its gray morass. Growing up on the East Coast, Jane had imagined California as mysterious, glamorous, sunbaked. She had not predicted this Los Angeles—antiseptic, asphalt, glitterless, and hard. Or how much of Hollywood felt like an enormous ad agency.

Still, she knew she was lucky to be here. Lucky to be having this meeting with this particular producer. She'd read about him last night on her laptop. Hampton Ford. The ink was still fresh on his multimillion-dollar development deal with the network. According to the article Marianne's office had forwarded to her, he had been brought on board by the network to create diverse content. The profile depicted him as a family man as well as a giant of the small screen.

In the photo spread that went along with the piece, he'd been dressed by a team of stylists in a tuxedo and top hat. He was posing in mid dance step coming down a white staircase smiling, though when Jane looked closely at his face, she thought his smile looked stiff, his eyes tired.

Lenny, beside her in bed, had leaned over to look at the screen. "That's the guy you're meeting?" He snorted. "Pitiful. All that's missing is Shirley Temple."

Jane had tried, a little defensively, to argue that the photo was ironic—that he was in on the joke.

"Never assume anything in Hollywood is ironic," Lenny said, rolling over and putting on his headphones to go back to his Japanese. "That's your first mistake."

Fuck Lenny and his platitudes. Fuck Lenny on his artistically pure high horse. She would not be here unless she'd needed to be here. She would not be here if she'd married a doctor. And yet, now that she was here, she couldn't believe she'd avoided this all so resolutely for years, in her Amish bonnet, quill in hand.

Anyway, those quaint novelistic days were over. Jane had been to three meetings already, with other producers: a short white guy named Doug at a production studio in Culver City, who wanted horror with a social justice edge; a blonde woman in Mid-City named Alison, who was interested in comedies about campus politics; a snappily dressed Korean American woman, also named Jane, who was looking for female-centric content. The conversations she'd had with each of them had already faded into a blur of white noise in her head, pleasant but inconsequential.

That, evidently, was what "generals" were like, getting-to-know-you sessions. If you vibed, you vibed. If there was a spark, it might lead to something else. A second meeting. A one-night stand. A marriage of the minds even. But, like blind dates, mostly these generals went nowhere. All you had to show for your time was a free bottle of ice-cold water in a blue bottle. Could she take the bottle home with her? Or was it like a hotel bathrobe, something to be enjoyed but left behind for the next guest? So far, she had left them behind.

Jane's focus in all the meetings had been to try not to seem desperate, too Dickensian. Not to mention the failed novel the rapidly evaporating sabbatical, the child at home who needed help. None of the other producers had called for a second meeting. Her idea was possibly too vague. Or maybe it was that—as Lenny insisted—she was too smart for these fools and they had nothing to offer her, even as material.

She pulled out her phone to check her face. The makeup had not fixed everything—it had not balanced out what was fundamentally asymmetrical about her face—but she looked okay, as blank and poreless and presentable as could be expected.

Just as she was putting the phone away, the door swung open. It was the man himself—dressed not like Bill "Bojangles" Robinson but like a forty-five-year-old television producer with a seven-figure development deal at a major streaming network. Crisp white T-shirt. Expensively torn jeans. Bright high-tech sneakers. He looked slightly older than he did in the magazine spread, a little heavier, his face wearier. He wasn't traditionally handsome, but he had one of those big caricature-friendly faces that famous people often have. She would have recognized him in a restaurant, across a room. Or in a car next to her in traffic. She would have pointed at him, and said, "Oh my God, there's that guy. What's his name?" Because he wasn't quite famous enough that she'd remember his name. And Lenny would snort, and say, "I have no idea who that is." And pretend not to recognize the guy even if he did.

Jane stood up, flustered.

"Hey," Hampton said. "Have a seat. Thanks for coming in today."

His voice was soft and scratchy, younger than she'd imagined. Layla followed behind, carrying a Styrofoam container and a green smoothie in a plastic cup. Hampton sat down at the conference table and Layla placed them in front of him, along with a plastic fork and a napkin.

On the toilet last night, Jane had looked up his net worth. It felt strange to be sitting across from him knowing this information.

"Sorry to eat in front of you," he said with a bashful smile. "I'm just coming from my trainer and I'm starving." He opened the container and took his plastic fork and began to dive into a mass of pale gunk dotted with color—some kind of veggie egg-white omelet, from the smell. Layla sat beside him, scrolling on her phone.

Jane watched him, thinking how all the things he'd brought into the room with him were things she'd like to have in her life, or at least in her vocabulary: *egg-white omelet, green smoothie, trainer, assistant.*

"So I read your first book," he said. "Your agent sent it to me in Bali. I was on vacation with the fam. Read it on the beach. Wow, great stuff." Hampton eyed her across the table. "I mean, the story's really great, but I was vibing on your voice, Janet."

"Jane," Layla corrected him.

"Jane! Of course."

Jane told him she admired his work too, especially his latest series—which wasn't true. Lenny and she had tried to watch it but had found it unbearably messagey. It was about a family of wealthy Black people living in the Palisades. The parents were wildly successful film executives, and their kids were all beautiful and neurotypical. The catch was this: The mother in the family felt guilty for their good fortune and decided to foster a child. The kid they ended up with was a ten-year-old white girl from a trailer park in Norco, California. Her parents were both in jail on fentanyl charges. The vulgar but oddly charming character of the girl seemed clearly based on Honey Boo Boo. At first, the whole family was horrified by the sassy fat white child in their living room—but eventually she won them all over, and in the end, they decided to adopt her. The culture clash was the running gag—all the ways Cookie didn't understand which fork to use or not to use the N-word, all the ways she rubbed the rich Black family the wrong way with her lying and stealing and general trailer park hijinks. The show was kind of a reboot of *Diff'rent Strokes* but with the races reversed.

"It's so clever," Jane said. "I love the episode about the ferret in the toilet—"

Hampton crinkled his nose. "You did? I hated that show. It was total network schlock. I'm stoked to leave that shit behind. To be honest, Jane, I felt shackled. I'm going in a different direction here. All premium, edgy stuff. It's time."

His omelet was done. He pushed the platter away and wiped his mouth. Picked up the smoothie and took a sip, sneered. "I hate smoothies but my trainer says I have to drink them." He sucked at it for a moment, his eyes watering with disgust, then put it down. "So, tell me, why would a literary writer, I mean, a real, full-grown professor—you're a professor, right?"

Jane nodded. She wasn't officially a professor, but her students called her Professor Gibson. They didn't know the difference.

"Why would a professor like yourself," he continued, "want to work in this TV swamp anyway? You know television is a swamp, right? Talk to me. Tell me what you're thinking."

Jane's answer came smoothly. She'd given it three times, rehearsing it with the producers she'd met on the other generals. She told him that she'd been realizing over the past few years that the greatest writing being done today was for television, not for novels. She repeated the line that had played so well with Marianne and Carrie, her observation that even English professors—people who had devoted their lives to literature—talked to one another not about books but about what they had watched on television last night. She said she'd decided that this was where her future lay, in this vibrant and collaborative medium, which was having a renaissance of sorts. She could see he was listening. She paused, took a sip of water. "Television is the novel of our times."

Hampton cracked a bashful smile. "Wow, you really think so? That's—that's wild. Well, I hope you're right! 'Cause I could never write a fucking novel. Now that shit looks hard."

"Oh, it is," Jane said. "It's—madness."

Together she and Hampton laughed, and she felt a surge of connection with him. Layla was still there, beside him, but so engrossed in her phone that it was as if she wasn't there.

"So tell me what kind of show you're thinking about, Jane," Hampton said. "I'm listening."

Jane launched into her pitch, the one she'd been trying to bring into focus over the past few weeks in the other meetings. It was all there in her doomed novel. She'd been wrestling with this material for so long that she could talk about it in her sleep. It was all about her people—the mulatto people—whose story, she explained, had been told up until now as tragedy. The mulatto had been depicted on the one hand as dangerously sexual, like the half-crazed mulatta harlot in *The Birth of a Nation* or the quadroon rapist Joe Christmas in Faulkner's *Light in August*. Or they were portrayed as sad and mopey, doomed to a life betwixt and between, like all those sad, bright-yellow girls of the golden age of cinema, the ones with odd names like Peola and Pinky.

Either way, the mulatto had been treated like a walking, talking predicament rather than an actual character. "See, I have this theory," she told Hampton. "Mulattos are like the queer people of races. Like gay characters, you might have noticed, who always kill themselves in movies. So do mulattos."

Hampton's expression while she talked was difficult to read. She couldn't tell if he was bored or interested. "I mean," she said, trying to wrap it up, "we usually end up offing ourselves by act two. But in the show I want to make, see, I want to show mulattos in a different light. Show us being, you know, just regular. Relatable." She hated the word *relatable*, which her students were always using, but it had come in handy here.

"Go on," Hampton said.

"So what I'm thinking," Jane said, "is we make a comedy about a kooky but lovable mulatto family. Present day. Not an interracial couple—that's last century's news, you know. But a pair of grown-up mulattos who have married each other and have given birth to two second-generation mulatto kids. Mulatto squared. A family with normal problems but with a mulatto twist." She was sweating. She took a sip from the blue bottle as she tried to read his face.

"Obviously, there's more to say," she said. "But we could get into the—you know—nitty-gritty later." She could hear that this still wasn't so much an idea as a premise, a place to begin—a situation.

Hampton nodded. "Yes, the nitty-gritty." He was watching her now, his eyes roving coolly over her hair and features. "Can I ask you a question?"

"Of course."

"What's your numbers breakdown? Like, percentages? I hope that's not offensive." He cracked a teasing smile. "It's just that I know all you mixed nuts like to spit into vials."

She laughed, not surprised or offended, only amused, because he was right. And Lenny was wrong about this guy. Hampton Ford was no imbecile. He was a very sharp student of her people. Because it was true, mulattos did like to spit into vials. She'd done it herself a few years earlier. She'd sent her saliva to a genetic testing company. Every mixed person she knew had done it, some to more than one company, hoping for a different result. Lenny had warned her not to do it, because her DNA would forevermore be in a database somewhere. But she had to know. Her quest to solve the quagmire of her background had been more important to her than getting away with murder someday.

The results had come four weeks later, with a pie chart that broke down her heritage. As expected, it was pure chaos, less biracial than rainbow pride flag. But it was an answer nonetheless to that ancient riddle, what's black and white and red all over?

"Thirty," she said now. "I'm thirty percent West African." She was rounding up by two points, but in addition to the standard disclaimer about margins of error, there had been a footnote in the results saying some indeterminable two percent of her was "unassigned," like a rogue seating situation, and could be from anywhere. She'd read that optimistically as extra African points.

But Hampton was still eyeing her, and she sensed he didn't believe her. "You got a family photo?" he said. "Mixed people love to carry around pictures of their families. I mean, you meet an old mixed nut, like seventy-five fucking years old, and she still got a picture of her parents and her siblings in her wallet in case somebody asks. Am I right?"

Jane saw what he was doing. He wanted proof. And she couldn't blame him. He followed the news. Every few months there seemed to be another white woman exposed for pretending to be biracial or Native or Latinx. Another white woman in mulattoface. They fucked it up for people like Jane, making her look like an imposter of—herself. It was an odd new twist in the "white people helping themselves to everything that isn't theirs" trope. And he was right too that people like her did tend to carry around family photos, sometimes whole photo albums in the glove compartment, always at least one in their wallet. They kept them handy, like yellow stars, to show people how they'd come out the way they had—people were always asking. She felt Hampton watching her as she scrambled to open her purse and wallet to find the picture. It was a snapshot from 1978, predivorce, a few years before the restraining orders and the custody battle. Her mother and father stood side by side, smiling brightly in the squalor of their living room, as if they still thought they were special for marrying outside the race. She and her sister stood flanking them, looking somber and dubious, as if they knew what was coming.

She handed the photo to Hampton. He looked at it and something softened in his expression. He showed the photo to Layla. "Look, doesn't her mom look like Patty Hearst? And her dad's got that Huey vibe."

Layla glanced at the photo. "Aw, so cute," she said, without much conviction, then turned back to her phone.

Hampton returned the photo to Jane. "So, you're like Quincy's kids. I get it." He took another grimacing sip of the smoothie. "Hey, I want to show you something. Layla, go get me that picture off my desk, the one of Doreen and Juju."

While she was gone, Hampton rose and went to stand by the windows. Jane took in his profile. It struck her that he had one of those faces that changed dramatically based on the angle of viewing; it almost appeared to be split down the middle. From one side, his expression was amused, almost laughing; but from this angle, he looked crestfallen, bereft.

"You want to know something, Jane?" he said. "I have never in my life slept with a white woman. I never wanted to go down that path. Never wanted to come home at the end of the day to an actual bona fide white woman. I just never understood that impulse. No diss on your pops, but damn, that generation of dudes really did drown in the buttermilk. No offense."

"None taken," Jane said. Was he cooling on her idea? She couldn't tell. Certainly none of the other meetings had gotten so personal.

Layla returned just then, carrying a framed photograph.

"Is this the one you wanted?"

Hampton took it from her, stared at it a moment, then handed the photo to Jane.

"Here they are," he said. "That's me with Doreen and Jujubean."

The photo was of the three of them at the edge of an infinity pool, laughing. The sky was technicolor blue above them, and all the colors—the white of the stucco on the house, the green of the lawn—popped like something out of the first color movie. Doreen was pretty like Dorothy Dandridge. Pretty like a Cotton Club dancer. Jujubean, beside her parents, wasn't so pretty. She glowed like some kind of phosphorescent sea eel, her red hair pulled into pigtails. She had freckles and the pugnacious features of an Irish clog dancer.

"You look surprised. And I know what you're thinking. Juju—she looks nearly white, right?"

"No, no," Jane said. "I was only thinking—" She searched for a line. "Your family is so beautiful."

Hampton didn't seem to hear her. His face still looked worried, drawn. "It's Doreen—she has some redheads in her family tree, going back to, you know, the Scottish fucking overseer."

"Got it," Jane said, looking between Hampton's face and the child's, trying to spot the resemblance.

"You ever seen that movie, *Rabbit-Proof Fence?* Australian flick about the Aborigines. There's this scene at the end where they show a wall of family photos spanning, like, four generations—and the faces, they start out Black, with those wide Aboriginal faces, wearing war paint, standing half-naked with spears out in the grasslands, but over the generations, the pictures keep getting whiter and whiter until there's nothing left but a couple of fucking Abercrombie & Fitch models, pink and blonde, standing beside a Land Rover holding rifles."

He walked back to the table and picked up the smoothie, swished it around. "My wife ordered us those 23andMe kits last year. She's like you. She just had to know what was in the mystery sauce. She bought one for me, one for her, one for Jujubean. Like, Merry Fucking Christmas. Doreen thought it would be fun. But I wouldn't do it. I wouldn't let Jujubean do it either." He turned so the laughing half of his face was showing. "See, I love being Black too much to want to find out that I'm, like, forty percent or some shit. Or any other . . . surprises."

"I get it."

"Jujubean has it all. She's growing up in the Palisades. We've got a whole village of Mexican help at our beck and call. We even hired a woman to sleep with her at night when she was a baby, like a human teddy bear. Now she's in one of those fancy-assed private schools that act like they can shape your child's destiny, make them into these perfect human beings even though the kids who go there are just like any other kids, maybe worse." He looked at Jane. "You want to know what that school is really teaching Jujubean?"

"What's that?"

"To grow up to marry a white person. Jujubean is gonna probably marry a white guy, and her kids will marry white people and I'll end up with some Abercrombie & Fitch motherfuckers for grandkids. It'll be a Quincy Jones Christmas extravaganza. I'm paying fifty-fucking-thousand dollars a year for my own extinction. If that ain't some volunteer slavery, what is?"

Hampton sat down at the table with a heavy slump.

"Maybe not," Jane said, still trying to save the meeting. "You never know. Maybe she'll marry a Ghanaian doctor and turn the whole ship around. It's been known to happen."

"Possible but highly unlikely. It's a numbers game. And the numbers are against us."

Jane was still holding the framed photograph of Hampton and his family, and when she looked down at their smiling, hincty faces, she imagined her own face there, and Ruby's face where Jujubean's was. Ruby and her having a mother and daughter moment, laughing in an infinity pool.

Hampton sucked at the dregs of his smoothie, then waved the green sludge in front of her. "See, race is like this smoothie here. This has probably got five different fruits and vegetables in it, six different supplements. But I couldn't tell you what. Because the more ingredients you add to it, the more it tastes like nothing." He took a sip and crinkled his nose. "I hate smoothies. They might lengthen my life, but they taste like vomit."

"You have ten minutes, Hampton." It was Layla.

Hampton stared at Jane. He still looked sad. "So, you want to make a comedy about mulattos." He said it deadpan, like he couldn't believe anyone would want to make a show about such a thing, much less a comedy. Jane swallowed. In the corners of her mind, a dark shadow was spreading, options narrowing, Tokyo looming. She knew that on real blind dates it was bad to look desperate, but she couldn't help herself now.

"I mean," she said, "it doesn't have to be about mulattos. We could go in another direction. The mulattos could just be sort of side characters?"

Hampton shook his head. "Are you kidding? I love your idea. I love everything you said before."

"Of course," Jane said. "I mean, of course it should be about mulattos."

"Damn right. It's perfect. A comedy about mulattos. Why the fuck not? Right? They exist. They're here. They're not going anywhere. If anything, they're multiplying like rats. So let's get there first. Let's get ahead of the issue. Let's make a show with a premium vibe—edgy—but not so out there that we lose the masses. I don't make shit that only appeals to, like, blue state hipsters, you know? I hate that childless lefty Sundance shit." He leaned back, clasped his hands behind his head. "Fuck. This could be the greatest comedy about mulattos ever to hit the small screen. You realize that? The Jackie Robinson of biracial comedies. It could be, like, *Pinky* meets—I don't know—*Modern Family*. *Imitation of Life* meets, like, *Everybody Loves Raymond*. I mean, why the fuck not? You all deserve it. I mean, this is America. Everybody deserves a show about people like them, right?"

A beep came from Layla's phone. "Your next meeting is waiting, Hampton."

"Argh," Hampton said, with mock annoyance. "These Nigerians will keep you on time."

He stood. "Now let me hear you say it: the Jackie Robinson of biracial comedies."

"The Jackie Robinson of biracial comedies."

He patted Jane on the shoulder, said his people would be in touch with her people, then she was being squired out of the conference room by Layla and led down the hallway back to the lobby, which had been empty when she'd arrived. Now there were two people waiting there. A young woman with Jane's own beige skin tone but with perfect ringlets gave Jane a steely smile as she eyed her up and down. A few seats away from her sat a young man—possibly Mexican—who was clutching a script on his lap. Jane tried to glimpse the title as she walked past, but he turned it over.

Outside, she was met by a wall of dry heat. This was what passed for spring in Los Angeles. Jane headed for the parking lot, thinking she would never get used to the parched and sweltering spring days, not as long as she lived here. But today of all days she understood all this heat and ozone was the price you had to pay. All that sunshine was said to be the reason the film industry had moved west back in the 1920s. Only in Los Angeles could they control when it rained and when it snowed. And the light here was, it was true, like no other light, perpetually effervescent, mirthful. Even on the brightest days, East Coast sunshine held a tinge of melancholy.

She found the Subaru in the covered lot, coated in tree sap and bird shit. The inside smelled strongly of fermented apple juice—one of the kid's juice boxes had turned to moonshine in the heat. She turned on the engine and checked her phone to find a flurry of texts from Lenny. Six of them, as if somebody had died. Guilt and panic swelled in her. But they were just a series of items he wanted her to pick up at Whole Foods on her way home. Potatoes. Milk. Yogurt. Gummy vitamins. Smart Puffs. Turkey burgers. She felt a prickle of resentment. For an hour, she hadn't thought about any of their needs. For an hour, she had not thought of her bank account. For an hour, she'd been distracted by the blind date potential of a general. By the possibility of another life, another self. Lenny claimed that she was a fool to turn her sights away from the novel— even for diversion, even for material. He wanted her to stay with him in the trenches of high art. He wanted her to keep banging away at her mulatto *War and Peace*. Believe in yourself, he'd said the other night, like he was parroting some kind of Whitney Houston song. But he wasn't staring the facts in the face. No book deal by August meant no tenure, no money for a house in Multicultural Mayberry, no Black lesbian neighbors, no transgender playmates for the kids. No book deal by August meant no stable life for their children.

To be a Melungeon was to learn to lie. She'd realized this during her research into that doomed tribe of nineteenth-century misfits who had, according to Josiah and Honor, taken up far too much space in her novel. That seemed so long ago now, the years she'd spent poring over dusty books and microfilmed articles about that mélange of tricksters who lived in isolation in the Cumberland Gap, that mountainous area where Tennessee, Virginia, and Kentucky converged. They were liars, all of them, from the beginning. It was a matter of survival. When they went down the mountain to sell and buy supplies, they lied to the white landowners, claiming to be of Portuguese ancestry, sometimes Turkish, depending on the day. Up on the mountain, away from the world, she'd imagined the Melungeons laughing about their lies with one another. Laughing because they knew they were the most American of people, a mix of "Injun, Negro, and white man." But they knew their fictional foreignness was all that was keeping them safe from harm, from the violence of white people, who had learned to fear them. To tell the truth of who they were was to consign themselves to death by association.

They'd seen what happened to their darker brethren, who had not been able to lie. They'd seen the scars and the corpses and the bodies hanging from trees. They'd seen the trail of dead Indians who were also their cousins and brothers and aunts and mothers. They lied to stay alive.

But lies are a funny thing. They don't stay where they're supposed to stay. They morph and mutate and spread like smallpox. A lie well told, often enough told, began to eat one's memory. And over time, it became harder to say where the fiction ended and the truth began. And maybe if you lied long enough, you became a lie. A walking, talking lie. If you lied long enough, Portugal would seep into your dreams.

In one scene she'd written, the Melungeon child called Roy began to cry in his bed one night, inconsolable. He told his mother he was homesick, that he wanted to go home. She laughed, confused, and told him not to be silly. This was home—this gap between states, this gap between people. The boy cried in great heaving wails and began to call out for Portugal, a country where he'd never been. The mother stroked the boy's back and told him to hush, but the boy only cried harder until finally she told him that she missed Portugal too, and that someday, someday, they'd go back.

LATER, after she'd finished the shopping and was on the freeway headed home, her phone began to buzz on the seat beside her. She assumed it was Lenny, checking where she was. But when she looked at it, she recognized the number as Brett's. She silenced the call.

10.

Jane stood in the kitchen preparing dinner. Lenny was seated on the sofa, his back to her. He was wearing his headphones, and at regular intervals, guttural, almost infantile, sounds emanated from his throat followed by silence, then more sounds. The children sat on either side of him, wearing their own smaller headsets and watching their own separate screens. Finn was watching YouTube videos of whirlpools. Ruby was watching *Frozen* again. They all looked like they were on a long flight somewhere.

The meeting with Hampton had felt so rich and alive inside of her in the immediate aftermath, had kept her buzzing all through that afternoon, through the fluorescent light of Whole Foods, through the slog of traffic and into the evening when she'd done something completely out of character and baked them all a cake, Duncan Hines out of the box but a cake nonetheless.

But now, two days later, the glow was starting to fade. The drudgery of mother life—the kids fighting, helping Finn with his homework, mending Ruby's wig where it had detached from the mesh cap—was beginning to make her feel that the meeting hadn't happened at all, that it was all some ridiculous daydream she'd had in the car. Hampton and Layla and the green smoothie and the egg-white omelet felt like something that had happened to somebody else.

Outside, through the glass, the garden lights blinked on to signal evening, and Jane contemplated the tasks before her. There was a slab of salmon on a plate. There was a potato. There was a pot of water on the stove. There was a plant-based burger patty sitting on a plate beside the microwave. Four dinners for four different people.

Finn was having salmon. Fish was supposed to help mend whatever thing was different about his brain. Ruby ate only carbs. Lenny was a vegetarian, so he ate a lot of plant-based meat substitutes, sausages and burgers that looked deceptively like the real thing but were made of soybeans. And Jane ate the way a lot of mothers ate, pretending not to eat. Often her dinner was dumpster diving the macaroni and cheese off a child's plastic plate. It had not been lost on her that she got the same number of calories that way as if she'd eaten a satisfying meal.

She had just put the potato in the oven when her phone buzzed in her back pocket. She pulled it out. Marianne. She glanced at Lenny's back and took her phone into the bedroom, where she sat down on the bed. She hesitated for a moment before answering, wondering if Marianne had been in touch with Brett yet. Was she phoning to call Jane out on her little lie? Jane forced herself to answer. To her relief, Marianne sounded excited and didn't mention Brett at all. Her news was all good: Hampton's people had called today to say he'd loved meeting Jane and wanted to meet her again. He wanted a second date.

"Hampton is on fire right now," Marianne said. "With his development deal, if he decides he wants to make something, he makes it. So, you wouldn't have to jump through so many hoops."

She said something about a merger and something about an if/come deal—if "they" got on board, "they" (what "they"?) would have a deal. About pitches and executive producer credits. And a bunch of other things that sounded like fortune knocking before she said, "But of course it's just a second date. Nothing to negotiate yet. No show yet. But I think you should go in with some solid ideas. Hampton's searching for a voice right now, and you could be it."

After the call ended, Jane lay back on the bed. She turned her head to the side and smashed her face into a pillow. No matter how many times they washed the sheets, they still smelled of Brett, something sharp and male. She wondered whether his idea for a mulatto comedy had really taken hold, and if so, how far along he was. Had he finished a draft for a pilot already? Would he be sending it to Marianne soon?

Lenny came in then, carrying two glasses of white wine. She sat up and took one, sipped. It tasted cheap. It was cheap.

"Where's this from?"

"Côtes du Ralphs."

"Yuck."

"Well, bottom's up. We drank all the others."

"All?"

Lenny nodded.

"We're going to have to replace them before we leave," Jane said, without much conviction.

Lenny laughed. "Sure. Those bottles were a little out of our price range, babe."

"Brett's gonna kill me," Jane said, half to herself.

"No, he won't. Dude's got money to burn. Remember? He'll call his wine guy. Rich people love having their shit stolen because it gives them something new to buy. That dopamine rush of consumption. We did him a favor."

Lenny crossed the room and went to stand in front of the glass, looking out into the courtyard as he sipped his wine.

"Was that Brett you were talking to?" he said.

"No. It was my agent."

"She dared to call you?"

Jane paused. He thought she meant Honor. "Yes." The lie came without thinking about it. An instinct. She let it hang there, more curious about its effect than remorseful. Everything was just abstraction at this point. Vague prospects. Nothing was real enough to matter, and in this sense, no version felt truer than the other.

"Did she apologize for being such a twat?"

"In her way, I suppose. She is suddenly very energized and—well, invested—in my book again, saying she wants to help me get it in shape. She says she had some lightning bolt last night about what was wrong with my draft." Jane paused, then said, "She thinks what I need to do is cut back on the Melungeon parts and fill in the Hollywood thread, bring it up-to-date. She says the Hollywood part should be the heart of the story and the rest of it is just backstory."

"Do you agree with her?"

"Weirdly, I see her point. But we both agreed I may need to do some additional research."

"Interesting. Well, I'm glad she's finally doing her job. Earning her fifteen percent. Do you feel better?"

Jane went to stand beside him, stared out at the garden. "I don't know. I wonder if it's worth the effort. Novels—nobody has the time or the attention to read them anymore."

"Are you serious?"

"Yes."

"Jesus, can't you just feel good for a minute? Take the win, Jane. You got positive news. Your agent is excited about your book. She wants to get it in shape and sell it. She's invested in you. Can't we just toast to that?"

He held up his glass. Jane clinked and took a sip. The supermarket chardonnay she used to chug happily was now nearly undrinkable. Disgusting.

"Lenny?"

"Yeah?"

"Would you still love me if I told you I don't want to look at that wretched novel ever again?"

"What are you even talking about? You've been working on that thing for a decade. Your agent believes in it. Why are you doing this? Is this your father or your mother sabotaging you?"

"It's a serious question. What if I told you the idea of going back into that cave, of sitting alone with the cluster of imaginary friends for a minute longer, feels like psychosis to me? Like, the little boy in *The Shining* making his fingers talk to one another? What if I told you that writing fiction at all feels bad for my mental health?"

"I'd say you're being a little dramatic. You're a writer. You'll get back into it now that you have some guidance—a goal."

"It's not just the writing. It's the publishing. It's what comes after. You finish this thing—then the book comes out and you have to go out on the road and peddle it. There's so much desperation involved in selling your own work. You have to cultivate a persona to hawk a product that, let's be real, nobody really wants. You have to be multicultural and wise. Be somebody with a position. You have to tweet increasingly inflammatory things about your vagina just so people will buy your book. A book nobody wanted or needed in the first place. Because they already have TV."

Lenny chuckled. He thought this was some kind of shtick. "Sweetie, you're self-sabotaging. I've seen you do this before when something good happens to you. You resist doing better than your family members. You're afraid of all those crabs in the barrel pulling you back down. So you try to jump down to join them."

He was repeating almost verbatim something Heidi had said last year.

"It's not that," Jane said.

He turned to her. "Honor wants to sell your book." He gripped her arms. Stared into her eyes. "Honor is going to sell your book! Think about it. That means you get to return to your department triumphant, shove the publishing contract in Mischling's face, tell him to tenure your ass right quick. Think how much fun it'll be to look down your nose at Kay Franken."

She tried to laugh along with him, but the way he believed in her made her sad, and she couldn't quite muster a smile. She wanted to take it back, to tell him that she'd made it all up—that she hadn't heard from Honor again. That she never would hear from Honor again. She wanted to tell him that the novelist he'd lived with for ten years was a fiction herself.

Finn appeared in the bedroom door. "Mama."

"Yes?"

"Something's burning."

She'd forgotten dinner. She ran into the kitchen, and sure enough, everything was ruined. She held a dish towel over her mouth as she opened the oven to a wall of smoke and pulled out the pan. She felt near to tears. Nearby, Lenny muttered that it was okay, he'd just order pizza.

IN HER DREAM that night, it was Brett, not Lenny, sleeping beside her. She leaned over his body, examining his features, the full lips and long nose and thick brows, the black curls springing from his scalp. Asleep, he looked less like a native California skateboarding screenwriter and more tragic and timeless, like Jean Toomer. She slid beneath the sheets and took him, felt him grow hard in her mouth. She slid up and climbed on top of him and they began to have sex, slowly, tenderly at first, then hard and fast. He was half asleep when they started, but as he woke, she could see his surprise that it was her, not Piper. He was inside the wrong woman. Yet he didn't stop. In the dream, she could tell he was finally understanding what he'd been missing. He was going Black and would never go back. In the dream, Jane too was recognizing her mistake. He was not her friend. He'd never been just her friend. He was more than her friend. And he was not just a California dude, light and airy. In the dream, he was from the same land she was from, a region ancient and contested.

She woke with a start, tangled in the sheets. She sat up, and as her eyes adjusted to the dim light, she understood that it was the middle of the night and she was alone in bed. She listened. She could hear a voice coming from the other room, a voice she didn't recognize. There was a stranger inside their house. She slid out of bed and went toward the voice, fearing what she might find. But when she got to the doorway, she saw it was only Lenny. He was seated alone on the sofa, shirtless, with his headphones on. "O-Genki desu ka?" he was saying in a strange singsong voice. "Otearai wa doku desu ka?"

11.

On the morning of her second meeting with Hampton Ford, Jane counted two good omens.

First, when she dropped Finn at his kindergarten classroom he went inside willingly, without tears, like a big boy. Maybe, she thought, he was finally adjusting to life on this planet. Or maybe Lenny was right, and there was no problem with him at all.

The other good omen was the rain. Late, unbidden, unpredicted, it poured down over the city in heavy streaks, sparkling like liquid silver, like something created by a machine or by the gods. She sat in traffic listening to its drumbeat on her windshield.

This time, Jane hadn't bothered to get dressed with any care. She didn't want to look thirsty. And she had remembered that Brett and other successful screenwriter friends usually dressed like they'd barely bothered to change out of their pajamas. So she had pulled on jeans and a dingy white T-shirt of Brett's that said BIENVENIDOS, and a pair of his limegreen PUMAs. She had always had big feet for a woman, and as she had discovered one drunken night in grad school when they put on each other's shoes by accident, Brett had small feet for a man.

What was funny was that she hadn't had to lie to Lenny about where she was going. She hadn't planned it that way, but the first lie—that Honor had called to talk about her novel, to encourage her to develop the Hollywood story line more, to make it more central to the story—flowed into the second lie, that she was going to have a few more meetings with Hampton Ford just to gather material. Lenny thought it was silly. He said she could make everything up; it was fiction, wasn't it? He pointed out that writing wasn't method acting. But since he wasn't a writer himself, she was able to convince him that sometimes writing did indeed require method acting.

Anyway, she wasn't even sure she was lying. Novel writing was funny that way. You never came to your material directly. It came to you. You had to have an almost religious faith in *process* if you were to write fiction. It was so much like dreaming. The subconscious held the answers.

She arrived ten minutes early. This time she parked her own car and made her way toward Hampton's building, which was tucked in the back corner of the lot—a modest pale-stucco two-story structure with no sign out front. On this gray wet day, it looked substantial but discreet, hidden behind bright-green tropical plants and overgrown succulents.

She passed an open hangar where a group of men—gaffers, tech guys, best boys (whatever the hell that was)—stood in a cluster smoking, staring out at the rain. They all wore the same graying buzz cut and the same faded jeans, the same combat boots, the same high-priced hoody—a sort of neo-Nazi chic that she found slightly hot. They nodded to her and she nodded back, and somehow the brief interaction made her feel important, part of the vast inscrutable city.

And yet, Jane hesitated at the door to the building, overcome for a moment by a bracing fear. It was her old fear, the one a therapist had once told her she'd been ingrained to feel as a child, the sense that everything good was bound to fail—because, deep down, she did not believe she was entitled to a world that seemed welcoming, warm. Now she did the thing the therapist had told her to do—she pushed past the feeling, through the door, and there was Layla, looking even prettier than Jane had remembered her, smiling in a yellow and orange head wrap.

"Sorry about this fucking weather," Layla said. "It's bumming me out. I mean, I'm a California girl. This is so not okay."

Jane had described Layla to Lenny the previous night, the Nigerian American beauty with the Valley Girl voice. She'd described her to Lenny as if she were a character that Jane was thinking about incorporating into the novel, which she'd secretly started to imagine was a bloated corpse now, swollen and ready to explode in Brett's desk drawer.

Lenny had launched into his theory about Nigerians. He said Nigerians were getting all the jobs and fellowships and creative positions that Black Americans had fought to have for more than four hundred years. He'd said white people preferred them because they had what he called the "arrogance of the never enslaved."

"They have that immigrant chutzpah," he'd said, while they prepared food together for the kids. "It makes them better at being us than we could ever be. I mean, think how pretty and poised we'd be if we'd come first class on Virgin Atlantic instead of via the fucking Middle Passage."

His theory would have amused her once upon a time. But she felt defensive—and she reminded him that Hampton himself, the man with the money, was as American as they were.

"You mean Stepin Fetchit?" he said. And she'd snorted, pretended to think it was funny and let it go. Because marriage was all about letting those little moments go.

Layla was not alone this time. A lanky white boy hovered behind her. "Jane, this is Topher," Layla said, turning to him. "He's our guy Friday."

Topher leaned forward to shake Jane's hand. He was very tall, she saw now, but he had such stooped posture she hadn't noticed at first. He wore baggy faded khakis, a Choate T-shirt, and Top-Siders with no socks. When he smiled at Jane, she saw that one of his front teeth was slightly brown, as if from decay.

"Topher will take care of you," Layla said, and she headed down the hall.

"Can I get you a coffee?" Topher asked.

"Sure."

When he went to make it, Jane looked around, noticing now that the office had been totally decorated since she'd last been here a week ago. Everything now gestured toward the producer's vision—Blackness, Blackness, as far as the eye could see. It was a specific California Blackness—boho mixed with California casual. There were mud-cloth throw pillows on the slouchy linen couch, a Beni Ourain rug. A gallery of framed headshots of Black television stars filled one wall—Kim Fields and Robert Guillaume and Roxie Roker and even Gary Coleman.

Topher emerged with her coffee and placed it on a coaster in front of her. "I love when it rains here," he said, going to the window beside her.

"Me too," she said. "I'm from the East Coast, so I suppose it makes me feel at home."

"I'm from Connecticut," he said. "I miss it. Some mornings I wake up and hear the sprinkler going outside my apartment and there's about five minutes where I pretend that it's actually rain. I pretend I'm back in Stamford. Do you miss the other side?"

"I used to," Jane said. "For years. But I guess I've adjusted. I like it on this side."

She realized as she said it that it was true. Maybe it was the rejection from the gatekeepers of the East Coast literary establishment, but it felt as if she had somehow finally cut the cord. You could act like a visitor for only so long. You could only resist the weird charm of this coast for so many years.

She'd always disliked the Buddhist saying, "The obstacle is the path." Or maybe it was that she hated the people who said it, smiling tightly as she pushed deeper into Downward Dog. But now she thought there was some small truth to it. Her crisis had forced her—and not a moment too soon—to finally look around the city where she lived and see it for what it was—or for what it might be. Lenny didn't see it yet. But maybe she could help him see it, make him see it.

Topher didn't see it either. She could feel the New England homesickness emanating from him. Could see it in his insistence on dressing like Dickie Greenleaf under the hot western sun. She wondered how such a very white and mediocre preppy had ended up here in this shrine to Black entertainment. She played Forensics in her head. The kid's father had to be a bigwig who had done a favor for Hampton once upon a time.

It was as if she'd voiced this thought aloud, because just then Topher began to talk about himself in forensic detail. He spoke with his head resting on the window, gazing out at the studio's wet lot. "I majored in theater at Yale. I wrote plays. Some of them even got produced. I wanted to be my generation's Tom Stoppard." He paused, glanced at her. "You ever hear of Tom Stoppard?"

She told him that yes, she had heard of Tom Stoppard. It was a code question, a way of finding out if she was schooled in high art and whiteness, which she was, because her mother was as white as a mother could be. White enough that she'd gone off and married a Black man as if she were conquering another nation. But these days, both parents seemed part of some ancient, fading world that she could see drifting out to sea.

"Then I got into film," Topher said. "And I decided theater was dead."

Jane peered down the hall in search of Layla, but she was nowhere to be found.

"Then I decided I wanted to be the next Kieślowski. Did you ever see any of his movies?"

He didn't wait for her answer. He said his favorite movie was *The Double Life of Veronique*, though in some ways he liked the *Three Colours* trilogy better. He said he'd been obsessed with New Wave for a long time, but now he was really into watching silent films, Busby Berkeley. "I wanted to go to the writing program," he said. "But for some reason I switched my application at the last moment to go to the production program. Well, not some reason. It was Layla. I met her a few months before I came here, and she told me to switch. We became good friends, and I guess it was—I don't know. I don't know what we are to each other. Anyway, our final term, Hampton came to speak to our class. He was just a showrunner then. He was so funny, so charming, you know? He blew us all away. Afterward, he asked me and Layla to go for coffee with him. Just picked us out of the crowd. To be honest, it was probably Layla he noticed, because, well, you've seen Layla, and I was beside her. I don't know. We had this amazing time, and afterward, outside, he got our contact info and said he'd be in touch. This is the weird thing about Hampton. He usually does what he says he's gonna do. He offered us jobs a few weeks later. I swear everyone in our program wanted to murder us, even our teachers. Because we were the chosen ones, you know? We had jobs. With a big showrunner. We worked with him at the network. And he just kept rising. Higher and higher. And he said no matter how big he got, he wouldn't leave us behind. And he meant it because he brought us with him here—to all of this." Topher swept his arms around the office. "I graduated from that program five years ago, Layla and I both did. We've been with him for five years."

"That's great," Jane said, thinking there was something sad about the story that the boy couldn't see.

"You know, the funny thing is," Topher said. "I think sometimes I wouldn't mind being a novelist even though I know not many people read novels anymore. It still seems cool to me."

"Well, trust me, it's not cool," Jane said.

"I hope this dude isn't boring you with his life story." Layla had reappeared in the hallway.

Topher's cheeks flashed a bright sudden pink. "I better get back to work."

"Good idea," Layla said, with a thin cool smile. "That printer won't fix itself."

Topher lifted a hand at Jane and went to the front desk as Jane and Layla headed down the hall.

"God love that boy," Layla said in a low voice. "But he can be a real Debbie Downer. I'm always, like, get your ass some Lexapro."

Jane glanced back to see if Topher had heard them, but he was squatting down in front of the printer, lifting its cover.

"He does seem homesick," she said.

"Well then, medicate, dude," Layla said. "Or go back to Connecticut or wherever the hell he's from. I mean, we don't need those *Dead Poets Society* vibes in here. We got shows to make. Carpe fucking diem, right?" She sighed. "Anyhoo. Hampton's psyched you're here."

Then they were there, at the door to his office, and Jane peeked inside and saw she'd dressed all wrong again. She regretted dressing like some kind of fourteen-year-old skater boy. Hampton was wearing his usual T-shirt and jeans combo, but it looked somehow fancier than she remembered, and he wasn't alone. A white man in a suit sat across from him, a silver fox with expensive red-framed glasses, tan skin, big grinning teeth. Jane hovered in the doorway. Hampton was in midstory.

"So, I said to him, 'No, Tim, Black families don't celebrate Black History Month. That's absurd.' I had to explain to him it's a holiday created for white people. His mind was fucking blown."

The white man was smiling and shaking his head. "That's a great example."

"But see, that's the kind of thing that happens every day in workplaces across America—little misunderstandings that escalate into—alienation? Mistrust? And we have so much power here to create awareness. People will open their minds and really learn if they're laughing hard enough."

"Wonderful," the man said. "I can't wait to put you out front, Hampton."

There was a lull in the conversation—just a beat—and Layla gestured for Jane to enter. Hampton looked up and smiled. "Jane Gibson," he called out. "Come on in. We're just finishing up here."

Both men rose to greet her.

"Jane's the novelist I told you about. And this is the one and only Bruce Borland. I've told Jane about you."

Jane didn't recognize the man's name, but she acted as if she did. "So great to finally meet you, Bruce."

Hampton came around his desk to give Jane a hug. He smelled expensive, clean. "Jane and I are working on a show that's gonna blow your socks off, aren't we?"

"Amazing," Bruce said. "You landed in the right place. Hampton's got such a vision. And that's a rare thing in this town, vision."

"Aw, that's so nice, Bruce. Jane writes books."

"Impressed," Bruce said. "A real writer."

"Well, no more real than Hampton," Jane said.

"Hah," Hampton said. "You kidding? I couldn't do what you do for five minutes, much less years—sit alone in a little office, just making shit up."

"Please don't make me go back in that room again," Jane said. "I'll slit my wrists!"

She meant it as a joke, but they both stared at her, their smiles faltering. She laughed. "I'm kidding. I mean, I'm just happy to be here."

Hampton looked at Bruce, smiling. "She's funny, right?" Bruce nodded. "See," Hampton said. "I was explaining to Bruce my theory—that the mulatto American is where the money's at. The fastest growing group in America—and nobody's noticed y'all are here! You're begging for your own show, right?"

"Begging," Jane said, nodding.

"Beg no more!" Bruce said. "This is going to be great." He glanced at his watch. "Listen, Hampton, I gotta get shaking. Meeting with the team. But call me. Let's do lunch. Jane, can't wait to hear what you kids come up with."

Then Bruce Borland was gone, and she was alone with Hampton. He went to stand by the window, staring out at the parking lot. She was seeing his face from its tragic angle again, and it looked stormy, worried. "That's the man, Jane. That's the man we have to sell this shit to. That's the top of the network." He glanced at her. "We need to think up a show idea so great—so original—that Bruce will take one look at it and give us a season order." He came back to the desk, sat down, and picked up a stress ball, tossing it from hand to hand as he watched her. "Has anybody ever told you that you look a little like Jennifer Beals?"

"No, I don't believe so," she said, pleased.

"No, I guess you don't. Listen, you heard Bruce. He's stoked to hear our show. We have him listening, waiting. Rare moment. So, we need to make this fire. We need to make this bulletproof, okay? Now, I know you have no TV experience, so eventually, when this is sold, we'll find someone for you to work with on the ground level, blocking out scenes, cranking out pages. But that's getting ahead of ourselves. Right now, we need to figure out what this show is going to be about. Conceptual stuff. World building."

"So wait, our show, it's really happening?" she said.

"Well, we're happening. But we need a show idea. To home in on what this is about. It's gonna probably be an if/come deal, okay, Jane? That's okay with you?"

"Sounds great," she said, nodding, though she still wasn't sure what that was. She made a mental note to get Marianne to clarify it later.

"And you have time to work on this? Because I don't want to take you away from writing, you know, your next great novel."

"The novel is finished," she said. "It's actually perfect timing."

"Good," he said, sitting back, clasping his hands behind his head. "So let's get cracking. Come on. What in the world are we going to create here? Let's spitball."

JANE'S EYES TOOK a moment to adjust to the startling brightness outside. She had no idea what time it was or how long she'd been up there brainstorming with Hampton. She'd arrived in the pouring rain and now the pavement was completely dry, as if it had never rained at all.

She found her way to her Subaru and got inside, pulled out her phone. There was a text from Brett. Hey can you call me back? She stared at it, trying to decipher in the brief six words a tone. Then three dots appeared below the message. He was still writing, and it frightened her somehow—that he was there, so immediate. She held her breath, waiting for some terrible thing to be said, but then he only wrote: We need to chat.

She swallowed. She looked around the lot at all the shiny cars, overcome with a feeling someone was watching her, but she was alone. She texted back: Can't talk this sec. Finn's sick. Puking. UGH. Can I try you later? Three dots appeared again, then dissolved into nothing. She needed to calm down. The meeting had gone great. She needed to remember that good things were happening. She turned on her playlist of eighties R&B. It was all old-school crooners like Freddie Jackson and Alexander O'Neal and Ready for the World—the kind of music she and her sister had listened to over and over again in high school, sharing the same fantasy of a wealthy, mustachioed Black man who would pull up in his Eldorado smelling of Drakkar Noir to save them from whatever broke white hippie hell they were trapped inside. Lenny hated this kind of music. He called it *belly rubbing music*. He hated the synthesizers and the cheeseball lyrics, and whenever she dared play it in his presence, he made so many snide comments that she mostly only listened to it on headphones, privately, while washing dishes. Now she cranked up one of her favorite songs—something by a one-hit wonder who was now dead—and sang along as she started toward home.

COLORED TELEVISION

IN THE COMEDY she and Hampton had drummed up that morning—for a show as yet untitled, an idea she knew was still as fragile as a fetus—the main character would be named Sally, as in Hemings. She would be a writer of novels, like Jane, and she would teach writing at a college. She would be married to Kyle, a Black comic-book artist who, unlike Lenny, made money from his art. And together they would have two children, a boy and a girl. Only the kids in the show would be older than Jane's real ones because Hampton had said there was more drama to mine with the advent of puberty—even a possible spin-off. Who knew? The daughter, Schuyler, would be popular, pretty, and spoiled, a teenager who was secretly becoming a famous influencer from her bedroom. The boy, Chester, would be a middle schooler who, sort of like Finn, would know everything there was to know about the history of Godzilla films going all the way back to 1954. Only, unlike in Finn's case, all his oddities would be depicted as charming and remarkable rather than symptoms of a disorder. The family would not, of course, be called the Hemingses. They'd be the Bunches, and they'd live in a renovated Craftsman in Multicultural Mayberry, with a kitchen that had a Wolf stove and Carrara marble counters. Sally's best friend, Reebee, a Black lesbian spoken-word poet, would live in the accessory dwelling unit, a converted garage, with her child, Jiffy, a gifted transgender kid the same age as Chester. ("I love the trans angle," Hampton had said. "That's so prestige.") The tension in the show would revolve around universal marital disputes with a modern spin—like the husband's ongoing annoyance with Reebee, who would have a habit of walking into their home at inopportune moments saying some catchphrase like "Where that high-yellow bitch at?"

They would be a family just like Jane's, only this family would be the stuff not of struggle and strife—and want, so much want—but of jubilant, knee-slapping comedy.

12.

It was funny—everything about Jane's life looked just the same as it had before Hampton. She woke at the same time she always had, made the same brand of coffee, fed the kids the same breakfast, walked them to school the same route, then retreated to her office, supposedly to work on the book she'd been writing for ten years. She was existing on the same plane as she had since they'd moved to Brett's. And yet, Jane felt like a different person.

She'd left a message for Marianne after the meeting with Hampton, but it was Carrie who called her back. She explained that Marianne had needed to leave town abruptly—her father was dying, and it wasn't clear when she'd be back. Carrie would be point person for the foreseeable future. So Jane gave Carrie her report on the meeting, and Carrie said it sounded great to her and she'd follow up with Hampton's people to hammer out a contract. Even in these if/come situations, she warned Jane, the contracts could take awhile. Jane should just plow ahead and start working with Hampton because, she said, echoing Marianne, "He's on fire right now."

And that's what Jane was doing—working. Even as she waited to hear from Hampton's people about a next meeting, she started to flesh out ideas for episodes. That's what she did in Brett's office every day, working with a joy she hadn't felt in years.

She felt like a different person in so many ways now. Like an improved Jane. The differences between Jane the TV writer and Jane the novelist were subtle but profound: Jane the TV writer was already a better mother than Jane the novelist. It had only been a week, but she had noticed that she was finally, for the first time in years, maybe ever, fully present when her children came home from school. She listened when they told her about their school days.

Jane the novelist had always had a glass of wine while she cooked dinner. She'd needed that glass to be anesthesia, to numb her feelings of anxiety and despair, the source of which was the novel, beckoning her to come back to it and swim in it some more. Jane the TV writer found she didn't need a glass in the evening, not in the same way. It wasn't only that the wine they were drinking now was the supermarket variety—six-dollar bottles of Chilean chardonnay. It was also that she didn't feel the need to numb herself after a day of work; in fact, she preferred to be clearheaded in the evening in case she felt like working on show ideas later after the kids were asleep.

She and Lenny were also improved, happier, since she'd decided not to be a novelist anymore—which was ironic, since he believed she was more a novelist now than ever. A resilient novelist. In the week since her meeting with Hampton, they'd had another episode of rare and shocking morning sex—on a school morning, no less.

She'd never understood so profoundly how much being a novelist was at odds with domestic life, with sanity. But now she saw it clearly. To be a novelist was to be a dreadful parent. To be a novelist was to be a monstrous marriage partner. That kind of writing had no beginning and no end. It just crept around the house, infecting every element of family life. You couldn't live with it, you couldn't live without it.

In the mornings, Jane the novelist had procrastinated playing solitaire for hours on her computer, going to Starbucks to ask the barista with the nose ring and pink hair incessant questions about her artistic ambitions, as if she cared—or even cleaning the toilet. Anything to avoid going into her novel. When, finally, she entered it, she would sink into its swampy morass, and as miserable as it made her, she would have a hard time leaving it at the end of the day. Succumbing to the work always felt like a compulsion—like a bulimic episode or a bout of trichotillomania, that disorder where you have the urge to pull out your eyebrows. You did it but only after fighting against it. And what gloomy, lonely work it was.

Television writing was easy in, easy out. Jane was happy to begin working at the start of the day, and she was happy to leave it at the end of the day. She could merge seamlessly from the world of make-believe into the world of reality. The transition wasn't as jarring. What a surprise that a medium she'd looked down on for all these years, as if it were junk food, turned out to be so sanity-making and salubrious for family life.

Of course, she wasn't writing anything, not yet. All Hampton had suggested was that she come up with some ideas for episodes about the Bunches. He'd warned her not to get ahead of herself—they were just trying to have enough to pitch to Bruce Borland. The better the pitch, the better chance they would have of getting that coveted green light—a season order. She knew these terms now.

God, what a waste the last ten years of her life had been. Not just the writing of that doomed second novel but also all the therapy she'd had to have to live through the writing of it. She'd shelled out thousands of dollars they didn't have in a fruitless attempt to ward off what her father called the "Sticks," his term for the depression that ran through his side of the family. And now it turned out that it wasn't therapy Jane had needed after all. She'd just needed to quit writing novels.

Novel writing was too much. It was such a relief to dispense with the tangle of language—all those heavy blocks of prose she'd had to wade through to *world build* as they called it in workshop. Novel writing was too many different jobs under the title of one. You had to be all the actors, like Eddie Murphy in *Coming to America*. You had to be the character of the mother, the father, the son, and the daughter, the mailman, the dog, the murderer, and the victim. But it was worse even than that. Because you also had to be the set designer, the set builder, the gaffer, the lighting man. You had to make it rain and make the sun come out, describing every change in the weather so the reader could smell and feel it. And the only tool they gave you to do all this labor was language.

In this new kind of writing, she got to do less. She only had to offer up a skeleton, the notes for a world that Hampton himself would fill in with color. She imagined him like Zeus—some wizened god on a mountain who would take her ideas and snap his fingers and bring them to life. Already she felt less alone.

There was another relief too. A relief that whatever she wrote now was only supposed to *entertain*. Literary fiction writers over the years seemed to have forgotten how to do that. They had taken too many of their cues from poets—allowed themselves to become dreary solipsists driven by the prospect of awards. They'd become too swept up in the whole Marion Ettlinger of it all, thinking their writing needed to be as leaden and stone-faced as their author photos.

"Maybe I was wrong," Lenny said in bed one morning. "Maybe that meeting with Hampton what's-his-name was the ticket. It's like you seem eager to get to work now. It's like"—he paused—"you're actually having fun with your work for a change?"

"I really am," she said.

"That's all I've ever wanted, you know. For you to have fun with it."

It was early. The kids weren't awake. What day was it? Saturday. What month was it? In this city, she was always forgetting. It was only May. Was it a bad sign that she still hadn't heard from Layla about a follow-up meeting? She decided no. Hampton was busy. And it had been barely a week. Which reminded her.

"Oh, that reminds me," she said now. "I heard from his office yesterday."

"Who's he? You mean Lincoln Perry?" Lenny wouldn't stop calling Hampton that odious name. Lincoln Perry was the name of the actor who had played Stepin Fetchit—the one Lenny had informed her the other day had died the richest Black man in Hollywood. "Cooning pays!" he'd crowed.

"Yes, Hampton," she said now. She needed to put it in Lenny's head that her research wasn't over. Had to prepare him for that to happen. "They want me to come in again."

"But you don't have time for that, right? I mean, this is like our last month of work. And you're flying with the novel now. Don't get distracted by tomcoonery."

"Well," she said. "Those meetings are just a few hours. Not that big a distraction. If I think I need more from him, I'll go."

"More what?"

"Material."

"Hon, you're the one who's always saying fiction doesn't work that way." He stretched, cracked his back. "You're the one who's always going on about the dangers of too much research for a novelist. Don't you remember?"

She remembered. There was a lecture she gave her students every year about how to transform reality into fiction—the lecture she'd tried out on Lenny several times. She told them you shouldn't know too much reality if you were to invent something fully on the page. She always used the example of Henry James—how he came up with the concept for his masterpiece, *What Maisie Knew*. He had been sitting next to a gossipy old woman at a dinner party one night and she told him she had an idea for a novel he should write. She began to tell him a story about a family she knew—two awful, greedy parents who were divorcing and the child caught in the middle, their pawn—when James interrupted her and said he didn't want to know any more. He only wanted the briefest of details, then he was off and running.

"Well, maybe I was wrong," she said to Lenny now. "I mean, the process evolves with each new project, right? Maybe this novel requires more immersion in the world."

"Hey, you'd know. You're the writer here. I'm just a dumb painter."

Lenny climbed out of bed, naked, and she felt the warmth leave with him. She admired his body as he bent over to look for underwear in a drawer. Though ten pounds heavier, with a slight dad paunch in his middle, it was essentially the same physique she'd married, the same broad shoulders and wide chest, the same narrow ankles. Ten pounds in ten years wasn't bad. He didn't eat a lot of sugar and he played tennis with the white doctor several mornings a week. Plus, good genes. Plus, Black don't crack. She thought with satisfaction that she'd married the right man. Thanks to Wesley, the racial alchemist, she'd gotten at least one thing right. She'd married a man who wanted her to succeed as a writer. It was an unusual trait in a man. Too bad she'd had to fudge her story, to lie about what she was really writing. But he'd understand when she made some money. Because money meant freedom, for him as well as for her.

And the great thing was, it wasn't a lie she could easily be caught in. Creative work was creative work, and as far as Lenny knew—or Brett, for that matter, if the news reached him—she *was* just meeting with Hampton for material for her novel. That was the beauty of novels, she thought, despite her current hostility toward the form: anything could be part of them. You could make a soup recipe or an Amtrak schedule or a doctor's file part of your novel. You could make transcripts from a court trial a chapter in a novel. Maybe the television show notes *were* pieces of her novel. Some part of her knew this wasn't true, but if Lenny ever walked in on her working on the show notes, she could say it was all part of the book.

"Jane. Did you hear me?" He was dressed, standing at the end of the bed.

"Sorry. I wasn't listening."

"I was asking if you'd spoken to Brett about when he's getting back. It would be good to know the exact date. I mean, do we have a month here left? Or longer?"

"Right, I'll call him," she said, which of course she wouldn't—not yet. He'd gone blissfully silent since her text about Finn vomiting. Maybe he'd forgotten why he'd been trying to reach her in the first place. "I've been putting it off," she said now. "Brett's so relentlessly cheerful sometimes. It's a bore."

"You know what?" Lenny said. "Fuck it. Don't call Brett. Don't worry about the apartment—or anything. Don't get distracted by anything. You're on fire. I can feel it." He scoffed. "Shit, maybe you should meet Lincoln Perry again. I mean, it really did get you going. I got to hand it to that rich Negro—"

"What rich Negro?"

It was Ruby. She pattered in wearing her pink nightgown, followed by Finn, who was wearing his rainbow pajamas and clutching his filthy old stuffed giraffe. They climbed into bed and cuddled up on either side of her. She hugged them closer, relishing the moment, imagining her old self, Brooklyn Jane, the one she wanted to save, out in the damp morning, watching them through the glass.

"What rich Negro?" Ruby said again.

"This one," Jane said, pulling her phone off the nightstand and calling up a photo of Hampton to show Ruby. The sight of his face brought back a rush of warm feelings about the meeting. "This guy," she said.

Ruby pulled the phone out of Jane's hand and stared at Hampton's face. "He looks like Papa," she said. "Only fancier."

Jane laughed. "He does?" She squinted at Hampton's face. It wasn't true. They didn't look alike, not really.

"Great," Lenny said. "She thinks all Black men look alike. Good job, Mom." But he was smiling a little to show it was just mock anger for the kid's benefit. They loved it when he played angry.

"But he does look like you," Ruby said, smiling, taunting him now.

Lenny put his hands on his hips, made his face go stern. "What did you just say?"

Finn giggled too, wanting to join in. "He does! He looks just like you, Papa!"

Lenny dove onto the bed and began to tickle all of them at once, and the children squealed and tried to hide behind Jane, who screamed through uncontrollable laughter.

13.

Her phone kept buzzing, a muffled cry trapped between throw cushions. Somebody trying to reach her. She didn't move to check who was calling. It was probably Brett.

It was after nine. The kids were asleep, and Lenny had retired to the bedroom to shower and get ready for bed. Jane was sprawled out on the sofa watching her third straight episode of *Intervention*. On-screen, another white smack addict was trying to find his veins.

The phone began to buzz again. Annoyed, she pulled the pillows apart and found it, then forced herself to see what Brett had to say now.

But the texts weren't from Brett after all. They were from Hampton. She sat up straight, scrolling through them.

He said he and the "gang" were brainstorming in the office right now—did she want to join them? No pressure, but if she felt like it, they'd love to have her voice in the room with them. He knew it was late but he said he was v hyped on the show idea and he didn't know when he'd have another minute to meet. The next few weeks are gonna be crunched.

Jane didn't hesitate. She texted back, b there in twenty.

She considered the Lenny problem. How would she explain to him why she was heading out this late in the evening to meet a Hollywood producer along with the so-called gang, whoever they were? An idea came to her. She could say it was related to a scene she was trying to write for the novel. The actress in the book had been called out for a late-night meeting with the producer. Jane needed to describe the night drive over to Hollywood. Was there traffic at this hour or not? Were there stores open or not? What kind of street wanderers were out at this hour? And what did the producer's offices look like this late at night when everything around them on the lot was shut down? She almost felt sure it was a scene she was trying to write as she headed into the bedroom to find Lenny.

But she was thankful that he was asleep, snoring, his laptop open on his chest, a Japanese horror movie playing at full blast, his glasses still on. She watched him for a few moments to make sure he was fully asleep, then began to prowl around the room gathering clothes—a pair of her skinny black jeans, Piper's white cashmere sweater and low-heeled boots. In the bathroom she smeared on makeup and drew on some eyebrows and hot-combed her hair, then threw on Piper's tailored black jacket and added a spritz of Piper's perfume. She stopped by Brett's office on her way to the car and turned the lights on. Let Lenny think she was working out there.

At the studio, Jane parked in the VIP spot next to Hampton's Porsche. The front door was cracked open. Inside, the waiting room was dimly lit, but she could hear Hampton's voice booming out of his office. He was telling the same story he'd told before to Bruce Borland.

"This guy really thought Black folks were celebrating all February. Like, it's our special month to feel proud to be Black. He thought we had parties, actual parties, with cake and all, on the first day of February."

Jane recognized Layla's laugh. "Oh. My. God. That's, like, so cringey."

Then Topher. "Yeah, that's, like, super fucked up. You must have been so upset."

"No, not upset, just—you know, perplexed. The things white people think about us. It's why I do this work, make these shows. I want to change the way people see each other, you know? So that white people don't have to keep asking dumb questions at work about our hair or our skin or our foods or what we celebrate." He paused. "How does my saying that make you feel, Topher? Does it make you uncomfortable?"

"No, gosh, I mean, I feel so honored," Topher said. "I feel like I'm getting the best education in the world."

"You are," Hampton said. "You're going to be, like, light-years ahead of the rest of the pack, Topher. You're evolving to another level of white man. You too, Layla. Because you may be Black but you aren't, you know, like us. You Nigerians have a lot to learn."

Jane knocked gently at the door.

"Well, look who we have here," Hampton said. "It's our favorite Halfrican Hamerican novelist."

He was seated in his leather chair, dandling a bottle of ginger kombucha in his hand. Layla and Topher were seated on the leather sofa in the corner facing him, slight looks of fear on their young faces. Layla smiled, as if relieved to see Jane. "Yay, she's here."

Topher lifted a hand and waved. Layla was wearing sweatpants and UGGs, and Topher was dressed in a faded green Black Dog T-shirt and khakis, loafers with no socks.

Jane immediately regretted her outfit. She'd broken the cardinal rule of Lenny's mother, the bougiest of Black mothers. "Act like you've been here before," she used to say to her children whenever she brought them anywhere nice. Jane had overdressed. She'd walked into a late-night meeting with a top-tier LA producer looking like Brooklyn Jane. How did she keep getting this wrong?

"I hope we didn't interrupt anything," Hampton said.

"I was on a date," Jane said, she wasn't sure why.

"A date?" Hampton said. "Aren't you married?"

"I mean, a date with my husband. But it's fine. We'd already finished dinner."

"Date night," Hampton said, smiling. "You still do those? Shit, whenever me and Doreen have a date night, it's our chance to go our own separate ways. We hire a babysitter so we can pretend each other doesn't exist for a night."

"Oh, well, I'm sure we'll get there," Jane said.

He shrugged, tossed a Nerf ball into the air and caught it. "Marriage with children is like being alone with somebody you got into a terrible car accident with when you were twenty. It's like you're both on permanent disability and now you avoid seeing each other because it's too fucking grim." He lifted his kombucha bottle to her. "But God bless you and your husband."

The jeans Jane had put on were too tight even though they were her own: last year's BMI. She felt them cutting into her belly as she took a seat across from Hampton.

"Seriously, though," Hampton said. "That's sweet that you still dress up for your husband. I want to meet him sometime. Meet the whole Jane family." He grinned, playfully. "When are you having us all over for dinner anyway?"

"We could arrange that," Jane said, just to say it, imagining how she'd explain such an evening to Lenny—Hampton, Layla, and Topher seated at their dinner table, eating fish sticks and mac and cheese with Ruby and Finn as part of her quest for "material."

Hampton laughed. "You look so scared, Jane. Don't worry, I'm only playing. We won't force you to feed us. But I do want to meet your dude sometime. I'm curious. Maybe we can go out on a double date, me and Doreen and you and your guy."

She nodded, still imagining selling that to Lenny. "Listen, seriously, Jane," Hampton said. "I'm so glad you're here. Layla was just about to tell me an episode she came up with for our show. Let's hear it, Layla. Let's hear what you've got."

Jane saw now that Layla's eyes looked puffy, from exhaustion or maybe crying. But it couldn't be crying. Her mouth was still frozen in a smile as she cleared her throat. She held up her phone and tapped it to bring up some notes she'd taken there. "Um, okay, so I was thinking, like, what if the mom in the family? She's a professor, right? What if she goes to her first day at work and she can't decide what table to sit with in the lunchroom. The Black professors' table or the white professors' table. And it's, like, awkward. And if her kid at school is having the same problem . . ." She shrugged. "That's just the beginning of the story. Obviously more would happen."

Hampton's eyes were fixed on the window. He sighed heavily. "Let's ask Professor Gibson," he said, glancing over at Jane. "Will you tell Layla what you think of her idea? I mean, is it believable that a biracial professor—of what, forty years old, fifty?—would be struggling with where to sit at lunch? Is that something that rings true to your experience?"

Jane felt a tinge of pity for Layla. She was smiling again, but it was one of those *Toddlers & Tiaras* smiles, false and strained, like she'd had to smear Vaseline on her teeth to keep it in place. Jane tried to make her voice sound teacherly, the way she sounded with her students when they handed her twenty pages of purple prose. She always started with something positive about the stories, no matter how bad, before she launched into what was wrong with the work.

"So, I really like the impulse to create a conflict for Sally Bunch in the first episode," Jane said. "And to establish her workplace dynamic. And to have her life mirror her kid's life, it's a cool idea. I mean, that's great, Layla. But—I don't think people of her age or her profession really worry about lunch tables anymore."

Layla nodded eagerly, looking grateful. "Right," she said. "I see what you mean."

"You're a nice person, Jane," Hampton said, tossing the Nerf ball from hand to hand. "That was very nice. But yeah, the lunch table thing, old or young, is really—like, done. We've seen it before. Awful. Boring. Let's move on." He nodded his head at Topher. "Doogie Howser, bring any plotlines to the table tonight?"

Topher's cheeks flushed pink. He had that Caucasian gene that turned his cheeks varying shades of scarlet at the slightest hint of emotion. He picked up his phone and tapped something, then swallowed as he looked at whatever he saw there. His hands were trembling slightly. "So, like, what if there's some kind of fight between the two sides of her family?" he said, his voice cracking. "Like, a racial brawl at a holiday dinner."

Hampton, still tossing the ball back and forth, rolled his eyes at Jane, but said, "Go on, Mr. Tonklin."

Topher cleared his throat. "Like, they have some kind of Thanksgiving dinner where someone, maybe, I don't know, the white grandmother, comes wearing an Indian headdress—"

Hampton stopped tossing the ball and turned to look at Topher, who had gone silent. "That is the dumbest idea I've ever heard. Indian headdress? That's not even the right fucking show. That's the Native American project. What do Native Americans have to do with mulattos?"

Topher's face had gone white again, as if it had reached the boiling point and the heat had shut off.

"I was going to get to that," he said, in a small raspy voice.

"We have thirty minutes to drive home our themes," Hampton said. "We don't have time to confuse the fucking paradigm. Jesus Christ."

He looked at Jane, then down at her lap. "What's that you're holding?"

It was her notebook—a cheap marbled drugstore notebook she'd bought at CVS after her last meeting with Hampton. She'd scrawled the word *Bunches* across the front in sharpie. Inside were pages and pages of her scribbled notes about the show she'd dreamed up.

She flipped through some pages, staring at her handwriting, nervous now.

"Wait, is that actual handwriting?"

"Yes," she said. "I think better when I'm writing by hand. Weird, I know."

Hampton sat up straighter. "Not weird. Wow, will you look at that, kids. A real live writer. See that? This is why we brought in Jane. Because she writes by hand and has fully formed thoughts that haven't been mangled by doom-scrolling on that fucking death box you two can't get enough of."

Jane shrugged. "I don't know."

"Of course you know," Hampton said. "Of course you fucking know." He pointed at Jane. "You're living the life of our main character. You're a real one, Jane. So let's hear it. Show these fools how a real writer thinks. A real mulatto."

Hampton was staring at her like she was some kind of genius or savior.

She opened the notebook and cleared her throat, then began to speak.

The episodes she'd come up with tried to walk a fine line between being all about biracial people problems to being about a family who just happened to be biracial. In one of them, the mother, Sally, forced the father, Kyle, to do DNA testing kits with her, against his wishes, and they both came out with ancestry numbers that didn't jibe at all with what they'd always understood themselves to be. Sally discovered she was more American Indian than Black, and Kyle found out he was half Irish—that both his Black sides were half Irish. The results shifted their behavior and thus the tenor of their marriage. They started to act out the stereotypes. Sally began to frequent casinos, and Kyle drank himself silly.

Hampton's expression when she looked up was unreadable. He was staring out the window at the night. He said, without looking at her, "Is that all you have?"

"No, I have some more."

His voice was soft. "Let's hear another."

She told him another—about a white documentary filmmaker who comes to live with the Bunches. He's a huge fan of Kyle's graphic novels and has gotten funding to make a documentary film about the "Black R. Crumb." Kyle is wildly excited to be finally getting famous. The filmmaker—Jane was calling him Harold—moves in with the family for a month, claiming he needs to gather B-roll and, well, craziness ensues. Boundaries are crossed, and in the end, it turns out Harold the filmmaker was a fraud. He was just an out-of-work white guy looking for a sofa to crash on. He was never planning to make a movie about Kyle, he never got any funding, but weirdly, his presence has made the whole entourage, including Reebee and Jiffy, the transgender wunderkind, behave more like their best selves.

Jane looked up. Hampton had his fingers in a prayer position under his chin and was nodding, his face still tilted away, staring out the window.

"I actually really like that," Layla said, nodding.

"Yeah," Topher said. "I think it's kind of . . . great?"

"I can tell you a few others I thought of," Jane said, encouraged. "They're just skeletal of course, but they give us an idea of where this family could go, you know?" She rattled them off then—an episode where Jiffy tests gifted while Sally's kid, Chester, just tests normal. "So she and Reebee get into a mom competition about whose kid is smarter, Jiffy or Chester—"

"That's awesome," Layla said.

"I can totally see it," Topher said.

They were smiling at her so Jane kept going. "I also have an episode where Sally gets accused of racism at work."

"Racism against whom?" It was Layla.

"Some white girls. She has these two white girls in her class and she can't tell them apart and they sit side by side, as if trying to confuse her—"

Hampton let out a loud groan. "Just stop. Okay. Those are not good, Jane. They're just not good."

Layla and Topher were no longer smiling. They were both staring down at their phones.

Hampton's expression wasn't angry or mean, the way it had been when Layla and Topher pitched their ideas. It was almost worse. He looked weary and a little saddened by what she'd presented.

"Bruce Borland is expecting something great from us. We gotta do better than this." He rubbed his face hard.

Jane flipped still more pages. "Okay, um, what about we open on Sally walking into a Black beauty salon carrying a picture of Angela Bassett she's torn from a magazine, saying, 'Make me look like this.' But of course, she looks nothing like Angela—"

"Stop it, Jane. Just stop it. I'm honestly freaking out a little right now." He sighed. "I don't want to pull the plug on this just yet, but these ideas are just mid. Really mid."

Jane's mouth was dry. She tried to swallow to create saliva. Her voice sounded hoarse, like she'd been screaming. "Wait, just hold on a minute, Hampton. I know those weren't it. I'm just getting started. This is my process. I—I have to do some bad ideas before I get to the good. Just let me try some more. You'll see."

"Maybe you're right. Maybe that's how real writers work. It's just we don't have novelistic time to spare here. That's the thing. We're on a totally different schedule here. Everything is sped up and—" He stopped, frowned, as if he'd just remembered something. "You know what?" He laughed a little. "I don't know why I didn't think of this earlier. We all need a little boost here. Right?"

He opened a drawer in his desk and pulled out a small lidded ceramic jar. When he opened it, she saw it was filled with tiny white octagonal pills. He popped a few in his mouth, then held the jar out to Jane. "Here, come on. Help yourself. Kids, you too."

Layla stood up, stretched, and walked toward the jar. She'd seen it before. She cracked her neck, and said, "How many milligrams are those again?"

"Ten."

Layla pulled out two and took them.

Topher shuffled over and fished around and took some; Jane couldn't see how many.

Hampton held the jar toward Jane.

"What are they?"

"Duh. Perkies."

Behind Jane, Layla was doing a yoga pose by the couch. "They're really great," she said. "Just, like, the best cup of coffee you've ever had."

"Yeah, you'll like it." It was Topher. He was sitting back on the sofa, scrolling through his phone.

Jane glanced at her watch. It was one in the morning.

Hampton winked at her. "I believe in you, Jane. I really do."

She took a pill and swallowed it without water.

Twenty minutes later, Jane felt a surge in her brain, another curtain opening. She had an idea for the pilot. She got up and started to pace as she spoke.

In the episode she thought up there on the spot, Kyle brought home a Labradoodle for Christmas, but Sally hated the puppy because she knew she would be the one who would end up walking and feeding the creature; none of the other motherfuckers would do shit. She fantasized about bringing it to Twentynine Palms and blowing its brains out. Then one day there was a suspect loose in their suburban neighborhood—a Black man. The police were swarming everywhere, searching for him. Kyle was scared to go outside, but Sally refused to have anything more to do with the dog, so he had to walk it. That's when he realized the magic of the Labradoodle. On his own, Kyle was a perp. With the dog on a leash, he was a family man, a father, an upper-middle-class nerd. He was Cosby, preaughts.

"The dog is like the great emasculator," Jane said. "Whenever Kyle, or Dwayne, or whatever we're calling him, walks Hercules, or whatever we want to call this dog, down the street, he becomes another kind of Black man—a soft, muted Black man. I mean, the Labradoodle is the canine version of a fluffy-haired biracial child. One of those always make you look less threatening. By the end of the episode, Sally comes to embrace the dog. She sees it has a purpose. The creature has allowed her husband to walk freely through the world. She does take the dog out to the desert in the final scene but not to shoot him—only to throw the ball for him. We end with them looking like a puppy-food commercial. That's our redemption. That's the show."

She stopped, her whole body vibrating slightly like a tuning fork.

Hampton began to clap, slow and steady. "Now that's the Jane I was waiting to meet. I mean, that's a fucking episode." He walked to the center of the room. "Not sure if it's exactly on brand for our show—but it's the voice I've been waiting for. Original and weird and prestige. Really good fucking stuff." He fell with a slump onto the sofa between Topher and Layla, and pointed at Jane. "I knew it. She's funny as fuck. I knew it." He glanced at Topher. "And you, you're just dead wood, aren't you?" He grabbed Topher in a headlock and roughly mussed his hair, biting his bottom lip with the effort while Topher squirmed around and tried to break free.

He finally let go and Topher sat up, his face beet red, his hair standing on end. "Cut it out, Hampton. That's not funny."

Hampton patted Topher on the shoulder. "I'm just playing. I love this kid. Now why don't you and Layla get the fuck out of here since you've contributed exactly nothing. Scram. Let me and Jane work on this alone without you dullards."

Jane was aware of feeling a small sense of triumph as she watched Layla and Topher shuffle out, yawning. She was alone. She'd been chosen.

"Now let's break the episode down," Hampton said. "Get the beats right. Add some more mulatto themes. See if we really have something."

For the next hour, they built a story line out of the fragments of her story. They added a whole subplot about the history of the Labradoodle. It was Jane's idea. She recalled hearing a podcast interview with the man credited with "inventing" the breed. He had been on a strange, late-in-life mission to smear the reputation of the designer mongrel he'd created. Jane's idea was that somehow Sally, in her hatred of the dog, ends up going to hear the guy speak at a local recreation hall and there's a surreal moment where Sally begins to hear his lecture as being about mulattos instead of Labradoodles. Hampton loved the touch of surrealism. "See, that's why we bring in the novelists. They take risks. They do all the crazy shit that'll earn you an Emmy."

They still weren't done. They kept working with an icy focus. They broke a scene. Then broke it again. Then patched it all up. They made everything lock together like a puzzle. When they were done with it, the outline was a gleaming machine of story.

The clock read 5:15 a.m., Pacific Coast time. Lenny would wake in an hour to fix the kids breakfast, to wonder where she was. She felt an ache for all of them, an ache to be the mother and partner she'd always longed to be. There was still time.

"I have to go now," she said. "I have to get home."

Hampton looked surprised, but then he nodded, his face a vision of calm and understanding. "Oh my God, of course, no problem. You did a great job, Jane. You had me scared for a minute, but I like where this is going. Now go home to your family, get some goddamn rest."

"You should too," she said, going to grab her bag and notebook from the couch.

He stood up and stretched. "Nah, I'm just gonna try to nap here. I got a nine a.m. with Will Ferrell. Can you believe it?"

He hugged Jane at the door. "We're gonna make magic together," he said. "I can feel it."

She made her way back down the hallway, noticing that posters had been hung on the walls since the last time she was here, a gallery dedicated to Black film and television stars of yore: Tootie grinning on roller skates, Kadeem Hardison in *A Different World*, Denzel in *Mo' Better Blues*, Halle Berry in *Jungle Fever* dressed up like a crack ho. *I'll suck your dick for five dollars.*

In the lobby, she was surprised to find Topher there, standing at the coffee machine, fiddling with the filter.

"I thought you'd gone home."

"Layla took off, but, you know, sometimes it's just not worth driving all the way home to turn around and come back."

"Oh." She watched him for a moment, remembering how Hampton had grabbed him and ruffled his hair, part jokey uncle, part something else.

"Are you okay, Topher?"

He flashed her a brown-tooth smile. "I'm great." He emitted a strange little sound like a laugh. "For someone like you, this probably seems crazy, right? It probably seems extreme."

"You just look tired."

He was babbling now. "And, like, sure, it must be cool to be real writer. Cool to be novelist. I bet it's great. But see, this is where the culture is made. Right? This is where you create things that matter, right? And, I mean, sure, all right, it can be bad down here sometimes. Sure, okay, the worst here is the worst you'll ever know. But the best here is better than anything you could ever know. It makes up for all the weird, shitty moments, you know, Jane? You taste some television magic, and you'll wonder why you didn't come down and join us sooner." Jane tried to remember how many of the pills he'd taken, but he had turned back to the coffee machine.

She made her way outside. She could smell fire in the distance. The season of burning was already upon them. She checked her phone and saw that Brett had tried her again. Her Subaru was where she'd left it earlier, next to Hampton's Porsche, still stained in bird shit and berries.

Inside the car, there were no messages on her phone. Everyone was still asleep. She found the podcast episode she'd been talking about in there—the interview with the inventor of the Labradoodle, Wally Conron. She turned it on and listened to it as she drove through the sleeping city toward the freeway entrance. The tone of the podcast was more ominous than she remembered. Conron, a retired dog breeder in Australia, was vociferous in his opinion that he'd created a monster. Like the inventor of thalidomide, this guy insisted that he'd had good intentions. He'd only created the first Labradoodle in 1984 as a gift to a blind woman who needed a hypoallergenic seeing-eye dog. In doing so, Conron had unwittingly created a demand for a dog breed that he claimed was grotesque, unstable. Conron sounded on the verge of tears as he said that he would never forgive himself for what he'd unleashed on the world. It was the great regret of his life. The interview ended on an up note—Conron saying he felt confident the world would eventually grow tired of the breed and they would all be euthanized.

As Jane listened to the episode, keeping an ear out for lines she and Hampton could steal, the perkie still pulsing through her veins, she imagined herself a part of the city in an exciting new way, industrious and practical, essential in a way she'd never felt as a novelist. She was a person with a job to do, a boss to please, a demand to fulfill.

14.

An hour later, Jane was standing in the kitchen fixing breakfast. Boy, what a breakfast. Asparagus and cheddar omelets. French toast. Fresh-cut mangos. Bacon. She could feel the pill she'd taken still coursing through her system, and below that, a jittery alertness, a profound exhaustion. She started a pot of coffee in Brett's German-made machine. As it began to burble and hiss, she was struck by the kindness of machines. "I love you," she said aloud.

"Who are you talking to?" It was Lenny, standing in the doorway, scratching his sleep-matted hair. He eyed the breakfast spread. "Why are you making all this . . . food?"

She halved another orange to put in Brett's juicer. "You know, some cancers begin when you're a child, at the breakfast table, with all those sugar-laden cereals. It might take forty years to show up, but it starts then, on a cellular level. I'm going to make organic vegetables a part of all our meals from now on—and by vegetables, I don't mean French fries."

"What were you doing all night?"

"I was working on my novel."

Jane couldn't read his expression. His glasses—the wire rims, the way the light reflected against the small lenses—made his eyes disappear. When he spoke, it was in a soft, preternaturally calm voice: "Your novel. You were working on your novel. That's interesting. Because it implies you were out in Brett's studio. But when I went to find you at three o'clock this morning, you weren't there. I almost called the cops to report you missing, but then I thought: (a) they'll probably suspect me and shoot me. And (b) she's got her phone with her. It's a funny thing. If somebody has taken their phone, you sorta know they're not dead. So when I saw you'd taken your phone, I figured you were alive out there. What the fuck, Jane? Where were you?"

Jane had not been expecting this complication. She had been planning to tell him how she'd fallen asleep in the studio next to the pages of her opus. Later, she would decide it was the perkie that allowed her to pivot so seamlessly and calmly to another narrative.

"Here's the thing. The old way of working on this book wasn't working, Lenny. Surely you know that by now. I'm having to do things differently if I'm ever going to get it in shape to sell it."

"I don't understand."

"You're just forgetting. My research. I'm doing research for my novel. I was working with Hampton. But only pretending to work with Hampton. We've talked about all this before."

"Do you actually expect me to believe this?"

"Well, it's true. He texted late to say he and the gang were working on the show and he wondered if I wanted to join them."

"The gang?"

"Oh, just those two kids who work for him. I told you about them, the pretty Nigerian Valley Girl and the sort of perennially lost white boy. See, Hampton was trying to come up with some story ideas with them and they were just totally useless, so he wrote and asked me to join them. The biracial expert." She laughed because it did sound funny. "I almost woke you up to tell you, but you looked so peaceful." She sipped her coffee. "I mean, my first reaction was of course no way. I mean, I was in my pajamas. But then, I don't know, I realized it was an opportunity. I've been struggling with this scene where the actress goes to meet this producer late at night—and I thought, this is an opportunity. I can get all sorts of details about that part of the city at that hour of night, sort of soak up the aura of mania and dissolution. Anyway, my instinct was right because it was deeply, deeply productive. I was going to tell you all about it this morning, over—over—all this." She waved her hand toward the breakfast spread. It looked repulsive to her suddenly, a pre-bulimic-binge smorgasbord.

Lenny was still watching her. "You sure this guy wasn't just trying to do the nasty with you?"

"That's funny. Really funny. Flattering but funny."

"I wasn't trying to flatter you."

"Well, the answer is no, a definite no. He wasn't trying to fuck me. I mean, he can have any starlet he wants and look at me." She glanced at her reflection in the glass. "A man like him wouldn't hit on a woman like me."

She waited for Lenny to disagree.

"True," he said. "But it just sounds—weird."

"I know. That's because we come from the art world and the literary world, where a guy calling you at that hour to 'work' would mean only one thing, right? Hollywood gets a bad rap, but the truth is, there's something weirdly sexless about the vibe over there. Like, they're all too industrious to be having sex. They're not hedonists like novelists. Or poets. Jesus. If a poet asked me to meet him at that hour? I would expect to be assaulted. But this is different. The big turn-on in this TV world, the thing that gets them hard, is success. Seasons. Deals. There's something very antipleasure about this town. They drink water and green tea and see their trainers. And they work, Lenny. Really fucking hard. All night long. It's all going into my novel, Lenny."

"You're not acting like yourself. You're talking so fast. And you keep calling me by my name."

"This is me when I'm finishing a book. You've never seen me finish a book before."

"I have. Last month, remember?"

"But I hadn't. Not really. And some part of me must have known that it wasn't quite right. I think—and I hate to admit it—that Honor was right. It wasn't finished." She leaned back against the counter. "I really think I'm getting there, Lenny. It's all coming together."

"That's great," he said, still eyeing her strangely. He went to pour himself coffee. "Do you even have the energy for tonight? I don't know if I can even get the money back at this point."

Jane stared at him dully, trying to remember what he was talking about. Tonight. What was happening tonight? Time and space seemed to collapse into each other. Was this the fictitious date night she'd described to Hampton? The one she'd supposedly come to him from, all dressed up?

Lenny looked at her from behind his glasses. "You do remember our excursion, don't you?"

"Of course I remember," she lied, with a little laugh. "And of course I'll have energy for it. I mean, how much energy could it require?"

"Maybe I should have canceled," Lenny said. "But crazily enough, I've almost been looking forward to it all week." A faint smile crossed his lips. "Anything to break up the drudgery of fish sticks and frozen pizza and the fucking *Phineas and Ferb* of it all. I love our children but sometimes Friday nights here make me want to slit my wrists. The way they look like every other night."

"I've been looking forward to it too," Jane said with feeling, assisted by a last surge of chemically induced enthusiasm.

The kids came groggily down the stairs just then, rubbing their eyes.

"Are we having a party?" Ruby asked, taking in the elaborate breakfast spread.

"No," Lenny said. "It's just another school morning at the funny farm."

In the end, Jane was unable to eat any of the feast she'd prepared. Ruby and Finn didn't want it either. They asked if they could have Lucky Charms instead, and Jane didn't have it in her to refuse. They ate the cereal at the island with their backs to her, taking huge slurping spoonfuls of dyed cereal while the hearty food she'd prepared grew cold. When they were done, Lenny went upstairs to help them get dressed. Then he and the kids headed out together, shooting Jane nervous looks.

Lenny paused at the door to tell her he'd be away all day at the Japanese consulate, meeting with a guy called Yukio.

Jane nodded as he spoke, only half registering what he was saying. But she did hear him say, "We should leave at four. Be ready. This is your night."

Her night. She watched as he and the kids got into the Subaru and pulled away.

Hampton had not warned her about the comedown from the perkies. She guessed nobody ever thought of that next-day feeling when they got smashed or did drugs. That was why they told you in AA to put up that sign on your wall: *The night before is never worth the morning after.*

She could feel the chemicals leaking out, could almost hear a hiss of air escaping her brain. The hot-air balloon version of the self she'd been last night deflating.

By ten o'clock she was stumbling around the house, yawning so continuously that it was more like she was gasping for air. She kept banging into walls and chairs. By eleven, she had a knifelike headache in her frontal lobe. By noon, she was sitting under a Pendleton blanket on the couch in Brett's office, slack-jawed, watching episode upon episode of *Intervention* on her laptop. It felt like her brain was bleeding.

She texted Layla.

> Does it always feel this bad when the pill leaves your system?

No idea! LOL I keep taking them.

Okay but what should I do? I can't function.

U R so cute! If you can't get your hands on more perkies (which I highly recommend) just drink a lot of water and take a nap. It'll be okay! I promise! ♥

Jane closed her laptop, gulped some water, then fell into a long Savasana of a nap on Brett's sofa. She didn't remember if or what she dreamed. When she woke, the light in the office was dim. It seemed a long time had passed. A panic seized her—like that panic when you're speeding down the freeway and you realize you left your fourth child back at McDonald's. She jolted upright. Where were the children? Then she heard laughter drifting in from the yard and was suffused with relief. And yes, there they were. Out the window she saw Ruby laying out her row of dolls. Minus Addy Walker.

On her phone was a cheerful text from Lenny: I'm ready when you are. Let's hit the road!

Across the courtyard, she could see into the kitchen. Kathy—stout, white, fifty-five, with a brassy dye job—was talking on her cell phone with one hand and opening a bottle of wine with the other. Kathy, the worst babysitter in the world. Worst in a low-key but not dangerous way. She was terrible with children, but she was always available. They used her for date nights. So that was definitely what was up—a date night she had agreed to and forgotten about. She wondered what they had planned.

Lenny moved into view from the bedroom. He was wearing a linen sports jacket and carrying a small duffel bag. He looked jaunty.

It came back to her then. Of course. How had she forgotten? They weren't just going on a date night. They were going on the overnight date Lenny had planned months ago. He was completing his half of the final assignment Heidi had given them. Heidi had told them to each plan a date—an overnight date—doing something the other person liked to do—something that they themselves didn't naturally like to do. She'd explained that it would get them out of their comfort zone. Jane had seen the woman's point. Because, though there were things she and Lenny liked to do together—take walks in strange cities, watch survivalist movies in bed, talk shit about Black and mulatto artists who were more successful than they were—there were also great gaps between them.

One of those gaps was that Lenny loved nature, and Jane did everything she could to avoid nature. She simply didn't understand why you'd ever need to tromp through the wilderness unless you'd jumped out of a van after being abducted. She thought the point of being a human with an opposable thumb was that you never had to defecate in the woods. She didn't get the appeal of going off the grid. Nothing of interest happened off the grid, and if something of note did happen, it usually involved things best left to the pages of a glossy children's book—a grizzly bear or a mountain lion or a rattlesnake. Or a serial killer. Also, camping trips seemed like an elaborate excuse to buy expensive equipment you didn't need—a flagrant display of upper-middle-class white privilege so that you could pretend to live simply.

All of which was why, last spring, in those dying days of couple's therapy, Jane had thought it was the ultimate selfless gesture for her to plan an overnight camping trip at Joshua Tree—she and Lenny, alone in the desert. She was ignoring literally every one of her true urges. She was passing as a wholesome, mildly anorexic white woman with ruddy skin and sturdy, highly arched feet—an ecopoet, in other words. She even rented a Jeep Wrangler, the kind of car Lenny drove when she first met him, when he was still dating Lilith.

At first it had gone well. Lenny had seemed touched by all the details Jane had thought of. They drove out of the city blasting his favorites on the car stereo—Robert Johnson, Thelonious Monk, Ry Cooder, John Prine. Jane got a thrill when the desert sky opened and she felt the wind in her hair. She felt like a white girl in a Mountain Dew commercial.

The first part of their stay went okay—they hiked for a few hours, and Jane even attempted to climb a wall—but by nightfall she was bored and uncomfortable. Watching Lenny as he stood in the waning sunlight, whistling over his little camping stove, she felt the stirrings of resentment. Heidi had warned them this might happen. Notice it, breathe through it, she'd instructed. Remember, this is marriage. Two separate people coming together. This is part of the deal.

Jane noticed it, breathed through it. She ate the dinner Lenny made them on the dinky stove, slabs of ham and a can of baked beans. Afterward, she sipped a cup of hot cocoa while Lenny played her folk songs on his old guitar, which she'd remembered to pack.

It looked bucolic from a distance. If Jane had been on social media, she would have posted a picture of this moment and humblebragged about their weekend.

Lenny stopped playing. "I wrote that for you."

"It's beautiful," Jane said, raising her cup as a toast, though she hadn't actually been listening. She wondered if this scene had been in Wesley's premonitions when he'd guided her to Lenny.

Finally, darkness fell, and they retired to the tent. Jane thought with relief that it was all almost over. She just had to go to sleep then it would be morning. But that was harder than it sounded. The temperature lurched lower and lower. The cold out West was harsher than the cold back East; it really got under her skin, into her bones. She lay stiffly beside Lenny, buried in flannel pajamas, two layers of sleeping bags, a wool blanket, a ski cap, and gloves. Another incompatibility: they had totally different body temperatures. He was always too hot, and she was always freezing. She'd read an article once that said this was the kind of thing that could destroy a marriage. She looked at Lenny as he lay half under his sleeping bag, one bare foot protruding into the icy night, reading Goethe's *Theory of Colours* with a flashlight while Jane lay shivering beneath all her layers.

She wondered if there was any racial significance to their different body temperatures. Did it make her more white or more Black that she was always cold? Did it make him more European or more African that he was always warm? Before she met Lenny, the only people she'd ever known not to get cold were white hippies she'd met in college who took mushrooms and walked barefoot through the snow.

Lenny shut his book, turned off the flashlight, and leaned over to kiss Jane. "Today was fun."

"Sure," she managed.

"You know, if you're cold, you can join me in my sleeping bag."

It was probably an invitation to have sex, and Jane knew it was an implied part of the assignment to have sex, but sex would require pulling down her flannel pajamas to bare her ass to the icy wind. It would never happen.

Lenny must have understood this too, because soon he fell asleep. Jane waited until his breathing was deep and slow, then pulled on her boots and snuck out of the tent and ran gasping through the darkness to the Jeep. Inside, she turned on the engine and blasted the heat, rocking back and forth until she began to feel her extremities thaw. She put on earphones and listened to the songs she'd downloaded from her own playlist, music from another time and place: Mtume, Siedah Garrett, Evelyn "Champagne" King, Teena Marie, Ashford & Simpson. She set her alarm for five o'clock so she could go back to the tent then and pretend she'd been sleeping there all along, but the next thing she knew, she was awakened by a knock. She opened her eyes to bright light and Lenny staring in at her through the window of the locked car, the wool blanket draped over his shoulders. Jodeci was playing through her headphones and the engine was still running and the heat was still blasting.

Lenny shook his head, then walked away and began to take their tent apart.

Jane got out and followed him, watching him pulling spokes out of the ground in angry silence. "I'm sorry," she said. "I just don't understand the whole camping thing. Spending all this money to be temporarily homeless feels tedious."

"Well, then, let's get back to the city, Jane." Lenny said her name like he didn't know her very well. "I can't wait to tell Heidi all about our raging success of a weekend."

In the car ride back to the city, Jane racked her brain trying to remember, not for the first time, if there had been another funny Black man with West Coast kicks at the party the night they'd met—a different, possibly richer Black man, who had less bizarre ideas of what constituted fun.

When they got back from Joshua Tree, they didn't speak for a few days except for the most transactional of communications. The tension cooled off when they admitted to each other that they hated Heidi. She was a condescending bitch who didn't understand their issues and had no taste in furniture. They decided it was her fault that things had gone badly. She was a toxic influence. This was also the point at which Lenny's credit card was about maxed out.

They didn't wait for their next appointment, they just called Heidi and told her that the weekend had been a total disaster and that they needed to take a break from therapy because they could not afford her fee. She didn't argue, and Jane suspected she was glad to see them go.

They had been so over Heidi that Jane had forgotten all about the second part of the assignment, the date Lenny was to arrange for them, doing something Jane would especially enjoy. Something he hated to do and she enjoyed. But evidently Lenny hadn't forgotten, and he hadn't canceled.

Jane went to pack her bag. Automatically, she found herself reaching for Piper's blouse, the one she'd been wearing so much she'd started to think of it as her own. But she stopped herself, put it back on the hanger. She went instead to the part of the closet that held her own clothes. She pulled a dress off the rack, something she'd bought years ago on sale. She held it to her nose and inhaled. The scent reminded her of the dingy, cramped space where they'd lived before. She promised herself that someday she'd replace it with a new dress, a better dress, very soon. She'd replace everything just as soon as she could.

15.

A rebroadcast of *A Prairie Home Companion* was playing on the radio as they drove. It didn't seem like Lenny had chosen it deliberately; it was just the show that always seemed to be playing when they were driving alone together. They had always both hated Garrison Keillor, and as always, their shared hatred felt therapeutic.

Lenny said he'd booked a hotel he knew she'd like, not far from where they lived. He knew she didn't like to leave the city. He'd been trying to do as Heidi had advised, pretending to be a partner who liked the same things she did. In this spirit, he told her, he'd booked them a couple's special, with massages and foot scrubs planned in the morning. He was keeping the name of the hotel itself a surprise, but he told her it was in Beverly Hills, in the heart of the celebrity trash culture she so relished and he so loathed.

If they ever got there. It was almost five o'clock, and traffic had slowed to a standstill. Jane stared out at the orange sunlight that hung over the city. It took her a minute again to remember the season. It was spring. May. The rain from earlier in the week already felt like a figment of her imagination.

She checked her phone. There was a text from Brett. Are you even alive?

There were three dots as if he were still writing, but then they disappeared, melted into nothing.

Lenny glanced at her. "Text from Kathy?"

"No, it was just Brett."

"You can call him back if you want."

"Not right now," she said. She looked out the window at a passing mini mall and craned her neck to read the store name. PRINCESS NAIL WAXING EYELASH EXTENSION. "The thought of talking to Brett is exhausting. I don't know why."

"It's because he's Brett."

"I know. You think he's an imbecile. A hack. A neoliberal, race-neutral, sellout Uncle Tom."

Lenny laughed a little, keeping his eyes on the road.

"Honestly," Jane said. "I can't stand his dishonesty. He pretends to be so humble and mellow but he's always bragging. Did I tell you he's trying to write some cloying race comedy—about halfies? Not because he's ever given two shits about race before, but because he thinks it's suddenly a hot topic and he wants to jump on the bandwagon. It's like, sorry, Brett, what makes you think you have a right to this material? But Caucasians love him. All the flavor of a Black man without the calories. He's probably already sold the thing for a jillion dollars and is calling to rub it in my face." She let her voice trail off. She had gone on longer than she'd intended. This was supposed to be a fun weekend.

"Who cares," Lenny said. "I'm sure whatever he wrote sucks. Brett is a perfect example of energetic mediocrity. Fuck him."

"Yeah, fuck him." She squeezed Lenny's hand. "Anyway, I just want to be here with you."

"That's good. Because you are."

Jane tried to remember now the last time they'd gone away, just the two of them. Joshua Tree didn't count. That was an assignment. The time she was remembering now was prekids—in fact, Jane had been newly pregnant with Ruby. They'd driven up the coast to Santa Barbara for a long weekend. Jane remembered how infatuated she'd still been with Lenny. She liked his rugged style. She liked the way he referenced movies she'd never seen. She even liked the Jeep Wrangler he drove then, before they sold it and bought the Subaru. They'd spent the whole drive talking about baby names. That's when Ruby had come to them. It was the name of an aunt Jane had loved, a raucous, hard-partying woman from Alabama who had died young. Ruby. Yes. Lenny loved it too.

And now here they were, with two kids, two beautiful kids. A full if scattered life. They didn't yet have the house, the Labradoodle, the Carrara countertops, but it no longer seemed unthinkable that they would have those things.

"Thank you," Jane said.

"For what?"

"For tonight."

"Tonight hasn't happened yet."

"For carrying out the assignment."

"Great. I get a gold star."

Outside, on the wide avenue, it was late in the day but still sunny. She watched a woman pushing a stroller with one hand and pulling along a child of about four or five with the other. They were rushing toward a bus stop, but by the time they got there, the bus was pulling away, leaving her alone with the children in the blazing brightness.

Jane wondered what Kathy was doing with their children right now. Or without them. How many episodes of *Phineas and Ferb* had they already been allowed to watch? Had Kathy even bothered to glance up from her phone to see if they were okay? Admittedly, the kids had not died in her care. In fact, they had never gotten so much as a scratch on her watch even when she and Lenny went to Joshua Tree. Because they didn't move when Kathy was around. She was that kind of sitter. If there was a fire, at least, Jane knew, she would call 911.

A therapist had once told her that if she had a baby she was going to have to lower her standards. Otherwise, she'd be the only person she felt was good enough to care for her child, and her husband would get away with not helping at all. If you lowered your standards, the therapist told her, you would end up with a coparent who did some things very badly but some things well—and your kids would be better off because they'd have two parents who weren't resentful and overburdened. The same could be said about sitters. You had to lower your standards, or you'd never get away and replenish yourself.

They had arrived at the hotel. It was a good choice, about as far from Joshua Tree as you could be and still be in the West. The Beverly Hilton, dated but iconic with its sixties-style white stucco and red lettering.

"I love it," she said. "This is perfect. Just perfect, Lenny. I always wanted to stay in this place."

They left the car with the valet, and a bellhop came out to help them with the luggage. While Lenny checked them in, Jane waited in the lobby, wondering if he remembered that this was the hotel where Whitney Houston had died so many years ago. She would remind him later. Lenny didn't follow celebrity news, not the way she did. He probably had blocked out Jane's Whitney Houston thing, which had begun in the eighties when Jane was a teenager and Whitney was just a bright young thing singing "Saving All My Love for You" on MTV. It was a love she'd never quite outgrown. She remembered the moment she'd learned of her death. She'd been alone, stuck in traffic on her way to get Finn from school, switching around for the news but finding only Houston's voice playing on every station. That's how you knew when someone had died in this town. They were suddenly playing everywhere, beloved again, restored to their best selves. She'd sat in traffic with tears rolling down her face, then she'd turned and caught the eye of a large white woman in the minivan beside her, also shaking her head and crying. And to her right, an Asian man in a Lexus was also shaking his head and weeping.

THE ROOM LENNY had booked was a corner suite, bigger than Jane expected, fancy in a down-market Hilton kind of way. There were two rooms, one with an enormous bed covered with extraneous pillows, the other with a plush sofa and a massive television.

"Nice," she said. "Movin' on up to the East Side."

"Is it to your bourgeois satisfaction?"

"It is, it really is."

She watched him go to set their bags down on the bed and felt a wave of tenderness for him. She knew he hated this kind of place, and this part of town, and yet here they were. All for her.

She went to him and pulled him into a kiss.

"Hey."

"Hey." He paused, looked at her for a moment. "I want us to be happy together."

"Are we not happy?"

He smiled a little but didn't answer.

She started to kiss him. He seemed to hold back at first, but then relented, and they had sex the way Heidi would have wanted them to. It was nice. They were both tired from the traffic, the day, but as he moved inside her, Jane felt the heaviness of the past weeks—months, years—start to slide away. She kissed Lenny, thinking that Wesley the psychic had been right after all. This really was her destiny, her future. She thought about all that had pulled them away from each other, the teaching and the overdrawn bank account and all the moves from one crappy apartment or sublet or glitzy but evanescent house-sit to another. And their children, and their different ways of loving them—hers with fear, Lenny's with his steely masculine confidence that all was well. They had nearly died under the weight of that love. Because having children, she thought, was like a suicide pact.

"We did it," Jane said afterward, lying naked in the sheets. "We carried out the assignment."

"That we did," Lenny said, rising and disappearing into the bathroom for a shower before dinner.

Jane got up and, still naked, went to the windows. She could see the edge of the pool, and beyond it, the mountains. They were crisp, purplish, even majestic, like in the song. She fixed herself a Bloody Mary with the packaged mix she found in the minibar, then went to sit on the sectional, nursing her drink.

She thought back to that weekend in Santa Barbara nine years ago. Lenny and Jane had wandered the town holding hands, talking about their dreams for the future. They'd gone into a maternity store called Due. Lenny wanted to buy her a pretty maternity dress. Jane hadn't even known they made such stylish maternity clothes. She was still slim enough that she had to try them on with a fake belly strapped to her middle. Lenny had said that weekend that someday they would travel the world with their children, maybe even live with them in another country. They'd become bilingual, even trilingual. Their children wouldn't be parochial, like other American children. They'd be raised to feel free. Jane had smiled and nodded. She'd said that, yes, this was her fantasy too. She didn't say what she really wanted—a home, a real home, a patch of land in this California dreamland. She didn't say that she wanted the ground beneath her feet, not the air thirty thousand feet above the earth. She didn't say that she wanted to own a station wagon and a house in Pasadena. She didn't tell Lenny she wanted to live somewhere, not everywhere, that for her everywhere was the place she'd lived since she was born, always and already, and that the solid ground was new to her. She didn't tell him that the sky he longed for was inside of her already and she'd seen its limits.

Money—real money—was what they needed now. It would finish the story. It would give meaning to all the struggle of the past ten years. And money would give Lenny the time and space he needed to make his art. The thing about being a woman, a mother, a wife, was that if you wanted to be any more than those things you had to hire another wife. Somebody had to be the wife in a family. Rich women got to pay somebody else to be them—a stunt double to make it look like they were doing everything well when, in fact, they were doing only the fun parts. Money would grant her the help and the home she needed to raise her children and to do what she wanted to do, which was to tell stories—and age richly. That too.

Lenny emerged wearing a plush white robe. "You've got to see the bathroom," he said. "There's a phantom television hidden inside the mirror. It appears like magic when you turn it on." He went to the minibar and fixed himself a drink, then carried it and his iPad over to the couch.

She laughed. "See? You like it too. This is fun, right?"

"Sure. It's kind of a hoot, for one night."

THE WAITER LED them to a table under a heat lamp. Nearby, a group of men were laughing and passing a hookah between them. It was a bachelor party.

Lenny and Jane watched them in silence until the waiter came and they put in their orders.

Jane ordered an Asian stir-fry; Lenny ordered a veggie burger.

"Thanks for planning this night," she said. "Heidi would be proud."

"My pleasure." He was still watching the men across the patio. He looked like he wished he was with them.

"What do you think Kathy is doing with the kids right now?"

Lenny picked up his phone and did an impression of Kathy staring dumb-faced into her screen.

"She's such a dolt," Jane said, laughing.

"I know," Lenny said. "How does one so old remain such a dolt?"

The waiter returned with their drinks, and Jane held up her glass. "To the most amazing partner I could imagine," she said.

"And all that schmaltzy crap." He looked at her. "I'm proud of you, babe. For going back into the novel. I love that you're still at it and that you're finding your way through it even if your methods are—unusual."

She swallowed and fiddled with her napkin. "I hope it's worth it."

"It will be. I mean, people don't realize that the thing that separates real artists from wannabes is real ones finish what they started. Persistence. Commitment to a work nobody seems to want or need until you show them what it was they were missing. Like with my students, it's always how I can separate the wheat from the chaff, you know? There are some students who work with a relentlessness, an urgency, and cannot be swayed from finishing a piece. And there are others, some of the most talented ones, who are just doing it for the praise. And you sort of know they're not going to be artists, not in the real sense. They're going to give up, go into graphic design or advertising or whatever. Real artists are relentless." He smiled at her and held up his glass.

"To completion."

They clinked and drank. Then the waiter brought their food, and they were quiet, focused on their plates. She imagined what they must look like to men like the ones in that bachelor party. Were they like one of those middle-aged couples she'd noticed when she was young—the married couple out at a restaurant who sat together eating in silence, sometimes looking up to peer at the more boisterous tables around them with a kind of wistful boredom. She eyed the men across the patio a little more carefully. It wasn't what she'd thought at first. They were not straight guys at a bachelor party, they were gay guys—celebrating something, maybe a wedding, maybe a birthday, maybe just one another. They were flirting, dancing with each other, some of them making out.

Lenny, she could see, was watching them too.

Suddenly the men erupted in peals of laughter. Somebody had told a joke and the others were shrieking, hitting their knees, bent over in glee.

LATER, in the room, after they tried to have sex again and failed, Lenny turned his back to her. She thought he was asleep, but after a while, he began to speak into the darkness. She lay very still, listening.

Last week, he said, on the way home from swimming class, Finn had asked Lenny to drive him up into the hills. He was hoping to spot a deer or a coyote. "It was already well past six," Lenny said. "And I knew you and Ruby were waiting for us at home, but I figured we'd just take a quick drive." So they drove up into those winding hills near the Rose Bowl, and Finn kept asking to go higher, higher. The houses got bigger and bigger, more ostentatiously wealthy in that new-money-meets-old-money Pasadena way. It was getting darker, but Finn kept begging him—higher, higher. "Finally, we got as high as we could go, and he wanted to turn onto one more street. So, I turned down it, and it was only when we got to the roundabout at the end that I realized it was not a street, it was somebody's private driveway. This big bumfuck Spanish colonial mansion with a Range Rover parked in front. I could see lights on upstairs. I was about to turn the car around and head out when Finn shouted at me to stop and look. And when I squint into the darkness, I see it—two deer grazing on the land beside the house. And he asks me if he can get out and take a photograph on my phone to bring home and show you and Ruby. I say okay and hand him my phone. I watch him get out of the car and walk over to the house. It's almost dark now, that sudden darkness that comes here at night. And I'm watching Finn move closer to the deer. He's a few feet away when the deer stop grazing and look up at him. And it's so beautiful, because he's not even taking pictures now. Just staring back, totally still. They're watching each other. And nobody moves until a light goes on in the first floor of the house and I see a shadow appear in the window. The deer turn and bolt into the woods. Finn turns to see what scared them. And I can't even move as the door opens and this silver-haired, sixtyish white man steps out to see who's there on his property. And I see Finn for the first time through someone else's eyes. He's still so small. But I don't know if the man can see he's small. I see him as a teenager, the one he's going to become. And I don't know what to do. So I sit gripping the steering wheel, just watching, as the man says something to Finn, and Finn points at the car. I don't know if I should get out and explain our mistake, explain about the deer, or if I should just stay inside the car because if they see Finn as a danger, what will they see in me? The man isn't smiling at Finn. That's the weird thing. Finn is talking about the deer I guess and the man isn't smiling. What kind of person doesn't smile at a little boy on his lawn talking about a deer he just saw? We know what kind. And then I see Finn walking back toward the car. The man just stands on the lawn watching as he climbs inside beside me. I don't know. I don't know. And then we drive away and I realize I've been barely breathing the whole time. He made me listen to *Moana* all the way home."

Jane could feel Lenny turn over beside her, could feel him watching her, studying her face. She closed her eyes and pretended she was asleep, but he spoke again anyway. "Let's get out of this place, Jane," he said, in the same soft voice. "Let's leave this country. It's not going to go well. You know that. It never has."

Jane didn't move or answer. She lay very still, breathing deeply. She made her eyes move under the lids as if she were watching dreams unfold. And after a while, Lenny seemed convinced she was really out, that she hadn't heard a word, and he turned back to his side of the bed, facing away from her, hugging a pillow.

SHE WOKE THE next morning alone. They'd closed the heavy blackout curtains, and she had no idea what time it was. As her eyes adjusted to the darkness, she saw that Lenny wasn't beside her. He was seated in a far corner of the suite, fully dressed. He said that her phone had been making noises all morning and he'd checked to see if it was Kathy.

"Was it her?" She sat up to look at him.

"It was from your boy, Lincoln Perry."

"Oh."

He picked up her phone from the table beside him and scrolled through something. He spoke, his eyes still fixed on the screen.

"He says, and I paraphrase, that the Labradoodle idea isn't working. He wants you to keep thinking."

Jane was quiet for a moment, glad for the darkness of the room. She decided there was nothing in the note that didn't jibe with the story she'd told him. Nothing in it that did not add up. "So what?" she said. "You knew I was working with him on something. It's exactly what I told you."

"You also got a message from someone named Carrie."

Jane resisted the urge to reach for the phone. Instead, she said levelly, "She's from the television agency. The assistant to the woman I met with weeks ago. I told you about that. Don't you remember?"

"She says she's still working on your contract for the if/come deal with Hampton—but that she's met some hiccups." He put the phone down. "What's all this about? If/come?"

"If you can sell the show, then the money comes. It's like a speculative deal. I—it's too hard to explain. I had to pretend I was trying to get a TV deal."

"Jane. Are you even writing your novel anymore?"

"Why would you even ask me that?"

"It just sounds like you've gotten sidetracked." He got up and began to pace, hands shoved in his khakis. "I thought after Honor called with that great feedback that you had a new energy around it. I thought you were back into it."

"What makes you think I'm not?"

"All this subterfuge. Playing games. It's not how people write books."

"How would you know? How do you know this isn't part of my process? You're not a writer. You've never tried to write a book, let alone finish one. You don't know how this works."

"Calm down. I'm just—I don't know."

Jane slid out of bed and went to the windows, pulled open the heavy curtains, blinked at the bright light. It was later than she thought. She'd slept away the morning. There had been no mention of massages or foot scrubs. Down by the pool, there were men in uniforms moving around trying to fish things out of the water. The patio area looked so ordinary in the morning, more down-market, almost seedy without the glow of the string lights.

IN THE HOTEL BATHROOM, alone, she didn't shower as she'd said she was going to. Instead, she climbed in the tub and sat cross-legged in the cool porcelain. She looked at Carrie's email. It read just as Lenny had reported. Carrie had actually used the word *hiccups*. They were having hiccups in the deal. Apparently, Hampton's legal team hadn't gotten back to them yet about the proposed terms of the contract, but they had put in a call to that office, yada yada. Not to worry, not to worry. So Jane wouldn't worry. It sounded more like a delay than a hiccup.

Anyway, she was more eager to read Hampton's text. She opened it now.

COLORED TELEVISION

LABRADOODLE EPISODE NOT LANDING. TONE WRONG.
THINK HARDER. REMEMBER OUR THEME.

The tone was a little harsher than Lenny had relayed. Was he angry, disappointed, losing faith—or just rushed? Were the all caps something he'd pressed by accident or was he virtually shouting at her?

Through the door, she could hear Lenny practicing his Japanese. His voice sounded so strange whenever he practiced; it was mildly offensive, like a white man parodying a Japanese woman. She hugged her knees, thinking of Tokyo, the witness protection program lifestyle that Lenny craved for them. He didn't understand Finn's needs for specialists. He didn't understand Ruby's needs for a real friend. He didn't understand her needs either. She longed to be home. And right now, all she wanted was to be in Brett's office, alone down there, thinking about the Bunches. She was eager for this date to be over, and the realization frightened her.

There was a small puddle left from Lenny's shower last night. She could feel it seeping into her underwear. Whitney had been found in a bathtub like this, somewhere in this very hotel, floating belly up like a goldfish. She'd read somewhere that the tap had been left running and that it had overflowed and soaked beneath the door to the carpet on the other side of the door. The bathwater had been scalding, so hot that her skin was blistered when they found her. Floating in the water with her was the scoop she had used to put in a little olive oil to soften her skin.

There had been a cloud of suspicion floating around for months. Suspicion of foul play. Ray J had somehow been involved. Mary Jones was to blame; she should have never left Whitney alone to go get those Sprinkles cupcakes. Clive Davis should never have asked her to come to his Grammy party. Clive Davis should never have made her a star in the first place. And then there was Bobby. There was always Bobby.

Then again, maybe she'd been ready to go. The last interview Jane had seen with her, on *Oprah*, she'd looked better than she had in years. She was no longer the dancing skeleton she'd been on the Michael

Jackson tribute. She wasn't the blazing, fierce junkie she'd been when Diane Sawyer asked her which, of all the drugs she'd tried, was the biggest devil? Whitney had said, "That would be me."

A Prairie Home Companion was not playing on the car ride home. Instead, they listened to an interview with a memoirist who had written about her mother's dementia. The symptoms of her mother's cognitive decline, the woman said, were not what she'd expected. At first, it wasn't memory she lost but kindness. Her mother had simply, she said, become deeply mean. Apparently, kindness required memory. They were linked, the woman said. They were stopped at a red light on Beverly Boulevard. Outside was the giant windowless mall on the corner. On the opposite corner was the Sofitel hotel, where a French flag hung outside. Jane thought about how far they were from Paris, how opposite this place was. There was no coherence to the architecture in LA, no pattern to the faces that spun past them outside. California was the future and Europe was the past. Everything happened first in California. Everything happened last. Once, so long ago, she'd made a list of all the cities she'd lived in her life and the impression they'd left on her. Brooklyn to her was the grayest. London was the warmest. Paris was the coldest. San Francisco was the whitest. Atlanta was the blackest. Cambridge was the bluest. Los Angeles was the loneliest and the most free. She turned to look at Lenny, who was staring out at the street ahead, a distant expression on his face. She was seized by a panic, a tightening in her throat. She grabbed his hand and squeezed it. He squeezed back, faintly.

16.

The kids were not in great condition when they got back, still hopped up on Kathy's diet of Skittles and Sponge Bob. They were tired and hyper and clingy. They wanted attention—and to Jane's irritation, Lenny said he was exhausted from "not thinking" for the past twenty-four hours and needed to go out to his studio to work. Before she could protest, he was gone. Jane spent the rest of the afternoon in hard parenting labor, cooking the kids a nutritious lunch, taking them on a walk along the Monk's Trail that ran behind the house, playing a game of cards with them, cleaning the kitchen while she did laundry, then cooking them more food—steamed broccoli and pasta. Finally, it was evening and she could pour herself a glass of wine and, even better, turn on a big splashy Disney movie to plant the kids in front of while she began to relax.

But just as she was taking off her apron, the phone rang beside her. It was Hampton. She was exhausted but relieved to see his name. Lenny was still in his studio. She took the phone outside and walked across the lawn to her office.

"Jane, how the fuck are you?" Behind Hampton's voice, she could hear the whooshing of the freeway. "Sorry to call at dinnertime."

"No, it's fine. The kids already ate. This is perfect."

"Cool, cool. I'm driving. Jujubean is in the back seat."

"Hi, Jujubean," Jane called into the phone, as if she knew the kid.

"She can't hear you. She's wearing headphones."

Jane switched on a light in the office and sat down at her desk.

"I saw your text while I was away," Jane said. "The Labradoodle pilot. You're not sure it works."

"I don't know, Jane. It seemed funny in the heat of things, but yeah, I have some doubts. Listen, can I just freestyle with you for a minute? Just talk? I've just come from something—an event—and I think, I don't know, maybe there's something there we can use."

"Sure," she said. "Should I take notes?" She was happy to hear him say *we*. It implied she was on his team.

"I don't know. Yeah, sure. But can I just flow for a minute? Can I just free-associate here with you?"

"Of course."

"So listen," he said. "You ever really look at the Kardashian kids? I mean, open your computer and google that shit. The new generation. Kim's kids. And Kylie's. Rob's kid, and the big-boned sister's too. Just, you know, the mixed ones. I want you to look at them."

Jane sat down, opened up her laptop, and did as he said. Sure enough, her screen filled with a grid of butterscotch faces. There were a few white ones too, speckled in like dandruff, but mostly the brown ones were the faces she recognized though she couldn't have said who was who.

"You want me to work them into our pilot somehow?"

"I don't know. Just listen. We're in the early fucking stages of this, so anything is possible, right? Me and Juju, we just came from a party. A birthday party for one of those half-baked Kardashians."

"Which one?"

"I don't know. I don't even fucking know. Anyway, I'm just—I'm just spinning a little here. Let me spin, see where this goes. It might be the seed of an episode? Just listen. I came all the way out to fucking Calabasas today to attend this party with a bunch of four-year-olds. I only did it so Jujubean could have some Black friends. She dislikes every Black girl in her kindergarten class—all two of them. That alone should tell you how bad things have gotten. When you go all the way to Calabasas to find your kid some Black friends, you know it's a lost cause." He laughed at his joke. "Did you write that down?"

"Yes. I wrote it down."

"Okay, cool. So I walk into this fucking princess-theme party and the Kardashian sisters are out in full force with their enormous inflamed asses on display like goddamn baboons in heat. Looking all *King* magazine but white. Anyway, I end up standing there by the punch bowl with Kanye. Have you ever tried to have a conversation with that guy? It's awkward. Like, spectrum shit. Anyway, he asks me to follow him. I follow the guy. He drags me to this pool house where all the fucking Black fathers of all the mixed nuts are hiding—the special-victims unit. They are all huddled in there. Somebody hands me a blunt. I think it was Stormi's dad, that weirdo. He says, 'Here, try some Hoodoo.' I take a few drags of the Hoodoo just to be polite. It looks like a normal blunt but it doesn't taste like anything I'd tried before. After a while, I realize I've lost track of time. I tell them I need to go check on Jujubean. I go back to the party and I can't find her. So I start wandering around, looking for the red hair. I look in the jumpy house, on the merry-go-round, in the ball pit. And then I see her. She's standing in a circle of Black kids, being led in a song by this old-assed Disney princess. They're in a circle holding hands and shuffling in this weird dance, like a cult, and I just watch her for a while, thinking this is good, she's holding hands with the Black kids. This is good. This is why I came today. But the longer I stare, the worse I feel, and I can't figure out why. But then it hits me."

"What's that?"

"Not one of those kids was a regular Black kid. They were all mixed nuts. Every single one of them. Do you hear what I'm saying?"

"I think so," she said, but not really getting it.

"Are you looking at their faces?"

"I'm looking at them."

"I start looking around the party, trying to find one regular Black kid in the whole place, somebody who has two Black parents. Like, where the fuck are Willow and Jaden? Where the fuck is Blue Ivy? Nowhere to be seen. I'm trying to calm myself down, telling myself, 'It's all good, it's all good.' But this feeling is swirling inside of me, an epic bad vibe. Like maybe I'm standing on a Cherokee graveyard or some shit, like maybe the earth is about to open under my feet and suck me in. And I'm staring at this circle of singing mixed nuts, and I'm thinking, Jesus Christ, is there a single kid at this party who is not a goddamn biracial? I'd take a white kid at this point, a fucking Korean kid. But it's all biracial. It's remarkable how many biracials those white women have spawned. Like, a whole army. I haven't seen that many mixed breeds since I went to the Baldwin Hills SPCA." He paused. "Write this down: 'Black man wanders Los Angeles party looking for one kid who isn't biracial. He's desperate. He finally spots a white kid and sits on a bench beside them, starts up a conversation.' Did you write that down?"

"I'm writing it down."

"So my point is, I'm standing in the middle of this princess party and it's like, maybe it was the Hoodoo, but I'm hyperaware of all the dots, how they're connected. And I get this strange sense that time is moving backward. I'm back in 1994, and Nicole Simpson is gagging on her own blood, then it's later the same year, and Robert Kardashian is smiling in the courtroom next to O. J.'s big sociopathic face. And Sydney and Justin are at the funeral, looking traumatized as fuck. And Kris Jenner. She's sitting next to that sinister-assed Faye Resnick, who was clearly Black but passing. And I'm back in the present then, in the princess party, and I'm surrounded. I somehow find my way back to the pool house but it's empty now, and a Mexican cleaning lady tells me that all the fathers have left the party to go to a sports bar and watch the rest of the game. Motherfuckers left me. So I go back to the party looking for Jujubean again, but she's not in the song circle anymore, and I'm surrounded on all sides by white women with their big overfilled fake asses and their biracial kids. And I finally spot this red hair flying. It's Jujubean. She's in the jumpy house with a bunch of those kids. And I stare at her and think how weird that there's so many kids here who could be mine—and the only kid who actually is mine doesn't look like she could be. I mean, Jane. There were so many. Then they start cutting up the huge cake with the birthday kid's face on it. And I feel like I'm dying. I feel like I've gotta get out of here. But Jujubean is not in the jumpy house anymore. And when I find her, she's biting into a corner of the birthday girl's face." His voice dropped to a whisper. "Jane. Listen to me. If I die tonight, if me and Jujubean are found on the side of the road, know it was some Silkwood shit. Tell everybody."

Jane stopped typing. "Are you all right?"

"Yeah. I mean, I don't know what was in that shit, but I saw everything clearly tonight. I looked at everyone at the party and I saw into their souls. I could tell you everybody's past and their future. Like, Stormi. She's going to be the most normal one. She's the one who will be happy. And Chicago, she's the tough one. She'll persevere. She inherited her mother's steely reserve. She's going to own the whole family someday. Own them. And North. She's going to always be who she is right now—ruining Christmas photo shoots from here to eternity."

A child's voice interrupted from the back seat. "Daddy, where's my gift bag? Daddy, Daddy, did you forget my gift bag?"

"What? I thought you were getting it."

"You were supposed to get it, Daddy. The grown-ups were supposed to get them. One per kid."

"For real? Shit. Tell you what. I'll get you a gift bag. I'll call Stormi's dad and have him messenger one over. We're friends. He'll do it."

"What if they run out? We have to go back there *now*."

There was a sound of slight struggle, then Hampton's voice. "Stay in your seat. Put that seatbelt back on. I am not driving all the way back to Calabasas. Come on, Jujubean. Please, not this. Put it back on. Please. Here. Take this. There. Just take it."

A small voice. "Can I have it all?"

"Yes, you can have the whole goddamn thing."

Jane heard the crinkling of a package being unwrapped. Then Hampton was back. "Anyway, what was I saying? Where did I leave off? Saint. Did I tell you about Saint? Sweet kid. He'll be okay unless some Blac Chyna type sidles up to him, batting her fake eyelashes and swishing her weave around. Somebody needs to warn him. He's too sweet for his own good. Who else? Psalm. He's surrogate Sammy. He's—whatever. Too young to say. Who else?"

Jane scanned the faces on the Google image search. "True."

"True, True! Cute as a button. She looks like a friggin' living Cabbage Patch Kid. Problem is, she looks like a regular Black person. Not a mixed nut. And as a result, they treat her weird. I mean, her white mother insists on putting a do-rag on her head like she's Aunt Jemima." He laughed. His first laugh of the night. "True is gonna have major issues. Dysmorphia. We're not talking just some Beverly Hills nose job. We're talking a full-on Michael Jackson race lift. Ruin her sweet Nubian face so she can look like La Toya Jackson in a fun house. She will pay billions to wash the Africa out. I didn't even need the Hoodoo to tell you that. Look at her mother's face. Look at her aunts' faces. Look what they did to Armenia."

"Right."

"And then there's Dream. Look at that kid and tell me what you think."

Jane located Dream in the search engine. She looked to be four or five years old—pale, slightly anemic, but ordinary.

"She looks pretty normal," Jane said.

Hampton snorted. "Well, I've got five letters for you. F-R-A-U-D. If Dream tries to hand you her Discover card, don't accept. Stay away from Dream."

"So what kind of pilot are you seeing?"

"You're the writer here. That's your job! But what do you think? Is there something there?"

"I'm not sure. Were you thinking the Bunch family would be at this party or—"

Just then, a figure out the window caught Jane's eye. It was Lenny. He was standing in the middle of the lawn, his clothes covered in paint, his eyes wild, his hair unkempt, watching her. In the next instant, he was walking in long strides toward her, a crazy look on his face.

"I've got to go," she hissed. "I'm so sorry. Can we talk about this later?"

"Whatever, sure," Hampton said, suddenly laid-back, easy. "But listen, Jane, we've got to figure out what the fuck we're doing here. I'm not counting on anything from Topher and Layla. Apart from their coffee duties, they're useless. But I know you and me, we can do this. It's just we've gotta work fast. And it's got to be more prestige than the Labradoodle episode. Bruce is waiting."

Lenny was at the door to her office then, knocking. She said a rushed goodbye and hung up just as he was coming inside. She waited for him to get into it all again, everything she didn't want to talk about, her novel and her lies, but he surprised her with a smile.

"Can you come with me for a minute? I want to show you something."

He led her across the lawn into his studio.

"I think I just figured it all out. This is it. This is the Tokyo show."

He'd lined up rows and rows of paintings. He began explaining what he'd been doing all these months. The show was called "Light and Absence," something relating to Goethe's *Theory of Colours*. He'd used some interference colors—colors that don't look like colors, colors that appear on thin films, such as soap bubbles—that change with the angle of view. Jane turned in circles, taking in the paintings. They were beautiful and strange and oblique and terrifying. They were unsellable. She took in Lenny. He looked like a madman. A happy madman, a smear of yellow across his cheek, a drip of blue in his hair.

17.

Hampton had his face hidden in his hands so she couldn't see his expression. But she didn't have to see it. She'd done it again—disappointed him.

"Let's cut this short tonight," he said, finally pulling his hands away, revealing what she'd come to think of as his disappointed face. Everything drooped low. "I mean, what's the point? Just get out of here."

"You mean we can go home?" said Layla.

"Yes. Please. You two chuckleheads can get out of my face. Scat."

Layla leapt up and put on her jacket. "See you guys!" she said, and fluttered out the door. Topher trudged out behind her, turning to salute them.

Jane sat alone before Hampton. She wished she could erase the last hour. She had come in and pitched him the Kardashian idea, the one based on the story he'd told her two nights ago. She'd tried to take the raw elements and spin them into a pilot outline. In her outline, the Bunches were attending a birthday party for a celebrity biracial toddler very loosely based on Stormi Webster. When they arrived at the party, they found that the hosts had built an enormous effigy of the biracial toddler's head and all the guests had to walk through her mouth to enter the party. In the draft Jane had written, Reebee and Jiffy had tagged along to the event. She hadn't figured out yet how the Bunches' social circle overlapped with the Kardashianesque hosts'. In Jane's episode, Jiffy and Chester somehow went missing, wandering off into the canyons of Calabasas. A search party ensued. It had somehow seemed inspired in the privacy of Brett's office, but now she could see it was half-baked.

Hampton was right. It wasn't working. He was squeezing a stress ball at his desk, a despondent expression on his face.

"I'm sorry, Hampton," she said again, rising and putting her notebook away. He just stared at her, with barely contained disgust.

She'd dressed like a librarian tonight, in old horn-rimmed glasses, a ripped sweater, hair frizzy, unhip sneakers. She'd gotten it into her head that Hampton liked her best when she most closely fit his idea of a real writer, with her old-school frumpy intellectual ways. But he'd looked sort of horrified when she walked in the door. "What happened?" he asked. She blushed and said she'd been in a library, working, as if that explained the outfit. Once again, she'd managed to get it wrong.

She'd taken a car service here tonight. She knew she couldn't leave Lenny and the kids carless. That would be pushing her luck. But the car service cost money they didn't have. And now it was rush hour, which meant Uber would charge her extra to get home. But as she started toward the door, Hampton called her back.

"Wait, Jane. Listen, sorry I've been grouchy. I think I'm fucking hangry. This intermittent fasting shit is killing me. I need food. Real food." he said. "Want to grab a bite?"

Pleasure, relief flooded her. He was still her friend. He still thought her above the other two. She was the one he wanted to talk to, to collaborate with. He was willing even to be seen in public with her. She looked at the time, though, and hesitated, thinking of the kids and Lenny, waiting on her for dinner.

Hampton was standing, gathering his things.

"Come on, there's this little Italian place you'll love," he said. "I can drive."

"Okay, great, sure."

She followed him out the door, headed down the hall after him. It was good. It was all good. She had to do it. She knew how important these unquantifiable social moments of fraternizing with your coworkers—your boss—could be. This was where deals were cemented, true partnerships forged. And it was good luck the Subaru wasn't here, smudging up the scenery. It was good luck he wouldn't see what kind of car she drove.

Outside, as she slid inside Hampton's Porsche, she was aware of that old sensation of there being two of her. One Jane was seated beside Hampton Ford in this luxury vehicle while another her was back in the house on the hill, fixing the kids supper. She took out her phone and texted Lenny that she wouldn't be home till later—she was working with Hampton and they should have dinner without her. He didn't reply.

They were headed west on Melrose. Hampton turned on music. Tevin Campbell's "Can We Talk," a favorite of Jane's from the eighties, one of those belly-rubbing ballads Lenny loathed.

"It's funny none of us knew Tevin was gay back then," Hampton said. "I mean, dude was clearly special."

"It was a good song."

"One of the best," Hampton said. He glanced at her. "Music is where you really see where somebody's coming from. It tells you who they sat beside in high school, which is who they will be for the rest of their fuckin' life. Who were you in high school, Jane?"

Jane looked out at the Spanish and Korean words on the storefronts they were passing. "I was not one of the smart kids. I was regular. Everybody thought I was Puerto Rican. It was kind of like a code word for biracial girls who leaned more Black than white."

"I love that. Puerto Rican. Code word. I love that."

"My sister and I hated all the sad, lost mixed girls, the ones who only hung out with white people. We'd crane our necks to look at them in the hallway like we were staring at a car wreck."

"You give the mulattos a good name, Jane, you know that?"

She felt herself smile, and she turned away so he wouldn't see. He fiddled with his Spotify settings, and another song she loved crooned out of the speakers. Dennis Edwards with Siedah Garrett singing "Don't Look Any Further."

"You're killing me with the old-school, Hampton," Jane said. "This was my jam."

"I knew it would be." He reached over and gave her shoulder a friendly squeeze.

She felt her phone buzz in her pocket. She pulled it out, thinking it was Lenny, but it was Brett—a text from him that simply said Some friend you are. She put the phone on silent and stuck it back in her pocket.

They pulled into a strip mall at the edge of Koreatown, where there was a line of people waiting outside of a tacky-looking Italian restaurant. The other businesses in the mall—a dry cleaner, a nail salon called Pure Bliss, a UPS store—were shut for the night. The cars that were waiting for valet parking were almost all Teslas and Range Rovers and other Porsches, and the crowd was low-key glamorous, shaggy, golden, vaguely famous. When they got out of the car, Jane could smell the wealth. Hampton handed the keys to the valet and Jane followed him past the waiting crowd and straight inside, thinking this was one of the things she loved most about LA. It didn't care if it impressed you. It was a sleeper hit of a city. It knew it was winning. It knew it before anybody else. LA knew to act like it had been here before.

The host looked up at Hampton, said without missing a beat, "Hello, Mr. Ford," and led them to a table in the back. The red-and-white-checked tablecloth, the candle, the works. Keeping with the spirit, Jane ordered a glass of Chianti, Hampton a bottle of sparkling water. She could feel the people at other tables eyeing them, some smiling and whispering as they recognized him.

Hampton studied the menu. "My trainer is going to kill me, but I think I'm getting the lasagna. Is that too crazy?"

"Get it!"

But when the waiter appeared, he changed his mind and instead ordered the ribeye, medium, hold the potatoes. "My trainer would destroy me," he said to Jane. "But get whatever you want."

Jane asked for the penne puttanesca and another glass of wine. The waiter looked slightly startled.

Hampton, watching him walk away, chuckled. "Enrico hasn't seen a woman order pasta since the year 2000." Jane looked at the tables all around them and saw he was right. All the women were eating meat and drinking clear liquids. She'd read somewhere that tequila was the beverage of choice for skinny women. Wine was bad. Pasta was bad. Bagels were bad. Crackers and cheese were bad.

"I should have gotten a salad," she said.

Hampton waved a hand. "Live a little." He winked. "You know, LA has this reputation for being all about looks. And sure, there are some beautiful people here. But the thing is, Jane, if you're smart in this town, if you've got fresh ideas and the stamina to put them into motion, this town doesn't give a fuck what you look like, how old you are." He scanned her face, her hair.

Jane touched her hair. It felt brittle, frizzy. She wished she'd dressed differently, wished she'd gotten her hair hot-combed, her face made up. She couldn't remember her logic in dressing anymore.

"I'm tired, Jane. I'm so tired. Have I told you how tired I am?"

"You should get more sleep."

"Not that kind of tired. It's another kind of tired. You're from the ivory tower, the rarefied world of letters. Here—it's so do or die. You have to produce, produce, produce."

"That's a lot of pressure."

"I've got Bruce Borland breathing down my neck, waiting for me to hand him some Black and brown and yellow comedy. He's like this hungry monster. Diversity, diversity, diversity. And the thing is—if I don't do this really fucking soon, as in this minute, he's going to lose interest. The default is whiteness. They get this flurry of interest in us every few years, but if you don't strike fast and hard, they return to the tundra. You know how it works." He shook his head. "You novelists get to take your time, really develop things. But here, it's just like, hand it over. Now." He eyed her in the candlelight. "It must seem crazy to you. I mean, you're a real artist. You, like, slow cook that shit. Right?"

"Yeah, novels can take years. You have to let your subconscious guide you. You can't know too much about what you're doing or it doesn't work. You're at the mercy of your most mysterious impulses."

"That's beautiful. Wow. I admire you, Jane." He paused. "Hey, speaking of real writing, when's your new book coming out?"

"Never," she said.

"Never. What's that supposed to mean?"

She hadn't meant to confide in him, but he was looking at her with such warm, smiling eyes, and the Chianti was starting to take effect. She blurted it all out then—how her editor and agent together had turned against her, saying the novel she'd been so excited about, the pages she'd labored over, slaved over, even, were not even worth editing. She confessed that she'd arrived on Hampton's doorstep like a broken-winged bird.

"That day I came to you, I was desperate," she said. "I mean, I was, like, on the verge of selective mutism. Many Black writers, they give up after a few books. They can't continue writing into the void. I was at that point—then you came along." She laughed a little, remembering how he'd given her the first glimmer of hope that her voice, her precious voice, was not so unintelligible after all. "Who would have thought that television would feel like such freedom?"

Hampton shook his head. "Fuck white people. Fuck the literary gatekeepers. I want you to promise me something."

"What's that?"

"That you'll do something with that book. You won't just shove it in a drawer and push it out of sight."

"You sound like my husband."

"Your husband sounds like a smart guy," said Hampton. "I need to meet him. You got a photo?"

She pulled out her phone and searched her favorites until she found a photo of her and Lenny and the kids—not the somber one taken by the Serbian, but a different, cheerier one they'd had a stranger take one day on a trail in Griffith Park. They looked like a family in a television show or a clothing catalog. Prosperous and winning. She handed it across the table to Hampton. He stared at it for a long moment, smiling softly like a proud uncle, then handed it back to her.

"I love it," he said. "Black-on-Black love. It's such a beautiful but rare thing. Did you know Blacks are leaking more members than the Jews? And with them at least the Lubavitcher are trying to stop it. But in this town? Every Black dude I know has a Caucasoid spouse. And most of the women too. Mass exodus. Miscegenation proclamation."

Jane nodded, thinking about Brett and Piper—but also about Colton, the boyfriend she'd been with before Lenny. The last of the white boys. He was the breakup she'd been healing from the night she met Lenny at the party.

"Penny for your thoughts," Hampton said.

She had already finished her second glass of Chianti and couldn't stop herself.

And so she told him the story of Colton. She'd met him at a reading in Williamsburg. They'd chatted at the bar. She'd found his blandness— the sense that he was an almost interchangeable sort of man—weirdly sexy. It had made her feel like a much duller girl, which she'd found somehow thrilling. Early into things, she'd had the thought that they were deeply incompatible, but she'd been so tired of being alone that she'd shut such reservations out of mind and pretended to enjoy all the things that Colton enjoyed—the sound of Ira Glass's voice, the spindly secondhand furniture, the quirky indie bands with names like The Weakerthans and They Might Be Giants.

The worst was that Colton was frugal. He hated nice things. He was obsessed with food. He liked baking bread from scratch and kept a copy of a Michael Pollan book about food ecology or something on his nightstand. He tended a mason jar of a goopy substance he called the Mother—a live starter—as if it were a household pet. Jane pretended to enjoy the homemade bread and the frayed blankets and the porridge he made for her in the mornings with beans and seeds in it.

"I did that mulatto mirroring thing," Jane said to Hampton. "Pretending to like it all, you know, submerging my own personality into his. I just chameleon-ed out. But it was exhausting, months and months of eating porridge."

"I bet."

The waiter came then with the food, and Jane dug into the puttanesca. It was delicious. Across from her, Hampton delicately cut his steak. She continued talking as she ate.

"He had this toaster that was from, like, the 1980s, that was always breaking, and he refused to buy a new one. One day the thing lit on fire. It just ignited. It almost burned his whole apartment down." Jane had gone out for what was supposed to be a brief walk, just to get away from the smell, but she ended up meandering the city for hours, making excuses not to return. As evening fell, she headed toward what she thought was a hotel restaurant, where she hoped to get something to eat, a glass of wine, but it turned out to be a Restoration Hardware showroom. "And I just stood there staring at these miles and miles of sand-colored linen sofas and chandeliers and gleaming nickel faucets. And I was so tired suddenly." She paused. "Am I boring you?"

"Not at all."

She continued, explaining to Hampton how she'd sat down on a couch, a luxe model, super deep, so that her legs dangled like a child's. She'd felt like Lily Tomlin playing Edith Ann, the little girl in the enormous chair. She just sat there for a while, watching the people moving around her, families and children, couples, queer and straight. They spoke so many languages—French and Spanish and Farsi and Hindi—and she'd stared at their hungry multicolored faces, feeling very tired, the adrenaline from the fire in the apartment finally gone. She tried to lean sideways, just to rest her head on something, but toppled over so she was lying sideways, like a baby who hadn't yet gained control of its neck muscles. She lay there for what seemed a very long time, until a saleswoman came over and squatted down beside her. The woman had a faint Russian accent and wore layers of foundation, beneath which Jane could make out the mottled scars of acne. She was dressed in evening attire, a black and gold see-through blouse, slacks, stiletto heels, but when she smiled, her teeth were yellow and crooked, evidence of a poor childhood in a war-torn nation. She'd asked Jane if she was okay. And Jane had almost begun to cry as she asked the woman if she could just rest there awhile. The woman said she could make herself at home.

Jane could not say how much time passed with her lying there. At one point a family stopped and stared at her as if she were part of the display, then they moved on, speaking to one another in hushed Korean. Outside the giant picture window she could see the frenzy of pedestrians moving this way and that. Colton would hate the furniture here. He'd say it was too big. He was a man who liked couches with skinny legs, recycled furniture, NPR furniture. But lying there, she hungered for something huge, excessive, like this furniture. She longed for a man who would take up more space. These couches were intended for big lives, big asses, in a way that felt hopeful, democratic. And somehow, in that moment, she understood that she did not love Colton and she did not love living in New York. She hated eating home-baked bread and wandering the farmers market and cooking stew with kale, and she hated that healthy porridge. She hated considering food and its source for so many hours a day. She hated the mammalian feeling of Colton's beard against her face. She hated most of all the furniture in his apartment, which had never been comfortable, not like this.

"It was, like, this big aha moment, you know? Right there in that showroom I realized I wanted to leave Colton and New York and go somewhere new, and make a home for myself, with big furniture." She sopped up the puttanesca sauce on a hunk of bread. "A week later, I had this call with a psychic, who predicted my future. And a week after that, I met him, Lenny."

Jane was suddenly aware of how long she'd been talking. "Sorry, that was a lot. More than you asked for."

"Are you kidding? I could listen to you all night, Jane." He winked as he pointed a finger at her. "And look at that. You got your big life, your big house, your two point two kids."

Jane nodded, forcing a smile, thinking that she had only gotten some of that.

Her bowl was gleaming, clean. The noodles were gone. "Wow," she said. "I must have been starving."

Hampton chuckled a little. "I like the way you enjoy food, Jane. It's so refreshing. Doreen, like most women in this town, barely eats."

As they made their way through the restaurant, she could see the people at the other tables turning to watch them. Their eyes were mostly on Hampton, but some of them, she could see, studied her too. She could see them thinking that she didn't compute with him. Seeing herself through their eyes, she didn't think she computed either.

Outside, at the valet, he said he'd drive her back to the lot, to drop her at her car, but she said he could save himself the extra trip. She'd taken a car service and could order her ride home now.

"Fuck a car service," Hampton said. "You don't want one of those

Armenian crooks driving you around at this hour of the night. I'll drive you home. What's your address?"

The valet brought the car around and Hampton held the passenger's-side door open for Jane. Jane made one last feeble attempt at resistance. "You don't have to do this," she said. "I'm fine taking a car—"

"Get in, Jane," Hampton said. She got in. She gave him Brett's address.

"Oh, the cool part of LA," he said. He asked her how long she'd lived there.

She paused, considering telling him that it wasn't her house, but it felt too complicated, so instead she said, "Just a year." She paused while he buckled himself in beside her. "Seriously, I hate your having to go out of your way. You said you were so tired."

"No worries. This is actually perfect. We can brainstorm some more about the show on the way. See, I never stop. You want to know how you get rich in LA? You don't stop."

A few minutes later, they were on Melrose, listening to vintage Prince, the feathered hair and gold hot pants era. Hampton sang along beside her, beating a rhythm on the steering wheel, as she stared out at the smear of colors, languages, bus stop faces. Visitors from regular cities never liked LA. She didn't blame them. Even after ten years of living here, she still didn't feel sure she could say she'd been to LA. And yet, she had a sense tonight, sitting in this car, moving through the cipher of a city, that it was inside her. She hadn't found LA, but it was growing inside her.

Hampton merged onto the freeway. "So you got any other ideas for the pilot, anything besides that Kardashian shit? Something with a little more traction than the Labradoodle episode?"

Jane tried to think clearly but her thoughts were foggy. She was full of Chianti and gluten. She did have one idea—something that had come to her the other night while doing the dishes. She'd even gone down to Brett's office to scribble some notes. It had seemed like a great idea, hilarious for a minute, in the light of Brett's office, but just like all the others, it had lost its sheen pretty quickly. She wasn't sure she should pitch it, but she could feel a kind of gnawing hunger emanating from Hampton and she didn't know what else to do.

She began to talk, half making it up as she went along. Sally is desperate for money. Reebee convinces her one night to go in on a get-rich-quick scheme, a business they hatch called Some of My Best Friends. It's an escort service geared toward white liberals who want or need a Black friend—a Black person who will be seen in public with them at a wedding or school events, somebody to help them signal to the world that they are not racist. "But see, the escort is just an actor," Jane said. "Instead of sex, they just act like they like you, and like they've known you a long time."

She eyed Hampton. He was silent beside her, listening to Prince or her pitch, she couldn't tell. He was clutching the steering wheel and staring straight ahead, and all she could see was the sad half of his face. Her mouth was dry. She was suddenly very thirsty. She searched the front seat for a bottle, but there was none. She spoke again, her dry tongue flapping around in her mouth. "And each episode would open on a different white person in trouble. And then they'd call this company and hire a Black friend."

"Shit," Hampton said, slapping the steering wheel. "Fuck."

"Right, it needs fleshing out—"

"I'm almost at zero. Do you mind if we stop somewhere so I can recharge?"

Before she could answer, he was pulling off the freeway. It was already nine o'clock, and they were in Glendale. She felt a pang of guilt. She had said she'd be home to put the kids to sleep, but now she'd miss them. She took out her phone and saw a missed call from Brett. Lenny had texted her: You still alive? Finn is asking.

She wrote back to Lenny, explaining that Hampton had been giving her a ride home and they were in Glendale, looking for a station to recharge.

A moment later, Lenny wrote back: Ok.

Ok without the punctuation or an emoji—he was definitely angry.

When she looked up, she saw that Hampton was pulling into a place she recognized, the Americana mall. The fake Eiffel Tower was all lit up, and as they went in through the gate to the parking structure, she was surprised to see that the mall was mobbed. They drove up the ramp to the sixth floor of the parking garage, where Hampton pulled up at one of the charging stations. He plugged in the car and got back in the driver's seat. He leaned across her to open the glove compartment. There was a box of protein bars tucked inside. He took a bar and offered her one.

Jane demurred. She was still full of puttanesca.

"These things make you forget about real food," Hampton said, munching. "I've lost eleven pounds."

She could see the top of the dancing fountain beyond the wall of the parking structure. The kids loved this place. She loved this place. They could never afford anything but ice cream here, but she and Lenny would sit on the lawn and let the kids run around the choreographed fountain while Frank Sinatra belted from the speakers. Even with Lenny muttering about the frenzy of late-stage capitalism, she found it cheering.

She missed the kids, suddenly, with a kind of terror. She wanted to be home, to touch them, hug their warm, real bodies.

But Hampton beside her had lowered his seat.

"I'm gonna close my eyes, okay?" he said. "You don't mind, do you? This charging will take a minute."

"No, that's fine."

She listened as the sound of his breathing slowed. He was asleep.

The kids. What were they doing now at home? What were they eating? Someday they'd understand that she'd done all this for them, for their future, to get them to a better life. She glanced over at Hampton's face. He did look a little like Lenny in sleep, the same kind of slack arrogance. Lenny liked catnaps too. He could just fall out for ten minutes, deep REM. She remembered reading somewhere that one of the seven habits of highly effective people was that they take short naps throughout the day. Brain recharges, like a human Tesla. She'd never been able to nap. In the Montessori where she'd gone to preschool, the teachers had finally allowed her to sit in the playroom alone, banging blocks, while the other children napped. She'd been a puddle of tears by the time her mother picked her up, though. All that going and going until the wheels fell off hadn't done her much good back then. And it wasn't doing her any good now.

Despite the puttanesca, she was hungry again. She supposed this was why nobody ate carbs anymore, not in this town. You were hungry again so soon. She remembered the protein bars in his glove compartment and opened it up, helped herself to one. She was about to close it when she saw that a slip of paper had fallen out. It was the automobile registration. She looked at it and saw it was under Doreen's name. The mysterious wife. It also listed their address. She stared at it—Amalfi Drive—then put the slip back and closed the glove compartment. Hampton was deep asleep. While she ate the protein bar—which was strange and dry but not inedible—she pulled up Redfin on her phone and put in Hampton and Doreen's address. The sales and tax history of the house came up. It took her a moment to compute what all those zeros added up to. She scrolled down to the tax history and saw the house had been sold to them three years ago. It had six bedrooms and seven baths. She scrolled up again and swiped through the website's photos, admiring the sleek modern staging. She clicked on Street View and stared at the front of the house. She made the camera move up and down the street so she could see the other properties around it. Most of them, Hampton's included, were set back far from the street and concealed from it by giant hedges and gates. These kinds of people didn't need curb appeal. That was a middle-class concern.

"What are you looking at?"

He was awake, looking at her through soft, sleepy eyes.

She fumbled to close the image on her phone. "Nothing," she said. "I helped myself to a power bar. Thanks. Those are awesome."

"I told you they were good. That's fifty percent of my diet." He yawned, then pushed his seat back up and sat tapping the steering wheel. "Jesus, I really went out. I was fighting with Doreen until all hours last night. She always wants to process everything at, like, midnight. Knowing my ass has to be in meetings the whole next day. Things change in marriage, Jane. Kids change you. Jujubean, she changed things between us."

Yeah," Jane said. "That's hard."

He yawned. "Where were we?" He frowned. Then looked sad again. "What were we talking about? Oh right, the Black best friend shit."

"I mean, there was more to it."

"It's not that funny, Jane. And it's not a biracial show."

"I thought maybe it was, in a roundabout way."

"Fuck roundabouts. We don't do roundabouts in television." He turned his body and looked at her face on. "This is the big-time. If I fuck this up, I'm toast."

She saw a fear in his eyes she hadn't seen before. She felt a parental impulse to touch him, reassure him. "You won't be toast," she said. "And anyway, how do you know Borland won't like your ideas? Our ideas? Shouldn't we give him a chance to see?"

"You don't know television like I know television."

"But I know how to write, how to create," she said, enjoying the new authority in her tone. "You can't create anything great from a place of fear. You're Hampton Ford. You can make whatever show you want. You don't have to teach white people lessons. It's not Sunday school.

And to be honest with you, the whole biracial thing is played. I mean, Sally can be mulatto, sure, why not. But it only needs to come up when we need it to come up. The rest of the time, we just let weird, funny things happen to her."

"You're thinking like a novelist, Jane. Stop thinking like a novelist."

His eyes were great pools of terror. He looked like a lost child.

"There, there," she said, and put her hand on top of his, intending it as a comforting gesture to a friend, but it felt awkward as soon as she'd done it and she didn't know how to pull her hand away. They eyed each other, then the car made a cheerful beeping sound and Hampton said, "We're fully loaded." And the weird moment was gone.

Twenty minutes later, they were on top of the mountain. She felt a certain insider frisson as he pulled up in front of Brett's house.

"Hey," Hampton said. "I've heard of this house, the one without the windows. This is your place? Wow, you really did get your big life."

"Sure," Jane said, climbing out. "Yeah. Um, listen. Thanks for dinner. It was great." She stood beside his door, hands shoved in her pockets. "And I'm sorry about the show idea. That it wasn't better. I'd had that wine and—"

"Don't worry, Jane! Keep at it. I know you can do better. Keep the faith!" He peeled away.

THE HOUSE WAS A WRECK. Something sticky had spilled on the floor, and Chick-fil-A wrappers sat crumpled on the counter. Lenny must have been truly overwhelmed to do the unthinkable. She felt a pang of guilt. In the trial of the mother, she would not fare well. After she'd tidied up, she went upstairs to check on the kids. She stood in the darkness of Finn's room, sensing the now-familiar shapes of the toys, remembering the details of the pictures that decorated the walls. She and Lenny had not even given their children the essential experience of getting to choose their own favorite things. Max's objects were so much nicer than anything she and Lenny could have bought Ruby and Finn, and yet they were not their own. She went and picked up a toy dinosaur, a brachiosaurus. Finn had made sure she knew all the names. She turned it over in her hands, trying to remember if they had brought it with them or found it here.

She went into Ruby's room. Something was sticking out from beneath Ruby's bed. It was the box with the American Girl doll inside. Ruby had not, to her knowledge, taken Addy out of it again since the day of the birthday party.

Jane went to the bed and pulled out the box. She opened it and shined the light from her phone on it. The doll's face was so generic and smiley and dumb. Jane doubted any enslaved child in history had ever worn such an expression.

She had to admire Ruby's protest, if that's what it was. She would not love this doll until she had a multicultural mélange of other American Girls to go with her. Until then, Addy could stay entombed under the bed in darkness.

Jane returned Addy to her cave, then lay down beside Ruby on the single bed. The mattress shifted under her weight. Ruby woke as if she'd been awake the whole time, her eyes dark and piercing as she studied her mother's face.

Jane touched her cheek. "Hi, baby, go back to sleep."

"Is that you?" Ruby said.

"Who else would I be?"

Ruby didn't answer. She just watched Jane a moment longer, as if she were trying to figure something out, then her eyes flickered closed, and like that, she was out again.

"THE WILY MULATTO," Cavendish wrote, "has been known by so many different names: Creole, light-skinned, redbone, quadroon, brass ankle.

Sometimes it's a simple combination of Negro and white. This mix of two distinct races often does well for himself, rising to the ranks of the Negro establishment, becoming a leader and an elite class unto himself. But sometimes what we know as the mulatto is not really a mulatto at all, but rather something rangier and more complex, a blend of not two but three colors—Native, European, and African. These triracial oddities often deny they are Negro at all. Born liars, they've adopted the name *Melungeons* and invented a false origin story that involves Portugal. The overmixing of the blood has led to a deficit of character and a confusion in them about where they belong. While the traditional mulatto becomes a lighter version of the American Negro, the Melungeon, with all that blending and blurring over too many generations, looks strange and indefinable, neither Black nor white and perhaps not American at all. Whereas the standard mulatto is a proud and striving emblem of Negro pride, the triracial figure remains on the edges of society, unclaimed and unaffiliated, and all too often trapped in a life of petty crime."

18.

It had all been done in such a rush, the pulling on of clothes, the slapping on of jeans and deodorant and T-shirt and contact lenses and makeup. Now she sat in the darkness, waiting. Hampton was coming. To her house. To her studio. He'd called twenty minutes earlier to say he was on his way over. He had something he needed to discuss in person. Something urgent that couldn't wait until tomorrow. She'd been in her pajamas when he called, scrolling her phone for celebrity news. She'd offered to come meet him at his office but he'd said he wasn't far away and would drop by—he remembered where she lived.

It struck her then that the room didn't look right. It looked like the fake space of a fake writer. Somebody who played a writer on TV. It didn't look the way a real novelist's work studio should look. She searched the space for something to add a little novelistic flair, then remembered what was hiding in the drawer. Her novel. She could spread it out here on the desk, a prop. Hampton would be impressed. Alongside it, she placed a legal pad. But it was blank. What writer would have an empty legal pad on their desk? She scribbled some random words on the pad to make it look like she was working the way she'd claimed to write, painstakingly, by hand. *Platypus. Diametrical. Is it a man or is it a mask?*

That was as far as she got. She heard a car in the driveway, then she glimpsed his form making its way through the garden toward the main house, looking a little lost. She couldn't let him encounter Lenny. She leapt up and stuck her head out of the door and called out to him in a cheery, high-energy way, "Over here!"

He waved a hand and came toward her, smiling.

"This is awesome," he said, stepping into the office. "I dig it."

They hugged, stiffly, sexlessly. He smelled of almonds.

He glanced at the desk, his eyes taking in the manuscript, the pen, the legal pad covered in nonsense.

"This is exactly how I imagined it," he said. "A real writer at work."

She felt proud, as if it really were her office. He moved around, examining things. Every few feet, he plucked out a book, read the spine, put it back. When he reached Jane's first novel, he flipped through it, smiling, as if remembering his favorite parts. He put it back and turned to look at her desk. "So this is where the magic happens."

"Guess so," Jane said.

"Man, I would give anything to sit in a room like this, surrounded by books, free to write whatever the fuck I wanted." He walked over to the desk and she thought he was going to comment on her novel lying there, but instead he pointed at the portrait of Brett and Piper on their wedding day. "Wait, hold up. Is that—? Why do you have a photo of Brett MacNamara on your desk?"

Her stomach seized. She'd forgotten to hide the photograph of Brett and Piper on their wedding day.

"He's my cousin," she said.

Hampton picked up the photograph and squinted at the picture.

"See me?" she said, pointing at the tiny face in the crowd, Brooklyn Jane grinning in her stolen dress.

"Wait, are you related on the white side or the Black side? I guess with you half-nuts it could go either way."

She swallowed. "The Black side. Our fathers are—also cousins. So I guess we're second cousins? Something like that."

"That's weird you keep his wedding picture on your desk. I mean, nice, but weird." He put the picture back down. "Well, say hi to that dude. Tell him I want to work with him someday. He's hot shit. In the zombie world, anyway."

Hampton crossed the room to look out the window at the main house. Lenny was visible through the floor-to-ceiling glass, walking from the bathroom to the kitchen area. Hampton stared at him, frowning, as Lenny opened the refrigerator door, stood pondering its innards, pulled out something, stared at the packaging, put it back, and closed the refrigerator door. He went to the cupboard and pulled out a bag of potato chips. He threw himself down on the sofa and picked up a book.

"That the husband?"

"That's Lenny. Yes."

Hampton watched him in silence. She wondered what he was seeing. Lenny was about the same height and general build as Hampton, and about the same shade, but with hair he cut himself, a soft, unwieldy mop of curls. He wore cheap drugstore readers. Their expressions were utterly different too. Lenny's resting face looked hesitant, skeptical. Hampton's face had the two sides, the hilarity and the tragedy, but beneath both expressions was hunger.

"Lenny," he said, finally. "Lenny. Is he half Jewish or something?"

"No. It's just his name."

Hampton looked as if he were watching a television show, with an expression of anticipation, as if he were waiting for something. Maybe for Reebee to fly through a door and say, "Where that high-yellow bitch at?" followed by a laugh track.

"Does he make comic books, like the dad in the show?"

"Not really, no. He's an artist—a painter. Abstract art."

"Huh," he said, sounding slightly disappointed. "Wait, did you tell me he went to Harvard?"

"No, that's Kyle Bunch. My real husband went to Oberlin."

"Oberlin. He was born into money, I take it."

"Well, he was more middle class than wealthy."

"But bougie. The moody, alienated son of professionals. Right?"

"Pretty much."

"Yeah, I met his type. They were all over Howard. I hadn't even known about them when I was growing up." He turned to her. "You're like me, Jane, aren't you?"

She nodded yes, not entirely sure what he meant. Perhaps he was simply talking about money, the fact that neither of them came from much, or that they were children of divorce. But maybe he was talking about something more ineffable that they shared.

He put a hand on her shoulder and kneaded it for a moment, and she wondered again if he wasn't about to make an old-fashioned pass. He seemed to lose his nerve—or maybe interest—the last time in the car. But what would she do if he followed through this time? A small, degraded part of her wanted him to make a move—for the ego rush. At her age, to be sexually desired by a man who had a personal trainer and an electric Porsche, a man who was served egg-white omelets and smoothies by his beautiful assistant during meetings.

But Lenny was right there. Whatever was or wasn't going on with him these days, it didn't feel right to be having sex with a television producer just across the lawn.

And she couldn't help remembering that she hadn't waxed her bikini line in years. She knew that pubic hair was supposed to be in these days, but wasn't that for twentysomethings? And did they really mean it? She was almost positive that Hampton had never actually seen that much shrubbery. Not to mention that, like Lenny, she had gone a little soft around the middle. Which he had already noticed, she reminded herself, remembering his comment in the restaurant. She'd seen the picture of Doreen. She was taut, coiffed, pampered, a trophy wife with a standing appointment at a spa. But maybe it was all the ways Jane was different from Doreen that turned him on about her—maybe he craved the feeling of holding a fertility symbol in his arms.

Or maybe it was simply that he wasn't so superficial as to care about a little lapsed grooming, an extra fifteen pounds. Maybe it was her brain that was turning him on. Didn't he keep saying she was a genius? Hadn't he been intrigued by the latest episode ideas she'd pitched to him? Maybe it was the invisible things about Jane that he found so attractive.

She forced herself to meet his eyes and saw that he wasn't so much checking her out as looking *at* her face—at a particular spot on her face. His eyes centered, almost crossed. They seemed to be zooming in on the tip of her nose. She touched it, trying to figure out if something was there, but she felt nothing.

Hampton looked unsettled. He went to sit on the sofa. He closed his eyes for a long moment, as if meditating, before he spoke again.

"The public school teachers, they tried to break me," he said. "From the moment I started school they tried to crush my spirit. They tried to shame me and pathologize me. An army of white women, sometimes men, who literally thought it was their job to destroy Black boys. They sent me to the principal's office every day for no reason except I couldn't sit on my own little square on the carpet. I was always trying to mess with other kids. Normal little boy hijinks, you know? Pulling this girl's hair, giving that boy a wedgie. Nothing criminal. But when you're a little Black boy, that's what they do. They try to find a way to pathologize your ordinary fucking behavior. To get you in that pipeline. They really want to put you onto that track, you know, a life working at McDonald's or hard crime. Your pick. And I think that's what made me Hampton Motherfucking Ford. All that time spent in the principal's office and detention. That's where I discovered the fire that was inside me. The hunger to be, to persevere. I thought, I'm going to make sure these white people regret the day they ever tried to doubt me. It gave me this balls-to-the-wall urge to succeed. And now I'm running shit. I pay more for my cleaning lady than all those public school administrators make in a year."

"That's very inspirational."

"You're probably wondering why I came here tonight," he said.

"Yes."

"The network guys gave me a lot of fucking money, Jane. Like, more zeros than you and your husband will ever see in your life. Do you realize that?"

She caught a change in his tone—something sharp, scolding.

"Bruce Borland hired me to diversify the fucking content. He's aware and I'm aware that by the year 2050 the majority of this country will be mulatto. Which means every network is trying to get to the plate first, to launch their own little biracial juggernaut. What I'm trying to tell you is: this is no joke. We were supposed to get to it first, and biggest. That's why I called you in, Jane. That's what all these brainstorming sessions were supposed to be about."

"Of course."

"You were supposed to be helping me develop a biracial show. And instead you've been pitching me all these weird ideas about this random fucking family with all these random-assed issues." He shook his head. "The Black R. Crumb? The fucking Labradoodle Defense? The Some of My Best Friends escort service? It just feels so niche. Like, a little too inside baseball, you know? And anyway, what does any of it have to do with being biracial?"

"Well, it's just that the main character is biracial. The issues she's having are just, you know, her issues."

"Listen, if you didn't want to write a show about a character struggling with their mixedness, if you were hoping to write some random shit about a family as random as your own, this isn't going to work. I mean, Bruce will just hire some white writers to develop a white show with these same plotlines, because none of your characters even need to be biracial. Do you see what I'm saying? Every show lives or dies on its premise. Repeat after me: every show lives or dies on its premise."

"Every show lives or dies on its premise."

"That's right. And some characters are sociopaths who happen to be empaths. Others are sex addicts who happen to be germophobic. That's what television does. We find a little twist in our character's profile, some ironic twist. The character we were writing was going to be a biracial person but also funny. That was what the networks were waiting for. That was the twist."

Jane was still struggling to catch up. So this was actually a work meeting. Hampton had come here to give her notes. He was still talking. Telling her that it was going to make him look bad if the first show he brought before the network in his new role, under his new deal, was a pitiful weird little show that wasn't even really very biracial. He said it was fine, creatively—they could make the show about a fucking Smurf if they wanted to—but it would only die in the pitch room, and did she want that? "Every show lives or dies on its premise," he kept repeating.

He stood up and went to stare out the window again. She saw that Lenny had abandoned his book and was surfing through television stations, the crumpled bag of chips at his side.

"I mean," he said. "Maybe I should have hired Crystal Bookman. She was dying for me to pick her."

"Who's Crystal Bookman?"

"She worked with me on *Wally Spitko*. She's mixed too, though she never mentioned it to anyone until it seemed like she could get some advantage from it. That type. Everyone thought she was, like, Persian. White men are her jam. Now she's just dying to create biracial content because she sees where the wind blows. But see, I didn't want to produce some network shit. I just walked away from the fucking networks. I wanted something more premium. More prestige. And you being a novelist, I thought, that's the way to go. But now you're making me wonder, Jane, if I made the right decision." He turned around to look at her. "I mean, shit, forget Crystal Bookman. I might as well hire a white guy to develop the show. Because, trust me, there are a lot of them waiting it out in the bargain basement these days. Nobody would know the difference. You see what I'm saying?"

Jane nodded, her heart pounding. "I can make it more biracial," she said. "I can do that."

"I hope so, Jane. Just remember, we're trying to represent. That's the magic word here. *Represent.* You've got a real chance here. Don't fuck it up."

Jane picked up the fountain pen and wrote in all caps on the legal pad. *DON'T FUCK IT UP. REPRESENT.*

Hampton nodded, took out a pack of gum, unwrapped two sticks, and put them in his mouth without offering Jane any. He seemed relaxed now, and Jane allowed herself to take a deep breath.

"That your novel?" He nodded toward the stack of pages.

"Yep," she said. "The monkey on my back."

"Jesus. That's a big monkey. How many pages you got there?"

"Four hundred and fifty-seven."

He whistled. "Seriously?"

"Don't be impressed. Just because it's long doesn't mean it's any good."

"I don't believe you."

"Believe me."

"Where'd you learn this whole shtick, Jane? *I'm bad. My work is bad.* When did that happen?"

"Where else?" she said. "Daddy dearest. Mama dearest. Huey Newton and Patty Hearst. The interracial horror show. *Hating versus State of*

Virginia." She glanced at the novel. "The good news is I feel dead inside. The bad news is I feel dead inside."

"Jane—"

He rose and came toward her, and this time she thought he really was going to make a pass, but he just put his hands on her shoulders and began to massage them.

"This novel has been a real thorn in your side, hasn't it?"

"I try not to think about it most of the time."

"Maybe it's better than you think."

"No. It's pretty much unsalvageable."

"I don't believe you." He picked up a page and began to read from it. "'*She sat staring at the water, shivering. California nights were colder than she expected.*' That's amazing, Jane. Your voice is amazing—"

"Thanks."

He picked up another page and skimmed it. Whatever he saw seemed to draw him in, as he picked up the whole manuscript and carried it to the sofa. He sat down and actually seemed to be reading it—not from beginning to end, but flipping through, reading a page here, a page there.

"Listen, Jane," he said. "I'm about to say something I might regret."

She was afraid suddenly. It was about her book. He could tell from skimming a few pages she had no talent. The first book had been a fluke. She was a one-hit wonder—the Toni Basil of novelists.

"Fuck," he said, under his breath, still flipping through her novel. "Why am I like this?"

"Like what?"

"Listen, I don't have time to get a haircut, a massage, a motherfucking colonoscopy. But I consider you family. So, this is the deal. I like you. I like you a lot. So I'm gonna do you a solid, okay?"

"What's that?"

"I'm gonna take your novel with me to Vancouver over the weekend.

We're shooting season three of *White Kid in the Window*. I'll read it on set. There's a lot of dead time while the actors are in makeup. I'll read it and I'll tell you, fam to fam, Black creative to Black creative, what I honestly think. I'd do that for you. Jane, that's how much I believe in your voice."

"You don't have to do that."

"Shut up. I'm doing it."

"Well, let me email it to you then. So you don't have to carry all those pages around."

She could stall him. She could make it better. Or hope he'd forgotten this conversation.

"I'll never read it if it's electronic. It'll get buried. This is perfect." He was gathering the pages on her desk into a neat stack. "Anyway, you need a reader who gets your Don Cornelius references."

"I might need a minute to think about this," she said, trying to take the pages back from his arms. "I'll get you a better draft. A cleaner draft."

He put a hand on her shoulder, and said in a calming voice, "Jane, breathe, you can do this."

His tone reminded her of those drug counselors on *Intervention* who always told the addict they had to get on the airplane to rehab that very day, now or never, as if there were only one flight out of Norco, California, as if they were on the last ride off Gilligan's Island. She felt the same pressure those meth heads felt, surrounded by their so-called loved ones. The lucky ones ended up getting the "three months later" chapter where the show fast-forwarded to them ninety days sober, still living at the retreat, playing basketball, or walking ponderously on a beach in Florida or Southern California. They always looked chunkier without the substance, more ordinary, heading toward an energetic mediocrity.

Hampton straightened the manuscript by banging it on the desk, thwacked the top of it. "Okay, I can already tell I'm gonna love this."

Before she could stop it, he was carrying it with him out the door. Jane trailed after him through the garden.

"Seriously, it needs work. I've already changed some things. Let me take a few more days on it."

"Don't be silly," Hampton said. They'd reached his car. He turned to her, the manuscript under his arm now. "Listen, I want you to stop coming up with all these episode ideas, okay? You think you can stop?" She nodded. "Then I want you to take a step back and think about the larger premise of the show. Don't write anything down. Just think while you're driving, or cooking, or doing yoga, or whatever. Think—what is our premise here? What's the bigger picture? The elevator pitch. The twist. Because we've been doing it all backward. Okay?"

She felt very small, though she wasn't that small, as she stood before him, nodding.

"And remember, what does every show do?"

"It lives or dies on its premise."

"That's right, Jane. You got this."

"You really don't have to read that whole book," she called out one more time.

"Will you stop?" he said, holding out a flat palm. "Just stop. You gotta let go, Jane. Just let go."

He slid into the Porsche and slammed the door. Only then did she notice that there was another person in the car. Layla sat in the passenger's seat, staring down at what Jane imagined was her phone. And as the car pulled away, she glimpsed in the back seat, through the cracked window, Topher's pale face peering out at her, unsmiling.

19.

In the week that followed, Jane tried to do what Hampton advised. She tried to think about the show, but every time she did, she would wonder instead where he was in the novel, what part he was reading just then, and she was filled with a crippling, almost nauseating anxiety. She knew from experience that no creative work could be done when somebody was reading a draft of your novel. All one could do to survive that terrifying slowed-down time was to focus on something else. So she tried to distract herself by throwing herself into full-time mothering. Even when the kids were in school, she puttered around the house, cleaning up their mess, and doing laundry. When they finally did come home, she had nutritious snacks waiting, and she was game to help them with their homework or take them to lessons. She even made a meal schedule and posted it on the refrigerator.

Monday: Chicken à l'orange
Tuesday: Panko-encrusted salmon
Wednesday: Beef enchiladas
Thursday: Shakshuka with feta cheese
Friday: Impossible burgers and sweet potato fries

Lenny seemed taken aback by the meal calendar and the cleanliness of the house. He asked her what she was doing with her novel, and she said that she'd sent out a new manuscript to Honor and she was in a holding pattern as she waited on the response. Lenny was distracted enough by preparing for his impending show in Japan—packing the art, arranging for it to be sent over—that he didn't question her further.

One blazing hot afternoon, she took Ruby to the Grove and let her pick out a new American Girl doll. Not one to replace Addy Walker, former slave, but to befriend Addy Walker, former slave. Jane lightly suggested that Ruby pick Melody Ellison, the civil rights–era singer—but Ruby had her heart set on an Indian American doll named Kavi Sharma. Jane bought the doll on credit and afterward took Ruby to lunch and charged that too. When they got home, Jane waited to see if Ruby would take Addy out of the box under the bed to introduce her to her multicultural friend, but she didn't. She just sat brushing Kavi Sharma's hair while Addy remained in solitary confinement. Jane consoled herself that if Kavi wasn't Black, an American descendent of slavery, at least she wasn't white either.

The next afternoon, Jane brought Finn to a social-skills class in a mini mall "educational center" and left him inside while she stood outside in the heat drinking water and talking to the other beleaguered mothers of socially inept little boys who liked to bunny hop.

When Finn came out, she asked what he'd done in the class, and he said he'd played Connect Four. He seemed relieved it was over, relieved to be away from the other boys. He wanted to tell her about the differences between all the Godzilla films that had been released since the 1950s.

So this was active mothering, she thought. And the next thought was the same as always: Had Hampton gotten far enough into her novel to finally realize she was an imposter? And which part was she faking?

That she was a television writer or that she was a novelist? That she was Black or that she was white?

In those days of waiting, she looked up Hampton a lot on Instagram. From there, she could track his movements. First he was in Vancouver, then in New York City, where he was posing in the leather-upholstered booth of a bar with Justin Bieber and Puff Daddy. On that same trip, he was in the back of a taxi coming home from a party, holding his fingers in a V sign and sticking out his tongue. Victory is assured read the post. Then he was in LA again, by the side of his pool, in a pensive pose with Jujubean resting her head on his chest. Beside it he'd posted a Nas lyric: be more conscious of how we raise our daughters. He was close but so far away. She pictured him moving around his palatial light-filled mansion on Amalfi Drive, the one she liked to look at on Redfin when she was bored, and reading her novel, shaking his head. In awe or in horror? The vision switched back and forth between dream and nightmare.

One afternoon she got up the nerve to send a text to Layla. Hey lady, just wondering how things are going over there! Should we meet again about the show? Jane paused, then wrote: Everything okay with Hampton?

Three dancing dots appeared on her telephone screen—Layla was writing back. Then a series of emojis came through. A smiley face, a large nose in medium skin tone, a brown fist bump, a ball of yarn. And a little old man in a wheelchair.

Jane tried to translate them into English.

Smiley face: *She was happy to hear from Jane!*

Nose: *She thought Jane was being nosey. Or she thought Jane's nose was too big.*

Fist bump: *Hampton thought her novel was great!*

The ball of yarn: *Maybe she had more to untangle in the plot.*

Old man in wheelchair: *Hampton Ford has been in a terrible accident.*

Three dots appeared again, but after a few seconds, they stopped dancing, and there was nothing.

Jane went to her computer and googled *Hampton Ford accident*. If he was in a wheelchair now, she thought, he would have lots of time to finish reading her novel. She tried typing just *Hampton Ford* and hit "news." But there was no recent news about him, and no new images since the one at the pool with Jujubean.

Jane texted him directly. Hey dude! Should we get together soon? I have some thoughts on our premise! Also, love to hear what you thought of the novel, of course. But no rush!

She added an image of a curious emoji face, somebody who was just wondering.

He didn't reply. Which she took to mean he hated her novel. Which she took to mean she should not be a writer at all—neither for television nor for novels. Which meant she was good for only one thing: teaching.

What made matters worse was that she hadn't told Lenny about Hampton showing up at the house in person—about the pass that wasn't a pass but had turned into his reading her the riot act about the premise problem with the show then walking out the door with her manuscript.

The following Tuesday night, the house was unusually quiet. Lenny was out at his evening Japanese class in Little Tokyo—he'd outgrown the Berlitz tapes and wanted to speak to real live Japanese people. Finn was outside working on his Moon Mission project—he went into the garden every night with a notebook to record the phases of the moon. Ruby was watching some insidious tween dramedy on the iPad in her room. Jane checked Hampton's Instagram for the fifth time that day. There was a new post. It showed Hampton standing at a car dealership, looking skeptically at a bigger new electric. A Bentley. He'd written: Should I buy this car, Fam? #retailtherapy #saveourplanet #blessed #swirl #greenlight #seasonorder

He was buying a new car to swirl around town in. He'd gotten a season order on one of his many diverse projects. He was trying to save the planet. He needed therapy. Had he read her novel? Had he given up on their show idea? As she was processing all this, Finn came back inside and stood beside her, looking at the screen.

"He looks like Papa."

She turned to him. "He does not. Let's stop that little joke, okay?"

But he wasn't looking at the screen. He was staring out the window into the courtyard.

"Mama?"

"Yes, babe."

"There's a man in your office."

She looked across the lawn and saw that indeed the light was on inside her office. She must have left it on. But no. Behind the curtain, she could make out a silhouette of a figure moving around. Her first thought was *Hampton*. He'd come back in person to talk about her novel. He'd loved it so much he'd come to tell her in person. Or he hated it so much he'd come to tell her in person.

She pointed to her computer screen. "Did he look like this?"

Finn shook his head.

"Was he a Black guy, about yay high?" She was standing up now and held up her hand a few inches above her head.

"The sun is ninety-three million miles from earth. Did you know that, Mama?"

A prickle of fear. "What did the man look like, Finn?"

"I don't know. He wasn't wearing any clothes."

"What?"

"He was naked."

Jane peered out at the studio again. There was a naked man out there. And he wasn't Hampton. Or Lenny. A naked stranger in their house. Every Los Angeles crime story she'd ever read flooded her brain—the Manson Family, the Night Stalker, the Hillside Strangler, the Black Dahlia. Instead of hysterical she became very cool. That was, she understood now, the funny thing about real fear. When it washed over you, it felt close to a state of calm.

She rounded up Ruby and put both children in the bedroom closet with an iPad and told them not to move, no matter what, until she came back. Then she shut the closet door and went and got the biggest knife from the knife block in the kitchen, a gleaming Wüsthof. She opened the front door as soundlessly as she could and went across the lawn, clutching the weapon, feeling the strange bravery that came to mothers in times of emergency. She opened the door to the studio, and indeed there was a man in her office, though he was no longer entirely naked. And he wasn't a stranger. It was Brett. He stood shirtless, in sweatpants, rifling through his luggage.

"Oh my God," she said, "you scared the shit out of me." He looked up at her. She tried to smile, to look natural, happy to see him. "Hello, stranger," she said, and stepped toward him for a hug, but he stiffened and stepped away, eyeing her hand. She realized she was still holding the knife. "Sorry. Let me put this down. I thought you were someone else." She laughed as she put the knife on the desk.

Brett didn't laugh along. He just stared at her, unsmiling, and said, "I honestly don't know what to say to you right now."

HE WAS GETTING a divorce. He had been trying to call her all this time just to talk to her, friend to friend, about his life falling apart. And she had ignored not only his calls but also his texts. She was the worst sort of friend. A user. He'd given her the house and the year of living fabulously and she couldn't be bothered to talk him off the ledge in his time of need.

He looked slightly thinner but not unwell. He was golden brown from the beaches where he'd been surfing every day in Sydney. And he claimed to be glad to be rid of Piper. But he'd been through a lot and she was acting insane, he said, demanding full custody of Max, the house, the works. He'd left the wreckage behind in Australia.

He searched her face. "Where were you, Jane? I really could have used a friend."

Anyway, he'd been trying to tell her he was coming back early. Hadn't she listened to his messages? "I needed you, Jane," he said. "I mean, I was in a dark place. And you just fucking ghosted me. What was that about?"

Jane wondered where to start. With finding Marianne's card? She couldn't even begin to imagine how to explain it all—not now.

"I'm sorry, Brett. I've been a terrible friend. It's just, I was having a situation of my own."

"You and Lenny?" he said, sounding almost hopeful. Divorced people always wanted you to divorce too. And she'd never thought he liked Lenny much. Or maybe he had just sensed Lenny didn't like him. She shook her head.

"No," she said. "We're still together. Sort of. But it's my novel. My editor, my agent, they hated it. I've discarded it. Ten years and it's in the trash."

He blinked, surprised, and she could see some of the hurt and anger fall away. He felt sorry for her. And beneath that, maybe, she thought she saw a glint of pleasure, relief, in his eyes. He was glad her novel was dead. He was proving the universal truth about writers, any kind of writer: they enjoyed nothing more than hearing of another writer's failure.

"That's awful," he said, seeming almost sincere. "Shit. Jane. That was gonna be your big book. I'm so sorry."

"Thanks. But maybe I wasn't meant to be a writer, you know?" She eyed him, wondering now about that other question. What had happened to his mulatto comedy? She didn't want to know that he'd sold it. Not right now.

"So where's Piper?" she said instead.

"In Sydney with Max. She's talking about moving back to New York with him." He walked over and picked up the portrait of him and Piper from Jane's desk, stared at it for a moment. "It's gotten so ugly between us."

"I'm so sorry to hear that," said Jane.

"Are you? I always got the feeling you hated Piper. Did you?"

"Well—" said Jane.

A smile crossed Brett's lip. "You did. You did hate her."

"Hate is maybe too strong a word," she said, surprised it had been so obvious. "But seriously, are you okay?"

He shrugged. "I'll survive."

"I know you'll find somebody great."

"Actually," he said.

"You've already met someone."

"Her name's Lucinda. She really helped me through it. She's totally Piper's opposite. I think you'll love her."

"That's great. I'm so glad."

"Honestly, Jane," he said. "I can't believe I stayed with Piper so long." He spoke in a tone Jane recognized, a narrative rehearsed in therapy. "I wanted so badly not to be my father that I went the opposite direction. I succumbed to her joyless prison to try to make up for my dad's absence. The crueler she was to me, the more it felt to me like some kind of justice. But the moment I met Lucinda, I broke out of this trance. I mean, it was like a house of cards. Once you recognize one illusion, all the others become clear."

He was pulling objects out of his suitcase as he spoke. Now he stopped and looked around the office. "God, I've missed this town. To be honest, there isn't anywhere better than LA."

He pulled an expensive-looking leather dopp kit out of his suitcase and found a prescription bottle inside, popped a pill.

"Where will you stay now?" Jane asked.

"I forgot. You didn't get my messages. I'm home. I'm staying here. Lucinda's coming to join me soon. She's a set designer. That's how I met her. On the set." He began to stretch, cracking his back from side to side. "God, that flight was killer." He opened the mini fridge and found it empty. "You have anything to eat here?" he said. "I'm starving."

Jane remembered the children. "Oh God, I have to go tell the kids they can come out of the closet."

"The closet?"

"It was a safety precaution."

She headed out the door and across the lawn, Brett followed her.

"Where's Lenny?"

"He's taking a night class in Little Tokyo. Trying to learn Japanese."

"That dude. I love how quirky he is. He just does whatever he wants."

In the main house, she left Brett in the kitchen while she went to the bedroom. She opened the closet door, expecting the worst—her kids weeping, permanently scarred—and found them curled over the iPad, watching funny pet videos. Finn squinted up at her. "Can you shut the door? We're watching this."

She left them there and went back out to the kitchen. Brett was standing in the kitchen sipping a glass of wine, staring out at the garden.

"Is this one of my wines?" he looked unhappy with whatever he'd tasted.

She remembered the wine issue. "No, that's just something we picked up."

"The kids okay?"

"They're fine. They'll be watching YouTube clips at the end of the world."

"Max doesn't have screens," Brett said. "Piper believes they cause ADHD or some bullshit. One of the many half-baked ideas she forced on me."

"Well, she's probably right about that. But I'm too tired to care."

Jane fixed him a plate of fish sticks and congealed mac and cheese, and put it in the microwave while Brett walked around, taking in the room.

"Sorry I don't have anything better to offer. I wasn't expecting anyone." She put the plate of food on the table with a paper towel and a fork.

"God, I've missed it here. Nothing like home." He shook his head. "She's gonna try to take the house."

"She can't take the house. Can she?"

"I don't know." He came back to the table and sat down and looked at the plate she'd laid out for him, prodded the mac and cheese with a fork but didn't take a bite. He scrolled through his phone instead. She could see he was looking at cars. Fancy cars. He'd let go of the Tesla he'd had before he went to Australia—the lease was up—and he told her he was going to the car dealership tomorrow to get a new car. A Porsche or an Audi? He was of two minds. She told him to get an Audi so he wouldn't look too cliché. Divorced guy in a Porsche. He said that was a good point. He put his phone down.

"Where are you guys going next?" he said.

"We hadn't figured that out yet."

"I mean, you knew I was coming back soon," said Brett.

"I thought it was still a month away."

He watched her for a moment, concerned, then said, "Surely you have some leads though?"

"Sure. Of course we do."

"Oh good. Well, listen, I'm sorry, Jane, but I left you those messages. I thought you guys would have worked all this out already. And I need to be home." He took a sip of the wine again, crinkled his nose. "Will two weeks be enough?"

"I guess it'll have to be." She had been standing against the island, facing him, but now turned to busy herself with the dishes so he couldn't see her face. She thought of Hampton, reading her pages, and felt a swirl of nausea, hope, terror.

"Hey, did anything ever happen with your comedy?" she said. "The one you were writing about people like us?" She gripped the edge of the sink hard, steadying herself while she waited for his answer.

"Yeah. Well, no. I started it, and it was going okay—but the drama with Piper got in the way. Anyway, I think it's not my bag, writing quippy shit about race. I mean, I don't want to be pigeonholed like that."

"Makes sense," Jane said, turning brightly. She could bear to look at him now. "I mean, the mulatto game, it's never been your thing, right? You should do you, Brett. Follow your passion."

"I don't know if script doctoring is my passion, but the pay is insane." He rubbed his face wearily. "That's partly why I'm back. To take some meetings." He'd abandoned the kiddie plate she'd given him and was walking around, examining the house again. He called to her from the other room now. "Oh, I was meaning to ask you. Did you get in touch with my agent? Marianne? She mentioned something—"

Jane tried to think of a good story. She decided her best move was to play on his schadenfreude pity again. "Yeah, but, see, I can explain. I was in such a low place about my novel. I called her out of desperation—"

"No, that's cool," he called back. "You should totally work with her. Marianne is great."

Jane felt relief wash over her. He didn't care.

"But Jane?"

"Yeah?"

"What happened to all my wine?"

BY THE TIME Lenny got home, the kids were asleep, and Brett had stomped off across the lawn after they had it out about the wine. His pretty features had looked more petulant than angry as he bellowed at her across the kitchen island. He said he couldn't believe she and Lenny had actually finished every single bottle from the collection he and Piper had acquired over a decade. He couldn't believe they'd not thought to ask first. Now Jane sat at the kitchen island, staring out at the studio. She could see Brett's silhouette pacing back and forth behind the curtain, waving his arms. She guessed he was ranting to someone—Lucinda?—about her and Lenny.

"I thought we had another month to find a place," Lenny said, when she gave him the news.

"Apparently he left me a voice message alerting us he was cutting his trip short," Jane said. "Can you believe that? A voice message? Who listens to voice messages anymore?"

"Everybody," said Lenny. "Everybody does." He glanced across the lawn. "Can't he stay in a hotel? Brett can afford a hotel."

"He wants to be here. He wants to be in his home. He's licking his divorce wounds."

"How can he do that—just evict us for no reason?"

"It's not an eviction. We have no lease. This was, like, a gentleman's agreement. Remember?"

"What a scumbag. What a dirty piece of shit. I told you we shouldn't have done this. We should have stayed at Linda's. At least we had a real agreement with her."

"You didn't want to stay there either," said Jane. "When I told you what Brett was offering us, you said yes. You were on board."

Lenny sat heavily on the bed, then fell back against the pillow, his eyes closed. "Maybe I agreed to it. But it wasn't my idea. I wanted us all to go to Tokyo. But you wanted to finish your"—he made quote marks with his fingers—"'novel' here."

"My 'novel'? What's that supposed to mean?"

Lenny was watching Jane with the same expression he'd worn staring at her through the window of the Jeep in Joshua Tree the morning that now seemed like a century ago. Disdain.

"Why are we still even talking about the novel?" he said. "Let's talk about something more salient. Like your friend Lincoln Perry. And the show. The one you were just pretending to pretend to write."

"What's that supposed to mean?" She'd learned to ask a question when she was accused of a mistruth. To stall with questions.

"It means a lot of things. It means I'm not dumb. I knew you were working on that show for real for months now. I knew you were slaving over the Bunches."

"How do you know their names? I never told you that."

"You left your notebook lying all over the house. Some of those episodes sounded funny. Probably too funny."

Jane sat with a slump on the bed.

"Why didn't you say anything? Why did you let me keep acting like I was still working on the novel?"

"Maybe I was hoping it was true. That you were only doing all this shit for material. Or maybe I was hoping it would eventually become true. You'd start to use the stuff you were doing as material. Take ownership over it. But it never seemed to happen." He shook his head. "Now, come on, tell me you're at least going to get paid for all those ideas. The if/come deal, whatever that is."

She swallowed, then explained it to him. An if/come deal—which she didn't even officially have yet, as a contract hadn't emerged—meant you didn't get paid unless you sold it to the network. You did all the work preparing the show for free with the promise you would get some money when and if it sold.

"That all sounds very cute for a twenty-two-year-old. But did you ever think maybe it was important for Ruby and Finn that you finish your book and sell it? So you could have a better job? I mean, ever think that instead of trying to be rich you should try not to be homeless?"

The air went out of her. Finn and Ruby. "They're not going to be homeless," she said quietly, so quietly that the words seemed to die upon contact with the air. But where would they go? In two weeks?

She had a yearning to be back in Linda's accessory dwelling unit. Had it been so bad? The neighborhood had been pleasant. The schools had been good enough. The kids had loved Linda's little schnauzer. If only they hadn't left on such bad terms.

"So where is Lincoln Perry?" Lenny said. He was standing, watching her. "Did you and he get into some kind of fight? Did you step on his tap shoes?"

"No."

"Well then, what was it?" Lenny said. "Did you do something to scare him away?"

Jane closed her eyes. She pictured Hampton walking across the lawn, flipping through the pages of her novel. It struck her that everyone who read that novel seemed to disappear from her life immediately.

"Are you still working together or not?" Lenny asked again.

"I can't tell. Are you wanting me to work for him now? Is that what's going on here?"

"I'd just like the truth for a change."

"It's complicated."

"How complicated? If you did work for this guy, you should get paid. That was a lot of screwball ideas you came up with in that notebook."

"You don't understand how Hollywood works. It's not like painting. Or writing novels. I mean, it's big time. It's grown-up stuff with grown-up money. So just because I came up with some ideas you thought were funny doesn't mean it was ready to share with the network. Every show lives or dies on its premise. And we were—we are—still trying to figure out the premise."

"God," he said. "You're worse than I thought."

"What's that supposed to mean?"

"It means, I don't know who the fuck you are anymore. I'm not sure if I've ever known."

"Oh, go to hell."

"I'm already there," he said, then he stormed off.

She watched him through the glass, striding across the lawn the way Brett had done earlier. Watched him get into the Subaru and pull out of the driveway. She couldn't imagine where he'd go. It was after eight. There was nowhere to go in LA after eight unless you planned it a week in advance. It wasn't like you could drive down the mountain and wander into some party or bar scene. Maybe he was going to sit in a parking lot somewhere, fuming. Or maybe he'd finally check out that dodgy "massage parlor" in the mini mall down at the base of the mountain, the one he was always pointing out from the car as they drove past and wondering aloud, "Do you think they give happy endings there?" Maybe he'd gone to get his happy ending from the lips or hand of some sad, defeated woman.

Jane could hear owls hooting in the distance, a coyote howling at the moon. She picked up a Pottery Barn catalog that was lying beside their bed and flipped through the pages, staring at the furniture inside, the cookie jars, the Holly Hobbie kitchens, the perfect children's bedrooms with the same wooden block letters of trendy kids' names that they'd seen in Multicultural Mayberry. Names like Ruby and Finn. Who were the same shade of brown as the kids she used to ogle in catalogs like this one back when she was living in Brooklyn, the shade of brown babies she thought would make her whole. People liked light-brown kids with wild-but-not-too-kinky hair the same way they liked Labradoodles, designer mutts that were a signifier of liberal middle-class civility. Nothing bad could happen to a family with a Labradoodle. She wrote the line down in her little notebook and promised herself to tell Hampton the line the next time they spoke. He'd laugh and all would be forgiven. He'd forgive her the bad novel and they'd be working together again on the Bunches just like before, only better.

Jane must have fallen asleep. She woke to find the light beside her bed was still on and she was still dressed in jeans and a T-shirt, but it was much later than she'd imagined. It was 3:33 in the morning. She headed into the living room expecting to find Lenny sprawled out on the sofa, asleep, but he wasn't there. She went outside, hoping to find him in Piper's studio, but it was empty, dark, and the Subaru was not back in the driveway.

20.

Lenny didn't return until late the next morning. He came in and didn't meet her eyes as he got himself a glass of water and drank from it. His clothes were rumpled, his eyes bloodshot. Later, after he'd showered and was fixing himself coffee in the kitchen, she asked him where he'd been all night. He said, his face averted, "Just driving. Thinking."

She had never wondered about Lenny's faithfulness. He had not struck her as the type. And anyway, where would he have found time for a side piece? But perhaps she was the one who'd been missing something.

This new possibility buzzed inside her, the thought that Lenny might have his own secrets. It was a dangerous thought, as dangerous as the wide cool space between them in the California king at night. The thought of his touching another woman made her feel a rush of ordinary jealousy, but it was more than that. It jangled some deeper part of her psyche—a sense she held, and had maybe always held, that her life out here with Lenny wasn't solid or even real, and that it could all, in one instant, evaporate. She found herself checking her face in the mirror sixteen times a day wherever she could, not because she enjoyed seeing her frizzy hair and eyes ringed by dark circles but because she wanted to make sure her face was still there. She itched to interrogate Lenny, but she couldn't. There wasn't time to unleash any secrets. They had a more immediate problem to solve together—where to live.

It was pretty clear they had to leave soon. Brett was going out of his way to make them feel uncomfortable. He mostly did it by pretending they weren't there. He wandered through the living room, shirtless in boxers, to grab something to eat out of the refrigerator, which he'd stocked with gourmet meals and snacks he'd made clear they weren't supposed to touch. He walked past the screen while they were trying to watch a movie, scratching his butt as he headed into the master bathroom to shower. He had restocked the wine cooler too. He'd gotten his old handyman to come fix all the things they had apparently broken. He stood in the yard in the afternoons, bellowing into his cell phone at somebody named Toby about whether the cold opening was working.

Three days into it, Brett's girlfriend arrived from Sydney and moved into the studio with him. Jane had expected an Australian at least, but Lucinda turned out to be just another American white girl. She looked a lot like Piper but younger, much younger, fresh-faced and slim, as white and blank as a sheet of paper. She wore her dark hair long, with heavy hipster bangs and oversize faux-nerd glasses. She was Piper before parenting and marriage and life's general disappointments. She exuded sex and privilege—a rapaciousness Jane had seen before in young white women who were the product of family money and progressive education. She prowled around the premises, waiting for this family of woebegone Negroes who were getting in the way of her future to be gone.

It added a whole new level of discomfort to have Lucinda around, especially as school was out now and the kids were around all day too. Lucinda and Brett couldn't keep their hands off each other. They'd be making out on the sofa while Jane was trying to braid Ruby's hair. Sometimes Jane thought she could hear them all the way from the studio, fucking early in the morning or late into the night. She wondered about Piper, whether she was feeling destroyed by the new reality of her life as a single woman or liberated. What did she feel about being replaced by a doppleganger? Whatever she suffered, Piper would stay wealthy, so her chances of recovering her dignity, her optimism, were high.

Jane had met wealthy women over the years who talked about how much better their lives were after divorce. They always seemed to be trying to convince Jane and all the other married women they knew to join their new religion. They had so much more time to themselves, for self-care. Coparenting was the dream—the ideal feminist arrangement so they could do things on those childless not-my-custody weekends without a husband lurking around. They could go to wine tastings with girlfriends, fuck that hot plumber or cute barista, do yoga and go to brunch and browse in bookstores—or just lie in bed scrolling on their phone for hours. They could miss their children in a healthy way. And when it was their turn with the kids, they could be evolved, rested, restored versions of themselves, truly present, good role models, especially for their daughters. Those rich women talked about split custody as if it were the greatest invention since the Pill.

Jane could imagine Piper evolving into that kind of divorcée. But—should it come to that—would Jane? No, she wouldn't. Without enough money for even a single home, the prospect of divorce looked a lot different. Both her parents' financial situations had deteriorated after their divorce. The moment Jane and her sister went off to college—each on full scholarship—Jane's mother had gotten rid of the apartment they'd all shared and moved into a communal situation in Somerville with strangers much younger than herself. It meant that Jane and her sister had had no home to visit anymore. On holiday breaks, she and her sister had to share a bed with her mother, as if they were small children again. There were so many house rules, and the shelves in the refrigerator, labeled with each of the roommates' names, were crowded with little morsels of food stored in bowls and balls of aluminum foil, meals for one person, pots of homemade yogurt that her mother warned them, with a kind of hushed gravity, never ever to touch. The yogurt belonged to someone named Connie, whom nobody in the house wanted to anger.

But Jane didn't have time to dwell on thoughts of divorce or what was going on with her and Lenny. They had to find a place and fast. They put the kids into a janky day camp at the YMCA. At camp, they could forget they were about to be uprooted. Only when they got home at five, stinking of camp activities, in blazing prison-orange T-shirts, would they see the boxes of their belongings, Brett and Lucinda leaning against the kitchen counter playing tonsil hockey, see their parents skulking around like squatters on the eve of eviction. The children understood the facts: that they were going yet again to somewhere unknown where they would be the new kids in a sea of unfamiliar faces. Like refugee children around the world, they understood implicitly that there was no time to cry or complain. Like first-world children, they numbed their distress by staring into screens. In the evenings, they sat inside the closet for hours, huddling together in the dark with their iPads, watching YouTube videos and God knew what else while Jane and Lenny packed and searched online for apartments they could afford. They didn't make the children come out until it was time for sleep. They were in survival mode.

In between checking the real estate listings, Jane checked Hampton's Instagram. Unquestionably, he was still in town. He posted a photo of his lettuce-wrapped burger at the Ivy. A random Black child running on the beach. Jujubean posing with North and Saint at the Americana mall. A close-up of a giant gold nameplate necklace that said HAMPTON. None were photos of him reading Jane's manuscript captioned with the hashtags #janegibson #blackgenius #nusunusu.

One night, sitting at the table across from Lenny while he trawled for apartments, she saw a photo of Hampton in a restaurant mugging with a group of Black actors from his hit Black family show, *White Kid in the Window.*

Lenny's voice broke through her stalker's haze. "Okay, I found a place in our price range," he said. He showed it to her. It was in Burbank on the edge of a freeway. It was hideous.

"I mean, can't we keep looking for the next few days? I was hoping we could find one in Multicultural Mayberry."

"No," said Lenny. "We can't afford that shit. You know that. And we don't have time to keep looking. Brett and the new Piper are going to want the big bed back."

His tone with her was cold and impatient, like he was a DMV worker explaining a policy to a person in line. Jane ignored it and launched into the same speech she'd been making for days now. She told him that if they moved to Burbank they would just end up moving again in a few months, and they had to think about Ruby and Finn. They needed to move to a neighborhood they liked, in a good school district. If they ended up needing to move again, they could do it within that neighborhood, and the kids wouldn't have to change schools.

"Well, I don't mind Burbank," Lenny said. "And this apartment is fine. It's as good as it's going to get given our current predicament."

Jane scrolled through the listing. The pictures looked like photos from a crime scene. She felt a scream building in her throat. In as calm a voice as she could muster, she pointed out that the building was next to the airport as well as a freeway, which would be bad for all their lungs, and that the school there was rated 3 on greatschools.org.

Lenny said that was only because the population was mostly ESL students from low-income backgrounds, Filipino and Russian and Iranian and Guatemalan and Mexican. Did she have a problem with those people?

Jane said no, those people were great, better than great, but she wouldn't even be able to speak to their parents to arrange playdates. She reminded Lenny she'd gotten a C in high school Spanish. She'd given him this speech before. She paced as she spoke while he stared at his laptop screen with a dead expression.

"If we were new Americans, immigrants, it would be one thing," she said. "But we're not. We're a Black man and a mulatto—some of the oldest Americans you can find after the people who were already living here. We've been here too long. We don't have that immigrant chutzpah—the hope and grit of those Dreamer kids. Our kids were born lazy, jaded, and ironic—like us. They need a bunch of mediocre white kids in the classroom with them or they'll perish."

Lenny got up and went to the kitchen. He looked in the refrigerator for something, then closed it and opened the wine cooler. He came back carrying one of Brett's new bottles.

"We're not supposed to be drinking that, remember?"

"Fuck Brett. What's he gonna do, kick us out?" He poured a big glass for himself but nothing for her. "What if I was to tell you that I prefer Burbank to Multicultural Mayberry? What if I was to tell you that Multicultural Mayberry makes me want to vomit? I hate that bourgeois crap."

"I'd say you were lying. You claim to want to live low-rent, but you don't come from low-rent. You're bougie as fuck. I come from low-rent—and trust me, you don't want that. You want Multicultural Mayberry."

"Will you stop with this poor Black child shit? You grew up a mulatto child of bohemian parents. Bread and Roses shit. All that cultural capital to go with your government cheese. Let's be clear about that."

His voice had risen a notch. The children. They were in the closet, thankfully, on their screens.

"Keep your voice down," she said. Then in a low voice, "I never said differently. The point was the government cheese. I wasn't special like you."

Lenny let out a laugh she'd never heard before. It was harsh, and he was watching her with small mean eyes. "But you were special," he said. "In that Peola meets Joe Christmas way. That quadroon crybaby where-do-I-belong-mammy kinda way—"

She interrupted him. "Where were you the other night? Do you really want to go there, Lenny?"

He looked away, a mysterious expression on his face as if remembering something or someone. When he spoke again, his tone was more gentle, reasonable, like someone who was trying to neutralize a bomb. Like someone who was hiding something. "All I'm saying is we can't afford Multicultural Mayberry," he said. "And we have to go somewhere. We have to live somewhere. Those are the facts."

THE NEXT MORNING, after Jane dropped the kids at camp, she kept driving. She drove all the way to Multicultural Mayberry. When she got there, she started driving along each of its streets, systematically, as if she were a driver for Google Earth. She couldn't live in Burbank. She just couldn't. The thought of it was putting her in the Sticks. She wanted to live here and she would live here. She just had to figure out how.

It was late in the afternoon, nearly time to pick up the kids, when she finally noticed the sign. How had she missed it before? She'd been on this street so many times, but her eyes had never taken it in—a gargantuan apartment building, one of the few apartment buildings in Multicultural Mayberry. A sign out front read THE GOLDEN EAGLE— NOW LEASING. It was deeply ugly, but so was the place in Burbank where Lenny was now threatening to put down a deposit.

She parked and walked up the ramp and through the sliding glass doors into a lobby that smelled of cleaning solution and something else that was familiar but that she couldn't place. An old woman in a muumuu and slippers sat in an armchair by the front door, reading a newspaper. She smiled at Jane as she came through the doors, then launched in, as if they knew each other, as if they were deep in conversation. "I just read the most interesting thing."

"What's that?"

"Poodles are the most intelligent breed. It says so right here. Isn't that interesting?"

"It is," Jane said, and kept walking. Ahead was a common room where she could see residents gathered, some around a table, working together on a puzzle, others on a sofa watching *Ellen*. She saw a door labeled OFFICE and went toward it. When she knocked, a voice called out, "Come in." Jane opened the door to find a woman seated behind a desk, putting on lipstick. She was blonde, with a cheap face and an unflattering turquoise-colored blouse. She finished applying the lipstick, then put the compact away and smiled at Jane with yellow teeth.

"Can I help you?"

Jane told her she was looking for an apartment in the neighborhood and had just noticed the sign out front. Was a place available?

"Is it for you? Or a parent?"

"For me and my family. For me and my two children and my husband," she said. "The four of us. We have no pets."

"Oh, well, I'm sorry. We don't serve families here." The woman shrugged. "This is a retirement community."

As soon as the woman said it, Jane could see it. She laughed a little at her mistake. She'd been so obsessed with finding a place in this area, any place, she hadn't even noticed it was a nursing home. She shook her head. "Oh, gosh. I didn't realize. I'm so sorry for the misunderstanding." She started to go, but at the door she was overcome with dizziness. She steadied herself against the wall. She tried to remember when she'd had anything to eat or drink. The room swirled wildly around her.

"Are you okay?"

"Can I just sit for a moment? I've been driving around all day looking, and it's so hot. And I—do you have any water?"

"Of course, sit down." The woman held out her hand and they shook. "I'm Renata."

Jane told the woman her name and then sat down and clutched the armrests for steadiness. The woman appeared before her with a paper cup of water. Jane gulped it all down and sat with her eyes closed, waiting for the room to stop spinning.

"Any better?"

Jane opened her eyes. The woman was still standing in front of her in that garish turquoise blouse. Her tone was so kindly that Jane felt suddenly overwhelmed with emotion. She began to cry as if the woman were her mother. "It's too much," she sobbed. "It's all just too much."

"What happened?" The woman seemed to really want to know, so Jane began to talk.

She told the woman she wanted very badly to live in this neighborhood, but she couldn't find a place her family could afford. She told the woman about Brett—how he'd jumped ship after *Lemon Rock*, his one and only book, and how she'd pitied him, but now she could see that he'd been right to jump, for literature was the *Titanic*, sinking below the surface, about to vanish utterly. And how Brett was so rich and the experience of living in his house had allowed them to see how the other half lived for a year, but that only made moving to Burbank all the more awful. She couldn't go back to that, she just couldn't. But what other option did she have? She told the woman, this stranger, about Hampton and the show idea and how she'd made the terrible mistake of showing him her novel and how the book seemed to be almost magic, the way it made people disappear from her life. How she'd come to think of her novel as being like the video in that movie *The Ring*; if you looked at it you'd die. How she had squandered her sabbatical on a book that was apparently jinxed and how the show she'd been writing, about the Bunch family, who had lived in this neighborhood, this very neighborhood, had never gotten out of development hell because it didn't have a premise or wasn't biracial enough and now she was coming to the end of time and money and her kids would have to move again. And probably again in another year. How maybe all the moving was why

Finn was so disconnected. Maybe that was why he couldn't relate. He wasn't *relatable*. That word again. And then there was Lenny. They were headed toward a split. She could feel it. It seemed clear they'd be living separately already if they had enough money.

"And see, the thing is, Renata, maybe, for a white woman of a certain income bracket, it's exciting to be divorced. Liberating to watch it all go to shit. But a single mother like me is nothing radical. I do it, and it's a statistic. It's not radical or cute or even interesting at all. I never wanted to be just a statistic. Because then, don't you see, they've won?"

The woman was watching her, nodding. She couldn't tell if the woman was white or just a bottle-blonde Mexican. Couldn't tell if she'd offended her with going on about white women again.

"I'm sorry," Jane said. "You've been so kind, Renata. Thanks for listening." She pulled herself together, stood up, and started toward the door again, but Renata called out to her. "Wait, you know what? Maybe I can help you. Edith Ann, one of our oldest residents, she died here last week. Her two-bedroom is open. Do you want to see?"

"I thought you said this was a nursing home."

Renata shrugged. "Technically, it's a retirement home. Which gives us some wiggle room."

The apartment had the bare necessities: two bedrooms and two bathrooms, a small living room, and a kitchenette. It was nothing to write home about, but it wasn't the worst place Jane had ever seen. Okay, so it had low cottage-cheese ceilings and a slightly dingy beige carpet and there was no natural light. And the kitchenette had cheap cabinets and an electric stove that could handle only the most basic of cooking tasks. You could boil or fry an egg, heat some soup. And the bathrooms had safety bars beside the toilets and in the showers. And there were no locks on any of the doors in the unit so the paramedics could come in and help you should you fall and not get up.

But location was everything. The building was right in the center of the beautiful liberal hapa heart of Multicultural Mayberry. Across the street was the public library, and there were cafés and restaurants and yoga studios within walking distance. There was most importantly a 10-rated blue-ribbon public school in walking distance.

Renata told Jane that she and her family wouldn't be the first non-seniors to live in the place. It had happened once before—a couple named Marc and Andy had lived in the complex temporarily with their children a few years ago while they were undergoing a home renovation. Everyone had been crestfallen when they moved out. Indeed, the place had fallen into a kind of collective depression. She thought Jane and her family would inject some much-needed life into the place.

As she walked through the lobby on her way out, Jane could see now what she hadn't noticed on the way in—that the crowd in the common room was very old indeed. Some of the residents were dancing together. They were mostly female.

The old woman in the muumuu was still seated by the front door. As Jane passed, the woman looked up from her newspaper and smiled brightly at her. "Do you know," she said, "I just read that poodles are the most intelligent breed."

BACK ON THE MOUNTAIN, Jane pulled into the driveway, but she didn't get out of the car right away even though Brett's new car, a gleaming black Porsche Panamera wasn't there—a welcome sign that he and Lucinda were out. She just sat there with the engine running, looking at the house. The lack of windows made it look ominous from the outside, but now, as she walked into the courtyard, she understood why the architect had made the choice. The fortress-like exterior only made the revelation of the inside, the courtyard, that circle of light and glass, more dramatic, especially at night. The mysterious home revealed its beauty to you like a gift.

Jane did not enter the house. Instead, she sat down at the little patio table in the courtyard. The house was all lit up, and behind the glass, she could see her family. Ruby sat hunched over the dining table, drawing. Finn was lining up Max's toy cars in order of size. Lenny was watching television, sipping on a cocktail. The remains of the dinner they'd eaten littered the kitchen island.

From this angle, somehow, with all the lights on, the room looked flat, staged, an imitation of life flickering before her. She remembered how much television had meant to her as a child of divorce, a child of the eighties. How she and her sister had watched it on those long, dark, custody weekends, moving between Patty Hearst and Huey Newton. Those television families—the Jeffersons and the Evanses and the Bradys, Mr. Drummond and Mrs. Garrett, Blair and Tootie and Natalie—had been their one constant. They'd watched those scripted worlds with a certain kind of hunger, studying them like refugees who had just arrived in a foreign land and were trying to decipher its language and customs.

21.

Before Jane knew it, the summer was almost over. She would start teaching again in a week. The department secretary had sent her the fall schedule. Jane had been assigned four classes—two creative writing and two composition. She'd have four the next semester as well, she knew. And four the next. And four the next. A four-four load, as they called it, from here to eternity. She could not pretend to be surprised. It was what she'd been expecting.

She went to her office early one morning in mid-August so she could begin to put together her syllabi. She had nowhere to work inside the Golden Eagle, and her office was where she kept all the craft books and anthologies of mediocre realist fiction. She'd left the kids watching cartoons, Lenny in the shower. The campus was quiet, like a sleeping beast. She headed into Chester Hall and went up in the elevator and down the soft carpeted hallway to her office. MAKE IT WORSE. Just as she was unlocking the door, who should come plodding down the hall but Kay Franken. She was walking barefoot on her reconstructed feet and carrying a toiletry bag. She stopped a few feet away from Jane.

"You're back," she said.

"I just came to work on my class prep."

Kay's skin looked strangely luminous, not so much youthful as freshly washed, bare, exposed. She watched Jane fiddling with her keys. "How did the sabbatical go?" she asked, with what seemed like real curiosity.

Jane considered lying, but she knew the truth would be out soon—everyone would know that Jane had come back empty-handed—so she just said in a low, flat voice, "It was not as productive as I'd hoped. I didn't get a contract. My tenure has been denied."

Jane waited for Kay's smile of satisfaction or mockery, but instead her eyes shone with sympathy. "I'm so sorry to hear that, Jane. Writing is so hard, isn't it?"

Then she came forward and opened her arms for a hug. Jane didn't know what else to do but sink into it. She felt exhausted. She closed her eyes as she felt Kay's hands stroking her back, heard her murmuring, "It's going to be okay. Four-four is not so bad. And we'll have each other. You know that, right? I'm here for you."

In the end, it was Kay who pulled away. She squeezed Jane's arm one last time and said a hushed goodbye then walked back to her office on her bionic toes.

The kids would be starting school in just a few days too. Public school in California started absurdly, cruelly early, under the ogling, maniacal late-summer sun. It really was another planet.

The air, even in Multicultural Mayberry, smelled of ashes. Jane kept the sun reflectors in her car so she could put them on the windshield when she went grocery shopping; otherwise the steering wheel would be too hot to touch. She kept a towel on the seat so she didn't burn the backs of her thighs. She wore a sombrero everywhere, and wraparound sunglasses.

Jane tried to convince herself that the weather in Los Angeles wasn't so bad. You just had to think of the hot months as a kind of winter, think of the sunlight as being like snow. After all, on the East Coast for all those years, she'd learned to stay indoors as much as possible during the frigid months, December through March. Here, she tried to think of her sunscreen and sombrero and wraparound sunglasses as the equivalent of the woolen hat, scarf, and mittens she used to wear back East. The air conditioner was like a fireplace you huddled around to stay warm. The thought exercise never quite worked, but she kept trying.

She tried to focus on the positive. They were living in Multicultural Mayberry. A town with money was a town with money. Ruby's school was a clean white-stucco Spanish Mission–style building on a street that looked like it could have been the setting for a network series called *Suburbia*. Whenever they walked or drove by it, Ruby peered out at it hopefully, her brown eyes drinking in the still-darkened windows. Children were born who they would become, their souls as unchangeable as fingerprints. Ruby was a resilient child, still that dandelion. She had started writing in a diary with a purple pen, gifts from one of those girls who had come for her birthday party that day in the hills. Jane had stumbled upon it one afternoon while cleaning their bedroom, found it splayed open under Ruby's covers. Before she closed it and put it on the nightstand, she read the last words Ruby had written: *Mama says she has a feeling this is the year I'm going to make a best friend. I wonder what she will look like and what her name will be.*

Another good thing: Finn had a diagnosis now. And with the label came access to special services, special places. They'd found him a new school that would be paid for by the school district. Jane had accompanied him for his assessment and to meet the two directors. They were both named Barbara, one Black and one white. Otherwise, they looked very much alike, zaftig women in their mid to late fifties with loose-fitting cotton clothes and broad, easy smiles. They reminded Jane of *Sesame Street*, public television, another era. They sat across from Jane in a small dingy classroom at the back of a Korean church, watching Finn play on the rug with a dreadlocked man named Taj who was not only a certified special-education teacher but also a trained therapist.

The school specialized in "high functioning" kids. High functioning,

Jane thought, only sounded like a compliment if you didn't think about it for too long.

Jane was surprised to discover she could not tell what race Taj was. The locks were confusing. He could have been a swarthy white man. Or maybe he was just a light-skinned Black man. She was also surprised to discover she didn't care. She watched him and Finn play. Finn looked comfortable, like he was having a good time, and she felt a small, dim, new kind of pride. Maybe she had done the right thing for once, bringing him here.

Lenny and she were still living together—were still officially married—but she couldn't say they'd ever really recovered. Lenny was still focused on Tokyo, his impending show there. All the paintings had been shipped, and now he was working on text for the catalog. He'd rented a room in the basement of a restaurant near the Golden Eagle to use as a studio.

Jane had cried the day they moved out off the mountain and arrived in the dingy little efficiency unit in this home for the elderly. Cried quietly as they unpacked the boxes they'd retrieved from storage, resurrecting the remnants of their old life—the Melitta coffee maker and the stained old sheets, the Billy bookcase from IKEA. But the kids had taken to the Golden Eagle immediately. Finn liked to take the elevator from the top floor all the way down to the garage. Ruby liked to lounge around the common room with the old women, watching *The View* and *Wheel of Fortune*.

And two months into it, Jane found herself adjusting as well. Once in a while, walking through the glass door into the lobby, she still got a bad feeling—a feeling like she'd skipped a reel in a movie and jumped right to the final scenes. But most of the time, she didn't mind the old-folks-home feeling of the place. It was peaceful, gentle. And as for that other life—their life up in Brett's house in the hills, her fling with Hollywood, even the novel she'd loved and poured her heart and soul into—all of it was starting to seem like a dream.

She wondered if Kay Franken ever felt this way—whether an odd, surprising sense of peace came over her as she made up her bed in her office. Acceptance. For what other choice did she have? This was the only reality.

From time to time, she looked up Hampton on Instagram. That's how she saw the photo of him in Canada coming out of a Tim Hortons, giving a thumbs-up to the paparazzi. He'd tagged it: #blessed #ilovevancouver #enddays #swirl #blackandwhite.

She felt a twinge of sadness that he'd not contacted her again, that their deal had remained an if—but also a muted pride; for despite everything, she still thought of him as an old friend she wished well. She was still happy to see a Black man getting paid. It still made her happy in a vague Black History Month way.

She hadn't seen Brett since they'd moved out. The few texts he'd sent were slightly accusatory. One asked if they had flushed anything besides toilet paper down the toilet. Another asked if she'd ever worn his vintage Bienvenudos T-shirt—it had stains under the arms that had not been there before. Jane reflected, not for the first time, that whenever a rich person did you a huge favor—loaned you money, loaned you their house, got you a job, cosigned a loan—the friendship essentially ended. It became a relationship of charity, missionary to a starving child. You could not unsee it once it had been seen.

But one evening, while she was making oatmeal for the kids in the kitchenette, she looked down at her phone and saw a text from Brett. Jane! Dude? You left some stuff here! Lucinda has put it all in a box. Can you come get it? Also—I have something to show you—you'll laugh. She felt relief at his old friendly tone. It struck her that she'd missed him as a figure in her life.

She drove up the mountain the next afternoon. The sky was just turning pink over the hills. She had a strange sense of déjà vu as she came in through the courtyard. She half expected to see her children playing there amidst the succulents, half expected to see Lenny there through the glass, listening to his Japanese-language tapes on the sofa. But there were no children, there was no Lenny, they were all where she'd left them in the Golden Eagle. Instead there was Lucinda in the kitchen, preparing something elaborate in a casserole dish on the stove. She was wearing Piper's muumuu, the same one Jane used to borrow, as she moved around, adding spices to the expensive crockery, playing house. Brett wasn't with her. He was probably in the studio, the one that had once felt so much her own. Jane headed over there and knocked at the door. When nobody answered, she pushed it open, half expecting to see her own form sitting at the desk, working on *Nusu Nusu*. But of course it was Brett, sitting where she'd once sat, wearing headphones, bobbing his head to some inaudible music as he stared at his laptop screen, which displayed what looked like a script rather than a novel.

She cleared her throat. This time he heard her and turned, pulling off his headphones.

"Jane! Hey. Is it that late already? I got so lost in work."

He was dressed scruffily, like a rich screenwriter—faded jeans, old lime-green Pumas, a silly T-shirt with a picture of a dinosaur that said ALL MY FRIENDS ARE DEAD. "Let me get your stuff. Sit down. Relax."

He began to rifle through his closet. "Lucinda put all your things together," he said. "Sorry I didn't call before. We've all been adjusting to—you know, the new normal." He pulled out a cardboard moving box. "I think all this is yours."

"Thanks," she said, taking the box from him. She glanced inside and saw some books, some papers, some of Finn's drawings of Baby Blue, a broken Tyrannosaurus action figure. Nothing of value except the framed portrait of her and Lenny and the kids that had been taken so many years ago by the Serbian. The picture where they looked like a family living under military occupation. She'd forgotten to take it down from the wall during the rush of packing and moving out. She pulled it out now and stared at this old version of them.

"You guys look terrified in that picture," Brett said with a laugh. "Even the kids look scared."

"The guy told us not to smile," she said, and laughed too, feeling an old affection toward Brett return.

"Listen," she said, "I'm sorry about how everything went down here. I'm sorry about the wine and the plumbing issues. Sorry about ghosting you. It wasn't right. I was just . . . going through something."

"It's okay. I was being an asshole too. It was a weird time. My life was falling apart." He sighed, raked a hand through his curls. "Piper's lawyered up," he said. "She's living in a house in Larchmont Village where she's joined some women's empowerment group, like it's the goddamn seventies. She's begun crafting a narrative, you know, spreading poison about me. She's trying to alienate Max from me. Which is unconscionable." He shook his head. "I never knew she was like that. All those years, I somehow missed that she was a monster."

Jane saw now that Brett had aged over the past year. There was a dusting of silver in his dark curls. He was still beautiful, but his good looks were the kind that looked best young.

"Never get divorced, Jane. It's hell." His eyes filled with tears. She felt a welling of pity and held open her arms.

"Oh, Brett."

He came forward for a hug. He held on to her tightly for a beat longer than necessary, and she could feel his heart beating against her own. When they pulled away, his face was cloudy with emotion.

"I love you, Jane Gibson. You know that, right?"

She blushed, surprised. "I love you too." She punched his arm lightly. "We mutts gotta stick together, right?"

She made a sound like a laugh—but he looked uncharacteristically serious as he studied her in silence.

"That's why I was calling you," he said finally. "You know that, right? All those months, I just wanted to tell you I loved you."

Jane swallowed. A new awkwardness descended over them. She took a step back. The light had shifted so that a shadow covered half his face.

"You look uncomfortable," he said. "I'm not trying to make things weird. It's just, I wanted you to know."

She peered beyond him at the house. She could see Lucinda pouring a glass of wine at the kitchen island, taking that first exquisite sip. She imagined herself standing where Lucinda was, wearing a silk muumuu. Imagined all this was really hers, the house in the hills and all that came with it, the accoutrements of a life well played. Hashtag blessed.

"Jane?"

She looked at him.

The clouds outside had moved again and the shadow on his face was gone. He stood in the sunlight, smiling at her now, the same golden boy he'd always been. "I was just having a moment," he said with a crooked smile. "Don't pay me any attention. I'm fine. Really. I'm good."

"Okay," she said, confused now by the shifts in mood.

"I better get back to this fucking edit. They hired me to fix this Marvel script. I have to pay the lawyers."

"Right, of course. I should get going too." She felt like an old lady, heavy and stiff, arthritic, as she moved across the room. At the door, she heard him say her name. She turned, searching his face for something, but it was already gone. He wore a lopsided grin.

"Dude, I almost forgot," he said. "The whole reason I wrote you. There's something I have to show you." He began sifting through the papers on his desk. "Super random, but my agent sent over this series doc for a new show that just got green-lit. She wanted to know if I was interested in directing a few of the episodes. Did I tell you I'm getting into directing? Anyway, I started reading it and—this is gonna sound weird, but it totally reminds me of your book. I mean, not exactly, of course. And you only ever told me bits and pieces about it. But from what I remember, this kind of reminds me of it. It's an anthology series called *Swirl*. Every episode is about a different mulatto character, but it spans, like, centuries. I mean, there's, like, an episode on Sally Hemings, an episode on some actress in Hollywood who's, like, passing as white. It's all your territory."

Jane could feel a smile on her face, but she didn't know how it had gotten there or what it meant.

"And the only thing linking them," he said, "is that it's all, you know, mixed people. People like us, living on the so-called color line. But wait, the funniest part is there's a few contemporary episodes in it, and the characters in that part remind me of you and Lenny and the kids."

Brett pulled out a stack of pages halfway down the pile. They were attached by a gold clip. "They sent me the bible."

"The bible."

"It's, like, the big book that tells you everything about a show." He flipped through a few pages. "It's not my kind of thing—I passed on it—but you should look at it. Just for shits and giggles."

He handed the pages to Jane. She stared at the cover page. *Swirl— Created by Hampton Ford.*

Jane stared at it for a moment in silence. "Can I hang on to this?"

"Sure. It's all yours."

Somehow, without breathing, she managed to say goodbye, to walk away, to get in her car, and somehow, still without breathing, to drive without incident back down the hill into the flatlands, back to the Golden Eagle.

Inside their unit, she laid the box of belongings on the kitchen table. The kids crowded around to see what she'd brought back. Finn began to pull out old LEGO pieces and Ruby unearthed some clothing at the bottom. "My dress!"

"Is Brett still being a little bitch?" said Lenny.

"No."

"Is he enjoying Piper 2.0?"

She didn't answer. She just carried the pages down the hall into the bathroom, where she closed the door and sat at the edge of the toilet, still not really breathing as she began to read.

Everything was the same but also different. It was four hundred years of mulattos in America, culled into ten episodes. It was her work, but it wasn't. It was like looking at a celebrity who's had major face work. She could see the ghost of the real person beneath the fillers and Botox. Hampton had thrown a huge bucket of sentimental obviousness into every episode. Every concept she'd kept hidden beneath the surface of the story had been dragged up and bold-faced and articulated with a kind of screeching clarity. It was unquestionably a show with a premise now. He'd included some mangled version of the Bunches in there too, the Goins: a family of nouveau mulattos in contemporary LA, a rebellious comic-book artist, no longer Black like the original husband, but made mulatto too, to stay on brand, she guessed, and his hapless mulatto history professor wife. It was, she had to admit, edutaining. It had the aura of prestige, the aura of Emmybait. It felt big. Sprawling.

Reading it, what Jane felt most overwhelmingly was shame. And she recalled a movie she'd watched with Lenny a few months ago. It was called *The Edge*, and it involved a group of people who get into an airplane crash in the arctic wilderness and are stalked by a Kodiak bear. Just after the crash, Anthony Hopkins warns the other two survivors that most people lost in the wilderness die of shame. They are so busy asking themselves what they did wrong and how they got into this situation that they sit there and die. Shame, he says, keeps people from doing the one thing that will save their lives. Which is what? *Thinking*, he says in his cool British lilt. Thinking. Shame or no shame, a few scenes later, the Black guy is the first to die. He's ripped to shreds by the bear while the two white men stand at a distance, screaming, helpless.

She was filled with such shame she couldn't think, so the bear would eat her. She heard Lenny calling her name, and the shame rushed over her more strongly now. She couldn't face him. He still didn't know about Hampton showing up that night. He didn't know she'd handed him the manuscript. She rose to look in the mirror, half expecting to see nothing but a blank space where her face should have been. But she was there—an ordinary person of no particular color. *Black don't crack but beige do age.* She was still wearing the odd smile she'd been wearing on the mountain, but she could see now in her reflection it was more of a grimace.

She carried the document into the bedroom and placed it on Lenny's pillow, face up. Then she continued into the kitchen, where she found Lenny fixing himself a sandwich. He told her that the kids had gone to the common room to watch television with the old ladies. Then he took a bite of the sandwich and paused midchew to look at her. "Are you okay?" he said, studying her. "Did something happen?"

How she loved this sad, funny, intelligent face—a face that was growing more attractive with age. How she wanted to tell that face . . . everything. But she couldn't find the words.

"I'm sorry," she said instead.

"Sorry for what? Wait, where are you going?"

"I need some fresh air."

"Did something bad happen?"

"Yes," she said. "It's on the bed."

He looked a little alarmed and started toward the bedroom. Jane knew she should wait to face him, but she didn't want to see his expression when he saw what had become of all those years, all that work. She grabbed her bag and headed out the door. On her way out through the lobby, she saw Finn and Ruby. They were sitting in the lounge on either side of Jeanie, a tiny elfin woman in the early stages of dementia. On the screen, Ellen was doing the Carlton dance across the stage to the hoots of the audience.

As she walked the streets of Multicultural Mayberry in the fading light, Jane found herself thinking about her father. The year she turned seventeen, he'd gotten fired from his job at the newspaper where he'd worked for years. He'd been their only Black columnist, their only Black anything. He'd had an ongoing conflict with a white coworker—an aging Irish American beat writer who sat on the other side of the cubicle. The conflict escalated to the point of no return until finally HR called her father in one day and showed him the object they'd taken off his desk as proof that he was violent. It was one of those giant balls of rubber bands. His cubicle mate had brought it to their attention, and they'd discovered, sure enough, that beneath the rubber bands was a small steel ball. They said it could be used as a weapon if her father really wanted.

Her father had fallen into the Sticks that year. He stayed home watching the news from bed. Jane's sister had already gone away to college. Jane bore down on her schoolwork the way her sister had, hard, the way children who have nothing to fall back on work hard. And it paid off, because one day she got the news that she'd been accepted into the college of her dreams, her reach school. She rushed up the stairs to give her father the news. It was still daylight, but his apartment was dark, the window shades down. She found him in the bedroom, seated before the glow of the television. He was watching the news, a recap of the Iran-Contra hearings, but the volume was on mute. Jane sat beside him on the bed. On-screen were the faces of white men in suits, their thin lips moving but not making sounds.

That was the apartment where Jane had truly been formed. This was where she and her sister had been made, the place her own white mother wouldn't enter. She just dumped her two brown girls there to figure it out for themselves. She'd assumed they could survive anything, and she was halfway right.

Her father smelled of sadness in those days. It wafted off him. She spoke to him from the edge of his bed, told him about her college acceptance. She told him she'd gotten the minority scholarship, so he and her mother wouldn't have to worry about the cost. She could do it on her own.

"Minority scholarship," he repeated, and she thought maybe he didn't understand.

"It means I'm going for free."

"Free," he said, pondering the word, as if he were trying to remember its meaning.

"A free ride," she said. "They only give this scholarship to three freshmen a year—out of, like, hundreds."

Her father let out a short laugh. "You think you're special now, don't you?" he said, his eyes still fixed on the television. "The white man said you're special, so now you're special."

"I never said that. I just came to give you my news. My mistake." She stood up to leave, but he called her name. When she turned back, he was staring at her, his eyes flashing, alive, the way they hadn't looked in a long time. "Remember they're lying when they tell you you're special," he said. "Just like they'll be lying later when they tell you you're a piece of shit."

WHEN SHE RETURNED from walking, she found the kids seated around the kitchen table eating cheese and apple slices. They had iPads propped up in front of them. Lenny was sitting on the couch staring at an old episode of *Mission: Impossible* with the volume off. The series bible Brett had given her was on the sofa beside him.

She went and sat next to Lenny. "Go on, say it."

"Say what?"

"I'm an idiot for sharing my novel with Hampton Ford. And I was gullible and a fool for having worked with this goon for three months for free. Say it."

"That would be a cliché. I don't speak in clichés."

"But it'd be true. And you know what? I'm going to sue him. I'm going to make him rue the day he ever called me in for a general." She was talking about plan C. She'd thought of it in the last hour. The answer to her problems was so obvious. She'd sue Hampton. And she and Lenny would get a hefty settlement—hush money—and they'd buy a house with it. A house like the ones she'd passed on her long walk. She'd get residuals off *Swirl* for the rest of her days and never have to teach another workshop again. Of course she hadn't meant for any of this to happen; she hadn't written the book in order to have it stolen—but it was, she'd decided, all things considered, a kind of luck that it had happened too. For now she had the chance to make more money off it than she would have from some publisher's paltry advance.

"I mean, think about it, Lenny. This could be our ticket out of here." She waved her hand around the squalid living room. "He messed with the wrong mulatto. Do you see what I'm saying?"

Lenny kept his eyes on the television as he lifted a fist and said in a weary voice, "Free people of color."

A FEW DAYS LATER, the phone rang just as Jane parked in front of the Golden Eagle. It was a 310 number—the West Side—and for the maybe eight seconds before she picked it up, she imagined it was Hampton calling. He wanted to apologize. To straighten the whole thing out. He hadn't meant to steal from her. Absurd as the thoughts were, her mind lurched to hope, redemption, forgiveness, and back again. She put on her headphones and answered the call. Of course it wasn't Hampton's soft scratchy lilt. It was one of the lawyers she'd reached out to. Tony something-or-other. She'd gotten him off a Google search.

"I've had a chance to read the letter you sent over," he said, and laughed a little. "I can see why you're a novelist. That was some read."

"Sorry it was so long," Jane said. "I just wanted to make sure you got a full picture of the situation. Did you get the attachments too?" She'd attached a copy of *Nusu Nusu* along with the bible for *Swirl* so he could compare them.

"Yes, I got it all. Though I have to say, I haven't had a chance to read your book, just the synopsis you gave me in the letter."

The lawyer was a straight shooter. He told her that she could certainly pursue litigation against Hampton Ford, but it would get ugly. "I'm telling you—if you go after this guy, a world of pain will rain down on your head. Hampton will become the focus of your life, like a blimp, taking over your imagination and your thoughts and your lifeblood. Enemies, they take a lot of work."

As Jane listened, she was watching a scene unfold in the driveway of the Golden Eagle. An ambulance had pulled up out front, and the glass doors of the lobby were opening to let Renata push Jeanie through in a wheelchair. A medic was waiting there and he talked to them from the side of the ambulance. This happened about once a week. None of them, not even Jeanie, looked the least bit panicked by the situation. There was a special lift already lowered for the wheelchair.

Tony was asking her how old she was.

She told him she was forty-six.

"Yeah. Well, listen. I used to be forty-six. And I know how this works. Your brain at your age is just beginning to fray a little. You sue this guy, and you won't have time for the things you love. Do you have kids?"

She told him she had two and that was why she wanted to do this. For them. So they knew that their mother had some dignity.

The lawyer laughed. "Dignity. That's an interesting word. Because here's the other thing. I googled you before I called. I saw your job. You're a nontenured faculty member at a B-level liberal arts college. Right?"

"Right."

"And it's been a pretty long time since your last book. Right?"

"Right."

"Then trust me, you do not have the resources to fight this guy. He's Hampton Ford. He has every top lawyer's top lawyer working on his behalf. There are people in this town whose sole job is to make sure Hampton Ford doesn't get his reputation besmirched by any bitter ex-employees. Do you hear what I'm saying?"

He spoke fast, hard, spitting cold truth into her ear. The if/come contract had never actually been sent back to her. Which meant it wasn't real. It was only something they had discussed. The agent would just avoid her. He'd seen it all before. And another thing: there was no paper trail. You had to be able to prove that the defendant had access to the ideas they were accused of stealing. Was he understanding correctly that all her episode ideas had been written by hand and pitched into the air?

Jane said a quiet yes, recalling how badly she'd wanted to appear like a real writer—different from the screen-addicted Layla and Topher—so eager that she'd written every idea by hand, like an Amish woman.

And furthermore, the lawyer said, she'd handed over the actual manuscript of the novel, a big pile of papers that could have been burned by now for all they knew. Hampton could claim he'd never seen her novel in his life. The show he made could have been inspired by any old mulatto's story.

"You see what I'm saying, Ms. Gibson? The proof is in the pudding, and there's no pudding."

Beyond the windshield, Jane could see Jeanie was being raised into the air by the lift. She was waving from her perch like a beauty queen in a parade. Renata was laughing at something the driver was saying, throwing her head back so the whole expanse of her pale neck was on display. Jane thought, not for the first time, that Renata was the kind of woman who would get murdered. She was the kind of woman who would be the subject of an unsolved-crime podcast. She had that murdered-woman aura about her. Jane squinted to try to see the medic more clearly, to get an accurate description in case she needed to give it later. Maybe she'd become a detective. Maybe she'd go back to school and become a crime-scene investigator. The options were endless.

"Ms. Gibson, are you still there?"

Her voice sounded different when she spoke, like somebody for whom English is not a first language. "Yes, I—I'm still here."

"I want to help you out. I really do. But I went through this whole shenanigan years ago. Fighting a guy by the name of Norman Lear. A comedian hired me to sue him. A Black comedian, I'll have you know. He claimed Lear stole all his jokes for *The Jeffersons*. Do you know where that guy is now?"

"No."

"Neither do I. Neither do I."

Jane shut off the engine. The car was dead quiet. The air still smelled of fermented apple juice. She could see dust freckling the sunlight. She found her voice again. "So you're saying I should drop the lawsuit," she said. "Crawl back in my little hole, let him get away with this?" She let out a gasp. "Did you even read my file? Did you see the verbatim details he used, stolen directly from me?"

"I saw it," the lawyer said. "And I want to help you. I really do. I think you got screwed." He paused. "Now if you could prove that Hampton actually screwed you, or tried to screw you, and I do mean sexually, then we'd have an easy case, no problem. We'd have the entire me-too industrial complex behind us. A thousand angry young white women, not to mention Twitter, on our side. But he didn't try any funny business with you—" He sounded activated now. "Or did he?"

Jane glanced at her face in the mirror, her frizz of hair that had new white strands in it. Her face was sun-weathered and she had the mommy-shiners—dark circles—beneath her eyes.

"Did he?" Tony asked again.

"Well, he molested my brain," Jane said.

She could hear Tony sigh. "I see," he said. "You got taken for a ride. But not that kind of ride."

He told her if she decided to pursue it, she would surely be able to find another lawyer who would take on her case if the price was right. But he was a grandfather now, and he didn't like to help people ruin their lives even for his own benefit.

They said goodbye. Jane stepped out into the scorching heat and headed toward the entrance of the building. Jeanie and Renata and the medic were still there. The lift was jammed, and Jeanie still hovered in midair, smiling dreamily while the medic squatted beneath it, rejiggering something.

IN THE FINAL PARAGRAPH of Cavendish's essay, he declared his whole life's work a failure. The mulatto people, he said, were a riddle that could never be solved. And yet, he acknowledged, maybe they didn't need solving, for, he predicted, they would soon be extinct. Like mules, from which their name derived, he said the mulatto was in some essential way barren. Not literally unable to procreate, as the slave owners had claimed, but figuratively barren. The mulatto, he said, would always be only halfway to becoming something else, and as such, they would either be swallowed into the great maw of the white world or transformed, by the peculiar alchemy of the one-drop rule, into real Negroes. Like Pinocchio, who existed for a time in the liminal state between toy and human, between imitation and real, the mulatto, Cavendish wrote, was perched on a threshold—a magical in-between state, a center that could not hold. Eventually one side or the other would get you—and then you would cease to exist.

"My life's work has been to try to define a people that cannot be defined or even located—for the mulatto is the only race in our nation's history that is perpetually shifting, changing colors, morphing into something unrecognizable. Is it any wonder they have existed only at the margins of history? It is only once in a rare while, perhaps every hundred years, that they catch the fancy of a man like me, becoming the subject of our fleeting fascination and speculation, our pity and our glee. But now, my dear friends, I am finished. I bid thee farewell—and the mulatto too. Goodbye, mulatto. You have haunted my dreams and my waking days for far too long."

22.

Jane left Lenny a handwritten letter on a legal pad on the kitchen counter, where he couldn't miss it. In it, she told him her final bit of bad news. Plan C—Project Sue the Bastard—wasn't going to work either. She told Lenny that she realized this meant they were never going to have enough money to buy a house in California—they'd live their remaining days in a nursing home, where they'd finally catch up to the residents around them, finally grow old enough to need that grab bar beside the toilet. She understood the future was the wrong kind of dark, and it was all her fault. The biggest devil was her. Tunnels were everywhere if you knew how to look.

She told him the other truth too: that he was living in an arranged marriage—arranged by Wesley the racial alchemist. But arranged marriages sometimes led to love, and this one had too, at least for her. The truth was, she couldn't imagine anybody else she'd rather be living with in an old-folks' home, which was the same as living in an apocalypse movie, only slower paced. She told him that ever since they'd met she'd been keeping a secret list on her computer.

THINGS WE HATE

That movie *Sideways*

The fake cultural sensitivity that makes American zoos give panda bears Chinese names, as if the pandas speak Mandarin or give a crap

Hampton Ford

Easy credit rip-offs

Scratchin' and survivin'

Black writers who have made it their whole mission to placate white guilt

Dignity

Earnestness

Gifted children and the mothers who brag about them

Bruce Borland

9/11 novels

White feminism

Hampton Ford

Swirl

Poetry readings

World music festivals

Jennifer and Sarah Hart

Hampton Ford

Redemptive endings

There was more. So much more they hated together. The list went on and on like that for almost twenty pages—she'd printed it out and tucked it behind the letter in the legal pad. She wanted to give him proof they were compatible and that he wasn't just a psychic prediction. She ended the letter, "I hate all these things, but I don't hate you. Love, Jane."

She didn't want to see his expression when he read the letter. So she left and drove west, not sure where she was going. She drove toward the beach, but when she got to the PCH, she turned left instead and drove up into the hills beside the ocean. It was as if the Subaru were guiding her, as if the Subaru knew. The higher she climbed, the farther apart the property lines sat from one another until there were no houses visible at all—only occasional iron gates leading to mysterious driveways.

It was only when she turned onto a narrow little dream of a street called Amalfi Drive that she understood where the car had been taking her. She'd looked at this street enough times on Street View to recognize it now. The address was seared into her memory. She parked on a shoulder about a quarter of a mile up.

The air smelled of ocean and jasmine. Expensive air. But when she breathed in deeply, she could taste smoke from some distant fire. She crossed the road and headed by foot down the side of the hill to where the sprinklers ended. Everything was already dead, baked into straw. The dirt was rock-hard, riddled with cracks. She went deeper into the hillside then—and when she was low enough down, she turned and headed back up the hill, this time at an angle toward the house at the top.

It was nouveau riche, faux Italian palazzo, garish, too big. There was the infinity pool she remembered from the photo he'd shown her so many months ago. The water appeared to be pouring over the edge of the canyon. Through the arched window she could see people standing around in the glow of the living room. Music floated out into the night. Hampton was leaning back in an Eames lounge chair, waving his hands around as he talked. Even from here, she could recognize the other faces—characters in a movie she'd seen before. So many nights of so much googling as she waited to pitch the show to Bruce Borland. The pitch that never happened.

And there he was, Bruce, the silver fox in expensive glasses, the white man who was still in charge, still pulling all the strings. Beside him, a small dark-haired man who had not turned up in her searches, and beside him, a tall steely blonde woman—Jane recalled seeing her on the website, the head of the comedy division. There were Topher and Layla too. Layla was stunning in an orange dress; Topher wore his usual wrinkled oxford, khakis. They huddled together by the wine bar, whispering like lost siblings out of a German fairy tale. Where was Doreen, the Black wife with the Dorothy Dandridge face? Had she left him for another man? Or did she find these work events dull? Doreen did not appear to be at the party tonight, nor did Jujubean.

On the couch sat a beige woman in a pink dress. She looked oddly familiar, and Jane saw it was the woman she'd seen in the lobby on her way out from her first meeting with Hampton. So that was Crystal Bookman. The beige woman with ringlets like Shirley Temple, perfect biracial ringlets, the kind Jane could never seem to master. She looked a little like Jane if life had treated Jane kindly. Jane with good doctors, good needles. The woman was leaning forward into whatever story Hampton was in the midst of telling. He made the mind-blown gesture—exploding his fingers around his head—and she burst into laughter.

Jane had wanted to be that woman, the chosen mulatto for Hampton's "Project Rebrand a Race." *Pick me, pick me, let me be your guide through the land of half-breeds.* Hampton Ford, she saw now, was pure catnip for damaged biracial souls. She'd been willing to give him everything he wanted—every sad story she held in her memory bank, every last page of her ill-conceived tome. She'd performed like a Labradoodle on steroids. *Pinky* played for laughs this time around. In the glow of his smile, it had seemed like everything she'd gone through in her life had been worth it, all the peculiar, watered-down, gauche caviar trauma of the biracial isolate. It could be packaged and sold in a bidding war if she just kept dancing.

The woman was still laughing at whatever Hampton was saying. Laughing so hard it looked like it hurt. Jane tried to laugh too, squatting there in the darkness. But the laughter died on her lips. There were so many different kinds of thieves. Those who come under the cloak of night wearing a ski mask and gloves. And those who did it in the light of day. They called it homage. *Represent!* She could no longer tell where her skin ended and the air began. She could no longer tell where Jane ended and America began. The therapist who had assessed Finn said he was lacking in something called proprioception, the ability to know where your body exists in space. Jane wondered now if she had it too. The sky above her was a canopy of darkness. It seemed to flow into her and through her. Finn had told her about his planet so many times, described it so often, she felt she'd been there too, and sometimes, like tonight, she was filled with a longing for this place she'd never been. On the Finn planet, he'd told her once, the butter grows from trees. On the Finn planet, you have to tiptoe everywhere, because if you step down too hard, you will feel knives slicing into your feet. On the Finn planet, it is always dark, always night. The rain is soft, warm, perpetual. On the Finn planet, people greet other people by touching their heads. On the Finn planet, people eat lamb, steamed carrots, and Lucky Charms. *On the Finn planet*, he'd once said, *I was happy. But then one day I fell into a hole. There was a pain all over me. I couldn't breathe. And then darkness. When I woke up, I was a baby, all red and wet, but they were saying words I could not understand. And the air around me was too bright and too dry. I wanted to go home.*

She could see through the picture window that Hampton was holding up a remote in the air as the music switched to Tom Jones's "It's Not Unusual." Crystal leapt to her feet and grabbed the hand of the silver fox, Borland, and pulled him into a dance. She swiveled her hips and shook her perfect curls. Borland had the white man's dancing overbite and not one iota of rhythm as he held on to Crystal's hips for dear life. Topher and Layla went into the circle to dance too. The other executives joined in, a trio of jerking, out-of-sync white people, while Hampton watched from his chair, a slight inscrutable smile on his lips.

IT WAS VERY LATE when she got back to the Golden Eagle. The lobby was deserted. As she walked down the hall, she could hear sounds of coughing behind the doors of the apartments, the soundtrack of ancient ladies wheezing alone in the dark. She was filled with the old terror. She was Brooklyn Jane, back in her fifth-floor walk-up. She and Lenny had never met that night at Stu's party. She'd never even left New York. And the children had never been conceived and had never been born. And the novel she'd spent ten years on—it too had never happened. She felt like a figment of her own imagination. She searched the lobby for a mirror, but Renata had taken it down. It depressed the old women to see how much they'd changed.

Inside the apartment, trembling, she went straight to the back bedroom, to the IKEA bunk bed. They were both there, Ruby and Finn, fast asleep. Relief flooded her. She leaned over Ruby's bed and placed a hand on the girl's back, watched the rise and fall of her chest. The American Girl doll was tucked in the covers beside her. At first glance, Jane thought it was Kavi Sharma, but no, Kavi was propped up on the nightstand, staring straight ahead like a watchdog. She pulled back the covers and saw it was Addy Walker in Ruby's arms. And Ruby was dressed like the doll's twin, in her matching post-Reconstruction nightgown. Jane's eyes stung. She'd missed it all somehow. She'd looked away and missed this moment when everything changed.

She reached up and felt for Finn on the upper bunk, found his hot body curled in a ball. A book was tangled in the sheets with him—a book about the solar system. Maybe Lenny was right and the diagnosis was all a scam. Another way capitalism sorted people, killed them off with words. Maybe Finn was and maybe Finn wasn't. She touched his warm body and no longer cared.

She left the children and found Lenny in their bed, snoring. She got in beside him and lay staring up at the ceiling. Now he knew everything.

The full story. He knew who she was and who she wasn't. Now he knew that to love Jane was to love a lie. To love Jane was to stay entangled in this place. She was part of the problem. She longed to go back to the beginning, to begin again. To start the story in a different place. But which place? And which beginning? Dennis Mulholland used to say every story has two beginnings. The first is page one—the place where you actually begin the story—but the second beginning comes later, the inciting incident. *And then one day everything changed.*

"So, did you kill him?"

Lenny was watching her sleepily, wearing an almost imperceptible smile. In the half-light, she could almost see what the kids were talking about—his resemblance to Hampton.

"Kill who?"

"Lincoln Perry."

"No. I left him there, celebrating, alive."

He moved closer, wrapped an arm around her.

"That's good. You'd never get off. Johnnie Cochran is dead and he's not coming back."

"Did you get my letter?" she asked him.

"Your hate letter."

"It was a love letter."

"Anyway, the whole panda part." He yawned. "They're actually gifted to our zoos from China. The reason they have those names is they're Chinese. It's not just some awkward multicultural gesture."

"Are you sure about that?"

He didn't answer. He was out, his arm heavy across her waist.

JANE PROMISED HERSELF she would never watch *Swirl*. But it was hard to avoid. The ads were everywhere. Still, she steered clear of it for the first few months after it aired. It wasn't until she was well into her first semester back teaching, coming through the lobby of the Golden Eagle with a bottle of cheap wine, that she heard the theme song blaring from the common room. She could no longer resist the pull.

Four old ladies sat on the sofas in front of the television. They were passing around a bottle of sherry. Jane stood behind them in the doorway, gripping her unopened bottle of cheap wine.

This episode was set in 1990s New York. A mixed girl named Zyzzyva had an ugly breakup with her lying white boyfriend and ended up getting locked inside a Restoration Hardware showroom wearing corduroys, like the bear in that children's book. She spent the night sleeping on all the various beds. It was a scene from Jane's novel. It was a scene from Jane's life. Hampton had put the stories she'd told him in a blender and smashed them around in a writer's room so it was impossible to tell where her voice ended and his began.

One of the old ladies looked back at Jane hovering in the doorway and asked if she'd like to sit down and join them. "This show is quite interesting. It's called an anthology series. Jumps around time and space, incredibly ambitious. It's all about mew-lattos throughout history. Did you know there have always been mew-lattos? From the very beginning of the human race?"

"Yes," Jane said, in a quiet voice. "Yes, I knew that."

She sat down with them. The common room used some low-rent version of Hulu that had commercial breaks. While a commercial for Ace Hardware played, Jeanie refilled her sherry glass, and said to the group, laughing, "This episode is a riot."

Norma nodded. "The actress playing the girl is very clever, isn't she?"

Jane cleared her throat. "You know," she said. "This show is actually based on my book. On a novel I wrote. This is my story. My vision."

The women turned and stared at her.

"Don't believe a word she says, she's a fibber." Norma said it under her breath, half to herself.

Jane was always trying to convince her undergraduates that the old people in their stories didn't have to be sweet. They could be awful and conniving or just ordinarily mean.

One of the other women caught Norma's aside and snorted a laugh. She gave Jane a disingenuous smile and asked, "Is your name in the credits?"

Norma and the woman exchanged unkind, amused looks. "Yes," Norma said. "Why don't you tell us your name again? So we can look for it in the credits."

"See, that's the thing," Jane said. "I didn't get a credit. I didn't get paid. But it's all based on my work. I mean, loosely. The guy who made this, he stole it from me. The details are mine. Most of them, anyway. The premise is mine."

Her voice trailed off. She could hear how it sounded. She could see how she looked.

"If you'll just let me explain," she said.

But the commercial break was over, and they'd turned back to the show.

LATER THAT SAME YEAR, in a future that had not yet arrived, Jane would watch Hampton accept an Emmy for Outstanding New Series along with that prettier version of herself, the hack with the bouncy curls. In their acceptance speech, Hampton, his voice thick with emotion, would speak about the *power of representation*. How the very fact that he'd made it to the top was proof that in this town anything was possible. He'd step aside to let the woman speak too—the cowriter—and she would say how inspired she was to be standing on the shoulders of so many *people of color* who had come before her and who had toiled in the television shadows. When they were done, the audience would rise to their feet to applaud.

Not long after that, Jane would come upon a small news item saying that Hampton Ford's wife, Doreen, had filed for divorce. In the picture of him that went along with the article, he'd put on weight. Jujubean stood beside him, huge and pubescent, wearing the sullen expression of a child of divorce. Hampton had said she looked white, but in this photo, she looked to Jane like just another freckle-faced octoroon in an ill-fitting dress.

After that, Hampton would keep producing diverse content, so to speak, but *Swirl* would be known as the pinnacle of his success. He would acquire the bloated look of someone who had passed his peak.

In the future that had not yet arrived, Lenny and Jane would stay together. According to statistics, arranged marriages have the same success rate as marriages of free will. And who is to say what free will is?

Lenny grew nearly fluent in Japanese. He took many trips to Tokyo. Together they watched Ruby and Finn grow tall and strong.

In their wedding vows so many years before, they had quoted Rilke; they'd promised to protect each other's solitude. They held true to that promise. But they also kept each other company. They took walks together each evening with the dog they found at the pound, a low-rent Labradoodle they named El Debarge. They talked about what they hated but more often about what they loved. Finn and Ruby.

The new book Jane started one weekend in Palm Springs would go on to be rejected by three different publishers. With a strange new sense of pride, she reminded herself with each new rejection letter that she'd once written something good enough for Hampton Ford to steal. It was a mind game she was playing on herself, but it worked. And she was a scrappy Gen X latchkey child of divorce, which meant she was nothing if not dogged. The book ended up getting published. And with it, Jane was promoted. Teaching got easier, and sometimes she found she even liked it. Every so often, a student would turn up in one of her classes, instincts fully formed, vision so urgent and necessary that it startled her awake. They would remind her of why she'd done it, why any of them did it, what they were after: a story as dark and clear as a mirror.

In the future that had not yet arrived, Lenny's career lurched forward. He'd kept it a surprise, or maybe a secret, but just before he sent his paintings to Tokyo for his solo show, he'd taken Jane's advice and drawn a tiny Black man's face, mouth open, screaming, in the corner of each of them. Every one of them sold the first night of the show. Soon after, a gallery in New York offered to represent him. Between them, he and Jane finally made enough to put a down payment on a house in Multicultural Mayberry. It was a fixer-upper, an old Craftsman that had fallen into disrepair. But it was sitting on expensive dirt, and they had time to improve the situation.

JEANIE COUGHED BESIDE HER. Jane was still seated in the common room of the Golden Eagle, binge-watching *Swirl* with four octogenarian white women.

On-screen, a security guard was unlocking the door to the Restoration Hardware showroom. Holding his gun, he approached the enormous display bed, the lump under the covers—the character they called Zyzzyva.

Jane tried to remember the face of the real boyfriend, the last of the white boys during that long winter of her mulatto discontent, but all she could see was the face of the actor who played him on TV.

In the final scene, Zyzzyva wanders the streets in the morning light. She stops at a street cart to buy coffee, then, improbably, finds her psychic waiting for her on a park bench. The actor playing the psychic wears a turban. He sits flipping through a stack of tarot cards. He tells Zyzzyva not to worry. He can see her future. It will be filled with sunshine and swimming pools, children and laughter. Zyzzyva believes him. And that last image of her face is so beautiful, so symmetrical, so perfectly amalgamated, it is easy to believe he is telling the truth. The credits roll.

ACKNOWLEDGMENTS

Thanks to Rebecca Saletan, my brilliant editor, the best of the best, for every hour you put into reading and considering this work with such deep intelligence—what a thrill and honor to work together again. To Nicole Aragi, my dream of an agent, for your deep wisdom, laser instincts—so lucky to have found my way to you. To the exceptional team at Riverhead Books who have tended to this book with such vision and care: Geoff Kloske, Jynne Dilling Martin, Ashley Garland, Bianca Flores, Nora Alice Demick, Michelle Waters, Delia Taylor, Lauren Peters-Collaer, Amanda Dewey, and Sharon Gonzalez. To Dana Johnson, Victoria Patterson, Rebecca Walker, Aimee Bender, Maggie Nelson, Leo and Dorothy Braudy, Maya Perez, Matt Klam, Brooke Ehrlich, Francine Prose, Brigette Dunn-Korpela—for your sustaining friendships. To the original tribe, my sister and brother, Lucien Senna and Maceo Senna, for your formative humor, love, and genius. To the Huntington Botanical Gardens, for the space and silence to work. To Sarah Shun-Lien Bynum, for your joyful presence, generous readings, and crucial insights along the way—this book is in conversation with you. Thank you, finally, to my family—M, P, H—I adore you beyond words.